WIZZY WIG

Tiffany Pitts

Cover Design by Renee Garcia
Edited by Magdalen Powers
Cover Photo by Rachel Calhoun

This is a work of fiction. Names, characters, places, brands, media, and incidents are either the product of the author's imagination or are used fictitiously. Any resemblance to similarly named places or to persons living or deceased is unintentional.

PRINT ISBN 978-0-9976520-3-1
EPUB ISBN 978-0-9976520-2-4
Library of Congress Number: 2015914778

"Tiffany, if anyone had ADHD back then, it was you."

This book is dedicated to Linda Sue Schoenharl.
I love you mom.

BRAZIL

HIS NAME IS Octavio Jacinto Agostinho Gustavo Natanael the VII.

Or maybe it was VIII. He was never quite certain.

This is because both his parents died while he was very young and his memory is fuzzy at best. It is also because Octavio Jacinto Agostinho Gustavo Natanael the VII (*poss.* VIII) is a Brazilian wandering spider, a species not typically known for its genealogical acumen.

The locals simply call him *Diabo*. Diabo doesn't give a *merda* about his lineage. He prefers to spend his time terrorizing the local population of banana ranchers with a game he calls *os Gritos*.

Every day, he selects a new tree on the plantation in which to hide. When the bananitos come to cut down the fruit, Diabo runs out at them, flashing his blood-red fangs and waving the spines on his legs. Then he drops to the ground, finds cover in the rotting banana leaves and revels in the screams of terror growing fainter as the men run away. Truly, that is his favorite part.

To date, twenty-nine bananitos have tried to kill him. None have succeeded. With an eight-inch leg span and a body the size of a chicken egg, Diabo is the largest wandering spider in the forest. He has never backed down from anything in his life. The surviving bananitos make sure the rest stay wary of *O Bastardo do Mal*. Diabo likes it that way.

So much does he love *os Gritos* that Diabo has been known to dedicate entire days in search of interesting places to hide. One time, he waited for hours inside their noisy, wheeled machine. It had been risky climbing into the cabin like that, but the way the man shrieked like a baby monkey when Diabo rushed out onto the dashboard *absolutamente* made up for it.

Lately, he'd been wanting to try something new. Piercing their hides with his leg spines might be an effective way to add more depth to their wailing. Venom collected in little droplets at the end of his fangs every time he thought about the shrieking that would surely ensue.

He found an unattended pile of bananas someone had carelessly left lying around, and tucked himself inside. There he waited in happy anticipation for the familiar footfalls signaling an approaching bananito.

But the sounds never came. Instead, the bananas shook with a startling jerk. Then the sun went out. Diabo did not worry about this. The more secure the men felt, the faster they scrambled when he ran at them. Even when the thundering growls of their wheeled machine shook his banana-sanctuary, he did not worry. They would find him eventually. And when they did, the screaming would be tremendous.

After an hour or so, the banana pile still had not stopped moving. Being the strongest wandering spider in the forest, Diabo refused to let a convulsive box of fruit scare him. He simply drew his legs in beside his abdomen and took a nap.

He slept for a very long time.

FRIDAY, OCTOBER 14TH

SEATTLE

"WHAT THE HELL IS THAT?"

"A fedora. Why? Is it too much?"

"Not if your name is Elwood, no."

"Should I not wear it?"

"That depends," said Jake. His eyes lit up with good-natured devilment. "Are you on a mission from God?"

"No, Deli and I are going to that party, remember?"

"Oh, well, in that case, you should definitely wear it." Jake smiled, but his eyes dimmed, and he sat back down at his computer.

"We're meeting some of her friends at Shorty's first. You *really* don't want to go?"

Jake tilted his head slightly. "Who are you meeting?"

"Nicole and Jo," said Carl. Then he shrugged in apology and added, "Sorry man, Deli tried to get her to come out with us but she's working a double."

Jake remained impassive.

"You should come anyway. Nicole thinks you're funny, and Deli would be happy to see you."

Carl and Deli had been dating since August. So far, it had been going pretty well. Jake liked Deli. She was smart and funny, and she never complained about Thursday gaming nights. Most importantly, she was friends with Kix Welty, the delivery driver for Pizza Joe's.

"That's okay. I'm good here."

"You sure?"

"I'm sure. I want to get started on this Christmas wash for the swamp zombies anyway. It's almost November, for chrissake."

"I thought you and Sacha were gonna start that tomorrow?"

"I don't trust him. He told me the other day that Santa Claus is a materialistic excuse for overindulgence. What is that about?"

Carl shrugged his shoulders. "He's *Jewish*, Jake. He's *allowed* not to believe in Santa Claus."

"That's BS. *I'm* more Jewish than that clown, and I've got a Catholic-guilt hotline."

He pointed across the room to an old, hotel-style phone and answering machine combo sitting on its own table. Ostensibly, it was for tenants to call if they had problems with the plumbing or heating but everyone knew that the best way to reach Jake was just to go downstairs and knock on the door. The only person who actually called that number was his mom, Gloria. She thought it was his cell phone number.

Carl nodded, conceding the point.

"Besides," Jake went on. "Santa Claus hasn't got anything to do with religion, man. Everybody knows Christmas is all about little kids and presents and blowing shit up on your computer all afternoon."

"You sure you don't want to come out for a beer?"

Jake leaned back in his chair, stretching his arms over his head. "Thanks, but I'm good. There's nothing like drawing tiny Santa hats on homicidal monsters to put the shine on a Saturday night." He did not add that he also intended to order pizza for dinner. Carl had probably figured that part out on his own.

"Well, if you change your mind, text me." Carl straightened his tie and grabbed his coat.

"Wait a minute," said Jake. He swiveled his chair to face the desk behind him. There were four screens, all lit in various themes of red and green. He dug behind the lower left one and extracted a pair of dark sunglasses.

"You're gonna need these," he said and tossed the sunglasses across the room.

Carl's hand whipped up and snatched the glasses from the air. He put them on. "Later." he said.

DINNER

"HEY, JAKE!"

Jake's ears thumped as his heart tried to climb out of his chest. They were officially friends now, but he still had a panic attack every time he heard her voice over the phone.

"Hi, uh, Kix. How are you?" He tried to get the right mix of I'm-calling-because-I'm-really-hungry and it's-nice-to-talk-with-you in his voice. Already, he felt like an idiot.

"I'm so *bored*. It is absolutely dead tonight. No one wants pizza. Everyone's at a Halloween party or something."

Jake tried to think of a witty answer, but Kix saved him at the last minute by cutting him off.

"Wait, isn't Beck having his shindig tonight? I thought you were going with Carl and Deli."

"Nah, I have a...thing I gotta do."

"Oh of *course*," She said. "You got a *thing* you gotta do. I should have known you had a *thing*."

He heard laughter in her voice, just below her words and the tension in his shoulders melted away. The corners of his mouth turned up. His eyes even sparkled a bit. They couldn't help it. Whenever she spoke, the world suddenly became a more interesting place. Jake suspected she may have super powers.

"It's for *TerrorCity*. I have some stuff that needs to get done."

"Oh, so you're like, *really busy*?"

Jake had to restrain himself from answering too quickly.

"Actually...no. I just wanted to get it started. Last year's deadline was tight because the Ad Department had to go back to Kansas to visit his grandma for Thanksgiving."

On the other end of the line, he could hear Kix trying not to laugh, but he wasn't sure if that was a good thing or a bad thing.

"Well, if you're not *super* busy, maybe I could come over? I think I have something you might want."

Jake turned away from his phone so that he did not cough directly into the receiver. Once he'd gotten control of his breathing again, he said, "That depends on what you have."

"Remember last week, you were telling me about that experiment you were trying to set up?"

"Which experiment?"

"The wave one."

"Intentional collapse of a wave function?"

"Yeah, that's the one. You said you needed something in a closed box, right? Something no one knew what was inside?"

He'd said a lot of things. But *that* particular thing was absolutely correct. How did she remember that?

"Yes, that's right."

"Well, I got to thinking about that. Do you think you could use a pizza?"

Jake's mind was working too fast for him to answer right away. "Yee-ess, that *could* work, but only if no one knew what was on it. But how could someone make a pizza and not know what's on it?"

"Aha! I knew it! I think you are in luck. I think you're going to want this."

"You don't have such a pizza, do you?"

"Yep."

"How did you do that?"

"Marco did it, actually. He's been hopped up on cold meds for a week because of his bronchitis. He's so dopey that last night he made an extra-large with Gorgonzola and anchovies."

"That doesn't sound too bad," said Jake.

"He used peanut butter instead of tomato sauce."

"Oh, wow. That's…that's really gross."

"You have no idea. It smelled so bad, we had to send the busboy out into the alley to throw it in the Dumpster."

"Poor kid."

"Not really, he's kind of a punk. But never mind that. The point is that Marco made another orphaned pizza. He has no idea what is on it. Eric stuck it in the box without looking and after all the other orders were filled, it was still there. Marco thinks Eric played a trick on him, but no one plays tricks on Marco because he's got no sense of humor."

"By the time they figured out it was an orphan, I already snatched it. Marco was pissed when I told him he couldn't open it." She paused. "But...that was *right*, right?"

Jake didn't know what to say. *Hell yes, that's right,* seemed a little overzealous. He'd only told her about the experiment because he was horrible at small talk. He assumed she listened to be polite.

Then why did she remember the details? asked his inside voice.

Jake smiled because sometimes his inside voice made good points.

"You are so awesome," he said, then blushed a brilliant shade of red as the words registered in his brain. He blushed more thinking about how stupid he looked. She couldn't even see him, and he was embarrassed. He needed to stop overanalyzing this.

"Do you, uh, do you want me to come pick it up?"

Kix laughed, and a lick of fear ran up his spine.

"Eric's covering the rest of my shift. Can you wait twenty minutes? I'll bring it over."

"Wow, yes! That would be excellent. Are you sure that's okay? I don't want to get you in trouble with Marco or anything."

"It's totally fine, Jake. You want me to bring anything else?"

"Just the pizza would be great. I think I have everything else I need." Kix laughed again, and Jake suddenly wondered what she meant by *anything else.*

"I'll see you in twenty minutes then?"

"Sounds *great.* And uh, thanks...Kix."

"No problem."

He disconnected the line, unsure of what just happened. Did she call him up and invite herself over for extracurricular science? In a million years, Jake could not imagine something so awesome ever happening, and yet his brain kept trying to tell him it was true.

Crap—if it *was* true, then Kix was coming over and he was not ready. He jumped out of the chair and ran to check the fridge. *Yes!* He had beer. And it wasn't even crappy beer! He grabbed one and cracked it open, then ran back to his room to change. Digging through his clean clothes, he found his lucky t-shirt and the one pair of pants that still stayed up without a belt. Then he checked that his hair wasn't too goofy-looking.

He stared at his reflection. A scar, shiny and pink, ran across his left cheek. Jake loved that scar. The day he got it would have been his last if Kix hadn't shown up. He thought about that often. Plus, being able to say, *Yeah, that's where I got shot in the face* was the best thing ever. It *never* got old.

He checked the time. Kix was coming over in less than ten minutes. She had never come here by herself before. She usually only came over when Deli was here. Maybe she was just going to drop the pizza off and go? Jake couldn't imagine her wanting to actually stay for the experiment.

Maybe he wouldn't do it. Maybe he would ask her if she wanted to watch a movie instead. Could he do that? Would that work? Probably not. She probably got off early so she could go to Beck's party. Why hadn't he thought of that earlier?

He did a quick sweep of the apartment for beer bottles and dirty clothes on the floor. In the end, it was still messy, but it looked more like he was incredibly busy than just an incredible slob. It would have to do.

With his heartbeat drumming in his ears, Jake sat down at his computer and started pulling up preliminary data (time, ambient temperature, elevation). He relaxed as the numbers consumed him. His heart stopped having girl-induced palpitations, and he drank his beer in a mathematical trance. He glossed through the entire wave function, decided which points needed adapting to a pizza-based calculation, and got to work. Once he had the data from the pizza box itself, he would choose an outcome and solve the equation backwards. He needed only a few extra points and he could do it. He *would* do it. His heart started racing again. This time, Kix only got every other beat.

PIZZA DELIVERY

JAKE HADN'T YET RECONNECTED the doorbell after Sacha reprogrammed it to Rick Astley singing *Never Gonna Give You Up*. So when he heard the click he didn't respond right away. Two seconds later he realized what it was and jumped up from his computer.

"Coming!" he said and felt stupid. Who says things like that? Idiots say things like that. He hurried to the door.

Kix stood on the doormat in her combat boots. Jake swallowed hard but kept his breathing even. She wore red and black striped tights under a pair of cutoff jeans and an oversized military-style jacket. Her long auburn hair was tied into a ponytail that danced down her back in the wind. She held a pizza box in one hand. The other hand hid from the cold in the pocket of her coat. For a second, Jake's mouth hung open and he didn't say anything.

"Can I come in? It's cold out here." Kix stomped her boots a few times. Jake came out of orbit.

"Yes, of course. Please come in." She gave her boots a final stomp and walked in.

"Can I get you a beer or something?"

"You got anything warmer?"

"I think I have some wine left over from the homecoming thing in the cupboard."

Kix crinkled her nose and smiled at the same time. Jake watched her and did not choke on anything. He was proud of that.

"I also have some whiskey?"

"That sounds perfect."

This time he did choke, but only just a little. Then he tiptoed to the pantry-cupboard, afraid of saying anything else stupid-sounding.

He rattled around looking for a clean glass. Did she want ice?

"Do you want ice?"

"Sure."

Oh nuts, did he have any ice? He checked the freezer and swore under his breath. All he had were those joke trays that made ice into stupid shapes. At least they were full. He popped three of the novelty ice cubes from the silicone mold and threw them in the glass.

She stood with her back to the kitchen, facing the living room. Jake watched her ponytail bounce back and forth as she searched around for an empty spot to set the pizza. He walked up behind her just as she started to yell.

"Hey, where can I put this thing?"

"I'll take it," he said. Kix jumped and turned at the same time, nearly dropping the box in the process. She made a squeaky surprised sound before surrendering the pizza and accepting the drink he offered.

"Thank you," she said and turned back to the living room to scout out somewhere to sit.

"Sorry, I've been busy working on *TerrorCity* for a few days straight." He stuck the pizza on top of the file cabinet and swept magazines and game controllers sideways off the couch, into a heap next to the wall. "I don't really pay much attention to anything else when I'm working."

"Don't worry about it." She sat down on the couch without hesitation. "I have four brothers. I know how you men live."

A small bolt of fear shot through Jake's stomach. "You have four brothers?"

"Yep," said Kix. "Youngest of five." She smiled, raised her glass to him, then drank half of it in one large gulp. She didn't even flinch.

"Wow." It was all he could say.

"Why do you think I started with the bodu kura? You don't grow up with four champion wrestlers and not learn a thing or two."

Jake mangled his lips into something like a smile. "No, I guess you don't," he said, then fled to the computer for his beer.

The console was designed with an economy of space as the prime directive. There were roughly twelve million cables and billions of individual computer-type things. Somehow, in a wonky, lopsided way, everything fit together resulting in a technological marvel both fascinating and terrifying to behold—and not only because it was apparent that someone was very good with braiding.

"Jake, why are there mustaches in my drink?"

Kix drew a handlebarred ice cube from her glass and held it up to her lip. She raised an eyebrow and giggled. The sound broke through his tension, and the world seemed to relax around him.

"It's all I had. Sorry. Thanks for the pizza. Did I already say that?"

"You did, and you're welcome." She dropped the ice back in her drink. "It seemed to fit all the requirements you told me about last week, so I grabbed it before Marco could. He got pissy and demanded I check it but I told him you had mad cow disease, and that if he breathed on it, he would get wicked sick."

"That doesn't make any sense."

"Neither does Marco right now, he's so doped up. When I left, he was on the phone congratulating his nephew for getting picked up by Bruce Springsteen." She made little crazy-swirls in the air with her finger.

"Is he a musician?"

"He doesn't have a nephew."

"Ah, right."

"Tell me again what you are doing with this thing."

"Okay," he said and swiveled his ergonomic computer chair toward her. He concentrated on his lap until the other part of his brain—the part dedicated to all the -ologies and -atics he could stuff in, took over. Then he faced her and took a deep breath. When Jake got himself on a scientific tear, he could talk a body blue.

"Do you know the Schrödinger's cat paradox?"

"Dead cat in a box."

"Uhh...kind of. There *is* a cat in a box but it only has a fifty percent chance of being dead at the end of the experiment."

"That's not a huge improvement."

"Inside the box there's a cat and a vial of poison and a Geiger counter."

"Do your roommates know you plan such intricate cat-murders?"

"It's just a thought experiment. You don't actually do it with real cats."

"How is that any better? I thought you liked cats."

"I *do*." Jake shook his head and started to raise his hands in innocence, but Kix's eyes sparkled and she smiled a lopsided smile at him so he blushed instead.

"No one has actually done this with a live cat that I know of. Trust me," he said. She giggled. Jake took that as a good sign.

"Okay, you know what? Forget the grisly murder part. Let's just say that at the end of an hour, the cat could be dead or it could be alive. You don't know which until you open the box."

"*Toesy* would be alive, right?" she said.

"Toesy *would* be alive," Jake agreed. "But he's not a regular cat. Anyway, here's where the thought experiment comes in. *Theoretically*, until you open up the box and observe it for yourself, the cat is both dead *and* alive."

"That's ridiculous. You can't have half a live cat."

"We don't see half-live cats everywhere, that's true. But before you look inside the box, there is a possibility, no matter how small, of having a half-live cat. And you can write that probability down as a mathematical equation. That equation is solved when you open up the box and actually *see* what's going on inside. The cat is either alive or it's dead."

"So what?"

"Well, what if there's a way to solve that equation *before* you open the box? What if I *assume* the cat will be alive, plug that answer into that wave function and solve the whole thing backward? —kind of like reverse engineering the outcome."

"I'd say that sounds like a low budget sci-fi movie." Kix reached down and started to unlace her boot. The black and red stripes of her tights made mesmerizing patterns against her legs. "Where do the aliens come in?"

"No aliens, I promise. Just pizza. I think I've got the preliminary equation blocked out. It wasn't easy because of the variables involved, but if I've done it correctly—which I would like to point out, is highly unlikely—then theoretically we should be able to make the pizza into whatever we want."

"So, you're like a pizza-wizard?"

Jake laughed. "Nope, just really bored lately."

Kix gave him a curious look. "Where's Carl? Deli says you guys are inseparable."

"With Deli."

"Oh, that's right, they went to that party tonight, didn't they?" She said then hurried on. "About this pizza…"

Jake thought she was asking for an example. "Sure. Say I wanted jalapeños on my pizza. If the toppings have truly been put on at random, then there is a possibility, no matter how slim, of having jalapeños on it. What I'm going to do is assume it *does* have jalapeños and solve backward through that probability equation. If I can get the math to work out, the pizza should have jalapeños on it when we open the box."

She smiled all the way to her eyes. "Yes, I got that part. I was *going* to ask if, at some point this evening, you plan on actually eating it."

"Oh. Yes," he said, feeling very foolish.

"And were you planning on inviting me to eat the pizza with you?"

"Yes, of course!" He said this much louder. It was more like a shout. "Uh, if you *want* to, that is. It might take me a while to get through this."

"You can't expect me to wait around that long for dinner, Jake." She snapped her fingers at him. "I want some pizza! Hurry it up, or I'm going to be forced to open that box." His eyes widened for a second, and Kix laughed.

"I'm totally kidding." She said, holding her hands up in mock surrender. "I can wait. What have you got to watch?"

She cleared a path across the room to a particleboard monstrosity covering the far wall and leaning precariously to the left. Its shelves were packed with two decades of film collecting, alphabetized by director's last name. Jake watched her tick through the titles, fascinated by the movement of her stripes, until she grabbed one and straightened up.

"Oh, wow, you have this movie?" She held it up for him to see. Of course he had that movie. It had one of the best fight scenes ever recorded on film.

"Actually, that copy is Carl's. Mine is the full Korean version."

"Oh, I *see*. The full Korean version, huh? Well, Carl won't mind if I watch the half-Korean version, will he?"

Jake scrunched his face up, wondering if he'd said something stupid.

"Seriously, Jake, you have to lighten up. I'm messing with you."

He wanted to lighten up. He tried lightening up. It was not easy. He offered her another drink instead.

"Only if I can get a porn-stache this time."

Jake hopped it to the kitchen. He returned to find Kix cross-legged on the couch, watching the beginning credits.

"I love the fight scene in the corridor. Did you know that was done all in one take?"

Jake fought with an overwhelming impulse to propose marriage to this marvelous creature. Instead, he tapped her shoulder with another whiskey and frozen mustaches.

"Thanks." She glanced up at him as she took the glass. "You can go have fun with your numbers. I'll be fine." Then she shooed him away with her fingers.

Jake didn't want to go away. He loved this movie. He loved that she loved this movie. He loved that she was sitting on his couch. He stood next to the couch, watching the first scene unfold.

"Jake," Kix said, turning her whole body to face him. "I don't know about you, but when I was a kid, I wasn't allowed to watch television until I finished my homework." Her brow furrowed as she gave him a look full of detention and KP duty. She raised a stockinged foot and gave his knee a gentle push towards the computer.

"Go! You wanted to do this. *Go.*"

"Yes, I did. I mean, *do.*" Jake hurried to his computer and tucked himself into a screen full of numbers and the classier members of the Greek alphabet. Maybe he could finish before the corridor fight scene.

He calculated, resurfacing now and again to ask Kix if she needed anything. She said she could get it herself, if that was okay. It was totally okay. She could drink all the rest of his booze, flood the kitchen, and erase the memory on his game console, and it would totally be okay.

ON THE COUCH

JAKE HAD A THING for her. She could tell. Actually, Kix found it surprisingly difficult to ignore. Jake was always trying to stifle a cough or catch his breath when they spoke. It was sweet.

At first, she wasn't too sure she liked him. The last thing she needed was for regular customers to start asking her out. But after all the drama from the summer, Kix had gotten to know Jake better. He turned out to be a decent guy—not nearly as asthmatic as she'd assumed. Plus, he was easy to be around. He didn't talk at her cleavage or make sarcastic jokes all the time. He still got tongue-tied occasionally though. Especially when she wore her combat boots. It was kind of adorable.

Across the room she heard the *click-clock* sound of Jake pecking away at his computer and felt comfortable. It was nice to be lying on the couch while he sat at his desk being weirdly smart. It wasn't something most guys would do. Not in front of Kix, anyway. Especially not if she was lying on their couch.

It wasn't her fault. Kix attracted men. She didn't do it on purpose. It was more about the way she filled out a t-shirt or how everything sort of *bounced* when she walked. No one thought of her as plain. They all thought of her as something, but *plain* was not it. Hell, even Deli had been surprised to find out she was single. But why wouldn't she be? Just because she attracted a lot of men didn't mean she attracted nice ones. Most of them considered picking up the bar tab a sound investment strategy.

Jake had never been like that. He treated her like a regular person with a regular-person brain. He talked about stuff he liked and asked questions about stuff she liked.

He had a genuine spark of interest that was never faked or blown out of proportion. Last week, when he'd described his wave function experiment, he got so excited about it his eyes went all shiny and he fidgeted around like a little kid that had to go to the bathroom. She'd laughed about that on the way home. She couldn't help it. His enthusiasm was so genuine it was contagious.

Kix yawned. Her eyelids grew heavy. Maybe she should get some water before the corridor fight scene? It might help her keep her eyes open.

PIZZA

JAKE LOOKED AWAY from the screen as he walked himself through the function one last time. On the couch, Kix was so quiet he assumed she'd fallen asleep.

He rounded out the data points. At a casual glance, they seemed correct. The phone started ringing. He ignored it and checked his numbers again.

They were more than correct. They were *right*.

He did it.

"You want me to answer that?" Kix said from the kitchen. Jake whipped his head around, startled for a moment.

"It's just the Gloria Phone. Don't bother."

He went back to the function, rechecking the last three lines of code. They were right.

"The what?"

"The Gloria Phone," he said again. "No one ever calls it except my mom, Gloria. She calls whenever I'm wrong about something. And on Sundays."

But Jake wasn't wrong about this. He triple-checked his numbers. They were still correct.

"That's kinda horrible and kinda handy," she said. He heard the soft hiss of the freezer door latching shut, then her footsteps crossing the kitchen.

"I did it." He said this in a near whisper because even though he'd checked everything four times now, he was still having a hard time convincing himself that he actually did it. The phone rang on.

"You figured out your equation?"

"Yes."

"The pizza really has jalapeños on it?" Her voice was louder now that she stood in the kitchen doorway.

Jake opened his mouth to say yes but found that he couldn't form the word. His brain knew it was right, but his tongue didn't want to say it. In his mind, he ran backward through all the long equation. It was right. He thought himself forward through the same numbers. They were right. When he got to the made-up part at the end, just before the answer, he felt a small mental block. Like two magnets being forced together, a little hump of resistance. It was as if the equation *wanted* to be right—all the numbers were correct—but it needed a little more convincing.

Maybe if he could look at everything slightly skewed, he could make the answer be all-the-way right. Maybe the bump would go away then.

Jake reached his thoughts out to find the block. In his mind, he felt for the edge of it, grasped at it with the logic of his argument. Once he had a hold of it, he...

... PUSHED

THE WORLD AROUND HIM slipped. For a second, his stomach lurched into free fall and Jake thought he might throw up. Then he felt a solid thud and it stopped moving. He sat at his computer, the half-Korean version forgotten in the background. The Gloria Phone rang on.

"Well, what do you think? Are you going to feed me or not?" Kix stood across from the kitchen, at the entrance to the hallway. How did she get there so fast? She had on one of those strappy tank tops that girls sometimes wore underneath baggy shirts. Jake found it incredibly difficult not to stare.

"Yes, of course." he said and opened the pizza box. He smiled a corny stage smile, held the lid open for her and waved his arm over the pizza like a magician. Nestled within the greasy box sat a large pizza polka-dotted with jalapeño peppers.

She crossed the floor in her stocking feet, stopping right in front of him. He could feel the heat from her skin as she leaned over—way over—and brought her lips right up to his ear. If there was a point to turn away, thank God he missed it.

"You want to know a secret?" she said. All of the bones in his body wobbled, and the skin prickled up the back of his neck. She threw her leg over his lap and sat down, face to face. His body reacted and for a second he was back in high school, afraid of the pretty girl laughing at him. But she didn't laugh.

Kix leaned forward, softer parts of her body pressed into him. Jake let go of the lid to the pizza box, and it closed with a soft swish. The scent of her, tropical and almost dangerous, washed over him.

He had no idea what to do with his hands.

He wanted to touch her somewhere, anywhere, just to make it real—but he couldn't figure out where. He finally settled for resting his hands lightly on the curve of her hips. In the background, the answering machine picked up.

Hey, you've reached Jake Denny. Leave a message…

She wrapped her arms around his neck and pulled herself into him. Her lips brushed his ear when she spoke.

"I'm not hungry for pizza anymore."

Hey, Jake!

"Um…" said Jake.

"I'm glad you got your homework done. But let's go somewhere else and watch the rest of this movie. Your couch is really uncomfortable."

He nodded several times, as enthusiastically as he could. Jake had the commendable habit of always double checking his data points. Right now, most of his data pointed to the bedroom but he still couldn't help himself.

"W-where would you like to go?"

Her finger trailed from his earlobe down his arm, all the way to his left hand, still resting on her hip. She took his hand and moved it up the side of her body.

"Your room," she said.

For a second, Jake's brain shut down. He woke back up with her tongue in his mouth, cold from the ice in her drink. Jake kissed her back. His hands, no longer bashful, laced behind her and pulled her up into his arms.

Something nudged Jake in the back of his mind, but no way did he care enough to pay attention. For the first time in a long time, Friday night was turning out all right.

... PULLED

KIX LAY ON JAKE'S COUCH, slightly tipsy from the whiskey, trying not to doze her way through the corridor fight scene. The sound of Jake typing in the background lulled her, and her eyelids started to droop. She should definitely get some water before she fell asleep completely.

Ring.

The phone woke her with a start. The corridor fight scene was long since over. Her mouth was bone dry. She sat up and turned to see Jake, plastered to his computer monitor, typing too fast to stop. Standing up, she shook the sleep from her arms and walked toward the kitchen to get some water. In the hallway sat an old hotel-style phone on its own little table. As she walked past, it began to ring.

"You want me to answer that?" she said.

Jake looked up to her briefly, recognition of words spoken. He smiled and nodded, then went back to typing.

Kix reached out to pick up the receiver but she was too far away. She stepped closer. Again she reached to pick up the receiver. This time her hand fell through it like a ghost.

What the…?

The phone rang again, impossibly loud this time. Kix's eyes flew open in surprise. She was still lying on Jake's couch. Across the room, movie credits rolled up the television screen. Her heart pounded through her chest, and she tried to calm down.

"You want me to answer that?"

Hadn't she just said that?

The voice came from the kitchen. It was undoubtedly female.

Probably it was Deli. She and Carl must have come back from the party already. Kix opened her mouth to say hello, but her nose began to tickle. She closed her mouth and tried to rub the tickle away.

"Are you going to feed me or not?"

Footsteps padded across the room. Kix froze in place, finger almost up her nose. That hadn't sounded like Deli. Deli wouldn't talk to Jake like that.

She heard the squeak of an ergonomic desk chair as it, and the person sitting in it, leaned back. Before she'd fallen asleep, she had balled up her jacket to use as a pillow. The same balled-up jacket now acted as her only screen from the organic noises coming from the chair.

Her first reaction was disbelief. That couldn't be what she was hearing, could it? But the music from the credit roll was quiet and those noises were pretty unmistakable. What else could they be doing?

"You want to know a secret?"

Oh crap oh crap oh crap oh crap, Kix started repeating the words silently in her head so she wouldn't have to hear any more, but that trick never works for long.

"I'm not hungry for pizza anymore."

One finger shoved up her nose to keep from sneezing, Kix stuck the other in her ear to keep from hearing whatever came next. How was this happening? She wanted to stand up and scream, *Hello, I am in the same room as you, you perv!* but she didn't because if she had to interact with Jake or whoever was currently trying to suck his face off, she might have to die.

She tried making herself as inconspicuous as possible and wondered if she'd read the situation all wrong. Should she not have invited herself over? They weren't dating, but she'd always assumed the only reason was because he was a total chicken and unable to ask her out. It hadn't occurred that he might be interested in someone *else.*

She lay there, paralyzed with anger, horrified at what Jake and Totally-Not-Deli were doing less than ten feet away. It didn't last long. Around the finger jammed in her ear, Kix heard the squeak of Jake's desk chair again and footsteps headed to his bedroom.

As they walked behind the couch, Kix's nose staged a full-on sneeze attack. She pinched down so hard it would surely be bruised in the morning, but at least she was quiet.

As soon as the bedroom door closed, she sat up, ready to scream or bolt or punch someone, she wasn't quite sure. Grabbing her boots, she jammed her feet into them and started lacing. She looked over at Jake's desk to hiss something unpleasant in that direction, but couldn't on account of her mouth being frozen shut and her heart sputtering to a stop. Her breathing took a short hiatus, too.

Jake wasn't in his room making out with some random woman. He was there, at his desk, slumped over his keyboard. He almost looked dead.

Was he dead?

Kix took a step toward him to listen for breathing. As she did so, he let out a light snore. It made her jump, but at least her heart started beating again. Then her breath came back. Her anger slowly thawed into confusion, but that was okay—she could deal with confusion. She must have been wrong.

That *must* have been Deli and Carl she'd heard. It couldn't have been Jake because he was right *there*, asleep at his desk. She didn't know why they would go to Jake's room and not Carl's, but that didn't matter right now. The only people it could have been were Deli and Carl.

All the same, Kix decided to leave before any more weird stuff happened.

JAMMIES AND BED

KIX LIVED IN THE ATTIC APARTMENT of a three-story house two blocks east of the community college. She'd planned to move when her lease was up, but after she told the landlord, he lowered her rent by seventy-five dollars a month and offered to buy a new water heater so she wouldn't move out. Apparently, quiet tenants who paid rent on time and didn't throw up in the landscaping were hard to come by in this neighborhood.

The path through the alley was dark and slippery with moss. It would be easier to go across the back porch. She checked the time on her phone. It was almost five in the morning—hopefully, no one would be up. She walked around the side of the house as quietly as possible. As she reached up to unlatch the gate, the rank odor of Cuban cigar filtered out from the backyard. Kix knew they were Cuban because Thad had gone to Cuba recently and wouldn't shut up about the stupid things. *Dammit.* The last thing she needed right now was an earful of that guy.

Let's get this over with, she thought and walked through the gate. There he sat, under the eaves in his stupid camping chair, trying to make smoke rings. He was either really drunk or spectacularly bad at smoke rings. Kix didn't care enough to ask.

"Hey, Chicka-boom-boom. Look what the cat dragged in." He said and blew out a great big puff of stinky Cuban smoke.

"Hey, Thad," she said, closing the gate behind her.

"You have fun tonight?" He wiggled his eyebrows and tried blowing more smoke rings.

"Actually, I worked pretty late."

"You missed a great party."

"Oh, was that tonight? I'm sorry," she said, knowing full well it had been tonight. It was the reason she'd requested the shift in the first place. She'd requested all weekend shifts this month, just in case.

"Yeah, well, Matt brought a bottle of Ketel One and *Hannah*, you remember I told you about Hannah? She's the spokesmodel for Pro-X Boards? Anyway, *she* came dressed up as Catwoman. Damn, is that girl is sexy. You want a beer?"

"No thank you. I'm going to bed." Kix drew her phone from her back pocket. She texted Jake as she walked across the porch (*I think I left my scarf. Maybe I'll stop by after my shift?*) so she wouldn't have to listen to any more about Hannah's talents. Halfway there, Thad stretched his legs out, casually blocking her path.

"Yeah, she's pretty into me. Did you know she's in med school? She was going to stay the night, but she's got rounds tomorrow."

"That's great," said Kix she hit send and looked up from the screen. "Have a good night."

"Hey, where are you going? Have a beer with me, little lady. Surely you got time for one beer?"

"Nope. I have to work in the morning. Sorry Dr. Spokesmodel didn't work out for you," she said and stepped over his legs.

"Oh, she'll be over again," said Thad. "It's hard to get enough of the Thad, *if you know what I mean.*"

"In fact, *I do.*" Said Kix. "I often find it difficult to get the right amount of Thad. Please excuse me."

Kix immediately turned back to her phone so she wouldn't have to continue the conversation. Jake hadn't answered her message yet. A fresh cloud of cigar smoke followed her up the stairs.

Kix's tiny apartment was covered in clothing. This was not because she liked fashion but rather because she hated doing laundry. She tried to hang work clothes away from her drafting table, to keep the garlic and anchovy aroma down. But she lived in a studio apartment, nearly a third of which *was* kitchen, so it never really worked unless she also left the window open. It was late October. The apartment smelled vaguely Italian.

Kix didn't care. She'd had enough energy to make it home but nowhere near enough to care about garlicky t-shirts. She slid the deadbolt on her door and threw her bag down in one swift motion, glad to be in her own space. This morning had been disorienting to say the least.

She undressed, pulled on an old pair of pajamas, and flopped into bed. Closing her eyes tight, she buried her face in the pillow and repeated the same explanation to herself that she'd come up with earlier. Jake had not gone into his room with another woman. That had been Carl. Jake had been asleep at his computer the entire time.

She tried to stop over-thinking with a little meditative breathing. It sort-of worked but when she finally did fall asleep, she had crazy, vivid dreams.

ASHWOOD SUPER MALL

BRAD PATROLLED THE PERIMETER of the mall with the intensity that all mall cops possess. It is issued to them during training, and they wear it like a badge; or rather, instead of a badge because Brad had never been issued a badge, even though he'd asked three times already. He wanted to ask again, but he didn't need to be on Paul's radar for anything. Paul was an asshole.

He took a left at the Kitchen Kitsch and walked on toward the east entrance patio where a few costumed freaks from the haunted house were hanging about. He managed to discourage them with a few choice words, *fuck* and *off* being the choicest.

At his hip, the radio crackled to life.

"Brad, where are you?" Paul the night manager shouted through on his walkie-talkie.

"East entrance, patio."

"I need you to get down to the Family Lounge. The manager at Gallery Plus says there's a guy in his store complaining about something weird he saw in the men's toilet."

Brad checked his watch. "Any particular something weird?"

"I don't know, do I? Something *weird*. Just go check it out."

"On my way."

Even though he was almost to the food court, Brad backtracked through the playground and around through the Fountain Walk. He always took the Fountain Walk, especially if it was dark outside.

The sidewalk was slick and cold with rain, but he didn't notice. He was focused on Peartree Athletics. The sales floor lights were still on, and he could see Karen standing in the front window. He checked his watch. She'd be done in about thirty minutes.

Halfway down the Fountain Walk, he watched as a guy approached her. They exchanged words, and both of them smiled. Then suddenly she busted up laughing.

Brad knew the guy. His name was James Dennison. He ran a background check on him when he'd been hired on at Peartree's but it came back disappointingly clean. Maybe he should conduct a little follow up interview; make sure James understood how things worked around here.

A PROBLEM IN A PEARTREE

"YOU NEED TO LEAVE," she said, shaking her head.

Danielle Peartree propped the security door open with her shoulder and held her skinny arms at her hips in an effort to block Brad's view of the store. It hadn't escaped his notice that Peartree Athletics had rolled their security gate down ten minutes early this evening.

"I know she's in there. I saw her. Tell her to get out here or I'm coming in."

"You come in here, and I'm calling the cops," she said, staring at him with her unblinking eyes. He hated it when she did that.

"Where is he, Karen?" he shouted around Danielle's shoulder.

"Leave her alone, Brad." She still wouldn't look away.

"She owes me an explanation."

"No, she doesn't."

"Let her tell me that herself then."

"She can't. She went home sick."

"Bullshit," said Brad, craning his neck around Danielle's shoulder to shout into the empty store. "I saw you two together, Karen. I saw you laughing at his jokes like he's some sort of comedian. Is that how he got you in the sack? Because you think he's funny? You're not going to get away with this. *I know you can hear me.*"

He grabbed the handle of the heavy door and opened it wider, meaning to step around Danielle into the store, but she was like a spider scurrying to the spot you least wanted her.

"You try that little trick again, and you'll regret it."

"You can't touch me," he said, holding his jaw up high.

"Want to test that theory? You aren't the only one who knows how to hack a security camera, asshole. I figured out what you did and put them all back." She pointed to the security camera near the ceiling of the back hallway.

Brad clenched his fists but refused to let her rile him up. Danielle was always full of crap—you couldn't trust a thing she said. Still, he took half a step back. It wouldn't hurt for her to think she'd scared him.

"I'll come back *later*," he said.

"You come anywhere near here again, and you're going to jail. Stay away from my store."

"What are you going to do, Danielle? I'm *security*."

"You won't be for much longer if you don't get out of here." She pointed to the camera behind him.

Brad remained absolutely still, even though what he really wanted to do was punch this man-hating bitch in the mouth. She was always telling people what to do. Karen couldn't take two steps without this harpy telling her which leg to use first.

"She owes me an explanation," he said. His lips barely moved.

Danielle's eyes narrowed, and she cocked her head to the side like a dog.

"No, she doesn't. She doesn't owe you anything. And I'm giving you two seconds to get out of here before I call some real cops. Not your loser security buddies."

That was *it*. His stepped forward and snapped at the air in front of her face in one, swift movement. He shouldn't have done it, but the suddenness of his movement made her flinch. Not much, maybe half an inch, but half an inch was enough.

Pleased with this reaction, Brad stepped back into the hallway. He glared at her as the security door slammed shut between them. She'd better not cross him again.

PRODUCE, LINE TWO...

HE WOKE UP GROGGY, with an unpleasant feeling in his cephalothorax. The world had stopped swaying long ago, but the cold night persisted. Diabo wondered, just for a moment, if he should have paid more attention to his surroundings. Everything felt different now, but he could not describe how. What little light he could see did not match his expectations, and the seeds of suspicion sprouted throughout his thoughts.

How long had he been asleep? Where had the bananitos gone? The answer to that came quickly, as his pile of bananas started to rumble and shake.

He tried rearranging his legs in order to spring out at the unsuspecting men, but his joints would not comply. The bananas, so sun-warmed and pleasant before, were now cool and clammy. The ache in his cephalothorax began to prey on his mind. It felt...empty.

Suddenly, the banana pile jerked, and a weak light filtered in. Though it brought a slight thaw in the temperature, the light did not seem to have enough color in it. It flickered with a nervous twitch— almost like the legs of a dying meal.

A meal. The more Diabo thought about it, the more he wanted one. Something warm and fuzzy would cheer him up. The unpleasantness in his middle grew to actual pain, and Diabo understood, for the first time in his life, the meaning of hunger. He groped about, trying to find his way from the cold bananas.

"Produce, you have a call on Line Two. Produce, Line Two, please."

Overhead, the call of the bananitos comforted him. If he could hear their warbling speech, he must not be far from his jungle.

THE END STALL

BRAD CUT ACROSS THE FOUNTAIN WALK to the loading dock. He wasn't supposed to use the loading dock of course—it being private property of Burdock's department store—but Brad didn't care right now. He needed to calm down, and the cinder-block walls of the loading dock made less noise when you kicked them.

Five minutes later, he was calm. It helped that he'd worn his steel-toed boots. He'd been wearing them a lot lately. He took the security hallway weaving his way from the side entrance to the men's room using a curious path. If anyone had been able to see him on the security feeds, they may have questioned it, but they couldn't. Not if he stuck to his path. He glanced at Security Feed Thirty-Seven. It did not blink any red lights at him. It did not look at him at all.

Brad held the door handle so it wouldn't make much noise and sidestepped into the men's room. All the stall doors stood open except the accessible stall at the far end. That wasn't unusual, but it did warrant a physical check. He bent down to look underneath the partitions, tiptoeing silently along, peeking through the doors into each stall he passed. When he reached the last stall, he put one finger in the middle of the door and pushed. It moved with his touch. He opened it a few inches and peeked in.

The first thing he noticed was that the last person in the stall hadn't flushed the toilet. He gagged and turned slightly to kick the toilet handle with his boot. That's when he noticed the second thing.

What the hell was it?

Brad stared at the wall and tried to comprehend what he saw. It was definitely a hole, except that calling it a hole in the wall would imply that it had an edge or a rim or something. It didn't seem to work that way. If he looked directly at the thing, there *was* a hole in the wall—but when he tried to look at the edge of it, his eyes couldn't focus on anything. And when he looked away for a second, the thing disappeared from the periphery of his vision entirely.

Frantic, he turned back to the wall, studying the broken plaster. There, in the crack between two subway tiles, was the hole. It yawned open, wider than before and drew him in. Brad stared into the bewitching blackness. It felt completely empty. Not the kind of empty that is left when someone leaves, but the kind of empty that suggested nothing had ever been there at all.

He stared into the darkness and wondered. In the whole age of the Universe, was he the first to see this void? Before him, there was nothing, not even light. But now he was here. The more he concentrated on the darkness, the more he was convinced that he could go there, into that darkness. That he *ought* to go there. He was *meant* to go there. The Universe had opened itself up and given him this power. He could go where *nothing* had ever been.

He reached out to touch the void. As he did so, a pinpoint of light pierced through the blackness, into his mind. The tiny white dot grew. As it got larger, Brad saw that it was not a white dot but a dot of many colors.

Ring.

It was technically against company policy to carry cell phones during work hours, but no one was stupid enough to leave them in their lockers. The phone in Brad's back pocket rang again, cutting through the silence of the void, shattering his trance. He blinked. The white dot disappeared.

He cut the call off without looking and focused back in on the blackness of the void. Soon the white dot showed up again.

Ring.

This time, Brad grabbed the phone from his back pocket. He did not look at the caller ID. He did not dare look away from the void before answering.

"What?" he said.

"What the hell are you doing?" Paul's voice was irritated, but Brad

didn't care. More and more of his senses focused back in on the bathroom. As they did so, the void grew smaller.

"I've been trying to get you on radio for twenty minutes." said Paul. The void disappeared entirely and Brad's attention snapped back to the bathroom. He stared at the empty tile wall, trying to find the crack in the subway tile. It was not there.

"Sorry," he said. "Must have gotten turned down by accident."

"Accident my ass. You check out that disturbance yet?"

My disturbance, thought Brad. *It's mine.*

"It's just graffiti. Looks like some punks drew a bunch of dicks all over everything."

"The guy that reported it was all freaked out all over a bunch of dicks? Jesus H. Christ, what an idiot. Okay, Velda is on bathrooms today. Tell her about it and head out to the south wing, we got closing."

"Roger that," said Brad. He holstered his radio and kept his annoyance in check. He searched again for the spot but could not find it. Dammit.

Working quickly, Brad locked the stall door from the inside and crawled under it to get out. He found the *Out of Order* sign underneath the sink and taped it up. Then he went to find Velda.

It wasn't very hard to convince Velda that she smelled gas. She didn't, of course. The Ashwood Super Mall was the least efficient mall in America and had no natural gas lines whatsoever, but Velda was a fat, stupid cow, and the mere thought of a gas leak sent her into fits of hypochondriactivity. It took less than thirty seconds for her to start complaining about a migraine. Brad thought that might be a personal record for her. She left without setting foot in the men's room.

He doubled back to make sure no one had gone in the stall. The sign was undisturbed. He would come back after closing. For now, he had something he needed to do.

He took the Fountain Walk to the food court, expecting to see Karen in the window rearranging the hiking equipment but Peartree Athletics was already empty. Only the security lights lit the sales floor. Brad made a note to report it as per Ashwood Mall Board Store Conduct policy. They didn't issue fines anymore, but they would at least tell Danielle's dad that she closed early. Maybe that bitch would get written up or something.

He stormed back to check on the bathroom. The stall door was still locked but Brad didn't want to take any chances. He headed straight for the supply closet where he found a pipe wrench. No one would question his *Out of Order* sign now.

CLYDESDALE MANOR
(*HORSEY HOUSE* TO THE LOCALS)

SATURDAY MORNING

THANATOS, DARK LORD OF THE UNDERWORLD, was not all that dark. He was more of a stripy grey color with patches of white on his back and legs. Neither did he reside in the depths of Hell. In fact, he lived in a third-floor apartment with the Mistress of the Can Opener, Delilah Pelham.

It was a source of endless frustration to Thanatos that, although he was an evil demon who quickened every heartbeat with fear as he walked past, Deli still insisted on calling him *Toesy*. So did all the other humans. This was because they still thought he was a cat.

Oh, he had been a cat at one point, but that was before he'd eaten the little metal bean. Toesy had no idea that he'd eaten a prototype nanobot designed to enhance the human body. To him, it was just a metal bean. But after he'd eaten it, Steve had appeared.

The advent of Steve had been the best thing to happen to Toesy, ever—and that included the time he'd found half a broiled salmon in the Dumpster in back of their old apartment building. Steve was a bona fide miracle. When Toesy got shot, Steve healed his wounds. When Toesy was stuck, Steve gave him answers. And when Toesy needed to open a door, Steve had given him thumbs. Toesy had finally reasoned that Steve was a manifestation of the Universe choosing him for spontaneous deification.

And why should it not? Had he not pledged his life to the Mistress of the Can Opener? Did he not defend her temple from all foes? Had he not sacrificed his life to save the Holy Man from the rabid Sock Pants monster?

Indeed, the Universe had made the right choice to give him the metal bean. And after he conquered the bean, he had become a demigod. Now he was *Thanatos*, Dark Lord of Clydesdale Manor, Defender of the Afternoon Napping Couch, and a scourge to all vermin within a twenty-five block radius (songbirds excluded).

If one considers the definition of a demigod to be a living being with supernatural powers then Toesy's theory was pretty much bang on. Cat or god, the fact remained that Clydesdale Manor hadn't seen the slink of a rat tail since he and his mistress had moved in. Even the cockroaches had decamped. Eventually, Toesy had to resort to moonlighting at an apartment building three blocks away just to keep his skills sharp. Last week, he spotted a mouse in a natural foods store near Broadway. He'd chosen this morning to do a little reconnaissance because the Tall Man was still around.

The Tall Man went by the name of Carl Sanderson, but Toesy always thought of him as *the Tall Man* because that is exactly what he was: tall. Carl the Tall showed up every afternoon, sometimes as early as morning, but usually not until after the birds had fled the window from the heat of the afternoon sun. Even as Carl knocked, Toesy's mistress would be shooing him out the door.

Toesy hated the shooing part. One time he refused, then later that night, he'd had to shoo himself out the window in a hurry. It had not been a good night. Since then, he'd found ways to busy himself on weekend nights, and he never returned before dawn. Still, he hated the ritual of it.

He followed his secret trail around to the front door. He had thought to check in on the Holy Man, as way of buying himself more time, but for some reason the door was locked. Even with his new thumbs, keys still gave him trouble. But the front porch was dry and sheltered and he didn't mind a little porch nap.

"Oh, dagnabbit!"

Toesy stretched out his paws in lazy fashion and turned a bored eye to the man who kept him from slumber. He carried two paper bags of groceries which he set carefully on the stoop next to him in order to pull a slim billfold from his pocket. From it he produced a fat square of white. He pushed his glasses up before unfolding the square.

Meeroooww, said Toesy as he stretched in the man's direction and surreptitiously tasted the air around him. The man smelled like shoe polish and bar soap.

"Don't think you are waiting for me, Mister Cat. Unless you live here, I am not letting you in."

The security keypad beeped as the man fed it the numbers he had written down on his square of white. Twice he hit the wrong button but only shook his head and tried again. On the third try, the security door buzzed its approval. The man held the door open with one shiny shoe as he leaned over and snapped up his grocery bags.

Toesy did not want to seem overly eager, but something about this man called to him. Perhaps it was the groceries. Who could say? Toesy did not question divine intuition.

He gave the man a generous head start before slipping in the door and following him up the first flight of stairs. At the top of the stairs, the man turned right. Toesy stayed hidden behind the banister and watched him walk down the hall.

Huzzah! He opened the door to 2C!

Connie Caulfield lived in 2C, and she had a little fluffy squeaky thing that was neither a squirrel nor a rat. Toesy dearly wished to know what it was, but he'd only gotten one good look at it before Connie had come in the room and screamed at him to get away from her *sugar glider.* He'd been so affronted that he left immediately and hadn't bothered with her since.

How dare she judge him so harshly? Toesy wasn't a senseless killer. He had no intention of eating it—whatever it was. With markings like that, it could be poisonous.

But still...

Was it really made of sugar? If so, did it have icing? Toesy liked icing, especially the kind that came on those chewy ginger cookies his mistress loved so much.

The man wrestled the key from the lock and stepped inside the apartment. Thanatos, Dark Lord of the Underworld and Grade-A Nosey Neighbor, waited until the door was almost closed before darting inside.

JAKE'S ROOM

HE KEPT HIS EYES CLOSED and checked himself all over. The bedsprings complained of old age, but everything else reported back good. Maybe a little sore in some parts but definitely better than normal. Jake smiled and rolled over. He hadn't had a dream that vivid since high school.

"Hey, you're awake!"

His eyes opened and continued opening as they focused in on the voice. She stood in his bedroom door wearing only a t-shirt. The probability of her wearing underwear was so low that he was tempted to calculate it. He refrained. Mainly because his rough estimate was about thirty percent, and that was lower than he'd ever anticipated. It took Jake a few seconds to figure out where he fit into this situation.

"So that actually happened?"

She tsked him. "You didn't drink that much beer last night. I watched you."

She walked over to the bed and crawled in, sliding her foot along the length of his leg as she tucked herself into his side. She was definitely not wearing any underwear.

"Don't you remember?"

Of course he remembered.

"I do. It's just…" How could he put it? "I didn't really believe it."

He sat up on one elbow and looked at her. How was it possible that Kix was in his bed? Jake found himself blinking two or three times in disbelief until she became real.

"What are you doing today?" he asked.

"I have to work at three," she said.

"Oh..."

"What are *you* doing today?"

"I'm supposed to meet Sacha to finish the Christmas wash for the Swamp Zombie platform in *TerrorCity*. Are you busy later?" he asked.

She smiled. "I'm not off until eleven."

"If you're not doing anything after, maybe you could come over here and hang out. We could watch a movie or something?"

"We did that *last* night," she said.

She rolled over to the edge of the bed and stood up. The sheet fell away, and again Jake had the vague feeling that none of this could be real. She was so beautiful it made him sad. She stood in the middle of his room, looking like a lingerie model. He wasn't sure if it was okay to stare.

"Besides, I can't. I've got something."

"What?" he said and sat up. "I mean, sure, that's cool. Don't worry about it. I just thought—"

But he never finished his sentence. Kix had found her underwear and as she shimmied into them, the connection from his brain to his mouth stopped working.

"...I don't know what I thought," he said at last.

"Look..." She picked her jeans up off the floor and sat back down on the bed. "I had a great time last night, I swear, but I have a bunch of boring paperwork and stuff I need to do and I don't know how long it's going to take. Plus, you said you were going to be busy anyway. I don't want to bother you if you're working."

"Oh, that's cool," he said. "Sacha has to get up early for an interview tomorrow, so we're probably not going to work late." This was a complete lie, but Jake didn't know how else to backpedal.

"What about your swamp zombies?"

"Christmas swamp zombies. They can wait. It's not even Halloween yet."

She sat down on the edge of the bed next to him. The smell of her made his thoughts go hazy for a moment. She smelled so delicious, spicy and sweet. Jake wanted to bury his nose into the sleepy tangle of her hair but he didn't know the etiquette for smelling girls and he didn't want to look weird, so he didn't.

"I'm trying to remember that level. Is that the one with the axe-wielding psychopath that looks like Ronald Reagan?"

"You remember that?"

"I like how when you kill him, he salutes you."

She saluted him, and Jake had a minor anxiety attack. Even though they'd had sex like, twice already, he was still having a difficult time getting over the fact that Pizza Girl was in his room, sitting on his bed. He wanted to touch her somewhere, to make it all real again. He wanted to, but he didn't.

"I didn't know you played *TerrorCity*."

"Brad did."

"Brad?"

She stood up to wiggle into her pants. "Look, I should probably go. I'll try to come by tonight if I can."

"Sure," said Jake, still wondering who Brad was. "I'd like that."

She ducked out into the other room, and he used the brief moment of privacy to throw on some jeans and overanalyze what she meant by *I'll try*. It probably meant she didn't want to come over but was trying to be nice about it. He should give her a way out. It would be easier than listening to the I-like-you-but-as-a-friend speech. Still, he waited a moment before walking out to the living room.

"Hey, you know, you don't have to worry about this evening if you're too busy. We can catch up later if you want." He smiled but couldn't quite meet her eye.

She tightened the lace on her boot with a flourish, stood up, and walked over to him. Jake froze, not wanting to make any awkward movements. Or maybe he was terrified. He really couldn't tell.

"I'm not giving you the brush-off. I honestly do have stuff to do this evening."

Then she leaned into him and kissed him on the neck, so Jake decided to believe her.

APARTMENT 2C

TOESY SLUNK DOWN THE HALL toward the smell. It was a bite-sized smell full of bug-eyed fear and wood chips. He loved that smell. The man stood in the kitchen arranging food in the refrigerator. He did not see a cat sneak past.

The formidable-looking door at the end of the hall posed no obstacle for Thanatos and his glorious thumbs, although this was mainly because it had a lever-style door handle.

Toesy stood up on his hind legs and reached out with his paw. From tip to tail, he could stretch himself over four and a half feet. He'd gotten quite good at door handles. It was locks that troubled him. Toesy pulled the lever handle down, pushed forward, and fell gracefully into the room.

Although it was daylight, the room was very dark. Heavy curtains blocked most of the sunlight from the window, but Toesy felt no fear. He saw better in the dark than most animals. He was getting a little thick around the middle because of it, too.

The scent of cedar chips saturated the air, and Toesy's eyes dilated in response. He stalked into the room, confident and slow. The squirrel-thing was in here. He could feel it.

In the blackness, he snuffled along the carpet toward the back wall. The room had little in the way of furniture: a small bed, a nightstand, a desk and chair. On top of the desk sat a bird cage. From this angle, Toesy could not tell how large it was.

As he approached the desk, a strange buzzing started up. Toesy stopped padding along the carpet to listen. It came from the floor of the cage.

A bark rang out. Toesy did not flinch, although he was quite puzzled. No dog lived in this building. The only dog near enough was that ridiculous German shepherd across the street.

From somewhere above came another short bark, followed this time by a hiss. Toesy looked up but saw nothing. Were he any other cat, he might have turned tail at that moment. But he was not. He was Thanatos, and Horsey House was his realm. He would not be intimidated by something that looked like a squirrel with racing stripes. He padded on.

At the desk, Toesy sat up on his haunches in order to see the cage better. From the floor, it looked enormous. From desk height, it looked too big to be allowed in the room. He took a tentative sniff around the water dish clipped to the side. It smelled strongly of skittering, twitching, and urine. The animal had been there recently. Toesy could smell the faint odor of its fur.

Suddenly, a grey shadow flew out of the darkness and dove toward his face. Toesy ducked and fell backward. The hissing started again. Sitting back up on his haunches, Toesy set his whiskers in a friendly posture and scooted slowly up to peek over the desktop again.

Inside the cage, he could see nothing. He stood another skosh higher. The air thrummed with tension, tiny vibrations of fury that might have been funny were they not so very serious. Toesy felt a thrill of something he hadn't felt in a long time.

He inched his way up farther and snuffled a long, slow snuffle. The scent of the squirrel-thing's distress made Toesy wary. He had seen fear this strong before. It did brave and irrational things. He could almost be scared of this fear.

He trilled a small chirrup of goodwill. The hissing deepened. He inched toward the cage, hoping to provoke it into showing itself.

Mrp? he said.

There was no response for a second; then the squirrel-thing exploded into fury. It hit the side of the cage, hissing and waving and dancing some sort of ferocious hula. Tiny claws, smaller than Toesy's teeth, waved a warning. Its miniscule feet twitched in frenetic circles as Toesy watched, entranced by the depth of its fear.

What in the name of Seafood Flavor was it doing?

He had no intention of hurting such a fascinating creature. Not quite a rat, not nearly squirrel enough, he wanted nothing more than to smell it up one side and down the other. Whatever a sugar glider may be, from where he sat, it did not smell like sugar. It did not even smell of pastry. It smelled more opossum-ish than anything. He remained far enough away for safety and took a great snuffle.

Opossum, but not quite....

It ate a lot of fruit....

And it was...female?

Toesy stayed still and kept his whiskers friendly until she calmed down enough to stop moving. Then he slowly scooted up to the cage and poked his nose through the bars.

A threatening hiss, followed by a flash of ivory, and Toesy felt a spike pierce his nose. She bit him! He sneezed and tried backing out of the cage but she'd grabbed onto the short whiskers nearest his eyes and would not let go.

"What in the world is all this noise back here? I thought you were supposed to sleep during the day."

The man walked in and switched on the overhead light. The sudden assault on his eyes made Toesy blink. The squirrel-possum used the confusion to get a better hold on Toesy's face. Her claws now stood a whisper away from his eyes.

The man gasped when he saw Toesy and the squirrel-possum locked in their curious standoff. "Don't you dare eat Pansy, you brute!"

Toesy took no heed of the man. All Toesy saw was the squirrel-possum. She was a lot of squirrel-possum to behold.

And her name was Pansy?

The black beads of her eyes followed his every twitch. Her tiny body shook with fear and undisguised wrath. If he so much as blinked wrong, Toesy was quite sure she would have a go at his eyeballs. In the background, the man shouted and leapt about.

"What in Our Lord's name are you doing?" he said.

"Let go of Pansy!" he said.

"Connie will kill me if you eat her sugar bear!" he said.

"Get out of here, you monster!" he said.

None of it did any good. The massive cat and the sugar glider were locked in some form of warfare the man could not understand. It was predator and prey. A battle of sexes. A war of worlds.

And Toesy didn't think he was winning.

FOUR MINUTES

THE TWO ANIMALS had been locked in some sort of weird trance going on four minutes now. Nick had jumped and shouted and pleaded and finally just sat down. They hadn't moved an inch.

He contemplated the inevitable disaster. Connie loved that stupid sugar bear. If the cat ate it, she would never talk with him again. His chance would be gone before he even had it. How did the horrible thing get into the apartment?

He sat, brooding over the dilemma until the air in the room grew itchy. He had no idea what was going on in the wild kingdom. Had he been paying more attention, Nick might have seen that the defenseless creature in this situation sat outside of the cage.

After another minute, something happened. Later on, Nick would swear he had seen nothing out of the ordinary. He probably hadn't latched the cage properly. He certainly didn't see the monster cat reach out with his forepaw and push the latch up slowly. He absolutely did not watch as the cat snapped the door open with a dexterity no cat should possess.

He held up the book, a compendium of Shakespeare's works, in case he needed to defend himself. If Nick was being honest with himself he'd have to admit that he didn't think it would have much of an effect on this particular cat, but he held it up anyway. It made him feel safer.

With glacial slowness, Pansy let go of the cat's eyelids and reared away. The cat backed its nose from the cage and sat upright on its considerable haunches. Neither blinked. They had almost started to relax when Nick opened his mouth and ruined everything.

"Are you both done?"

The crack of his voice shot through the tension, mobilizing the enemies. Pansy leapt from her sitting position in an impossible trajectory out the now open door of the cage. Nick watched in horror as the monster cat jumped to catch her.

Surely the thing would eat her. This cat was going to catch and eat his not-even-current-and-soon-to-be-ex-girlfriend's pet.

Nick lifted the book higher to bring it down on the thing's head but hesitated at the last moment. The cat did catch Pansy, but not in its teeth. Instead, it stuck out its neck and ducked down. Pansy landed on its back with a small squeak and grabbed onto its ears.

"What are you doing?" said Nick.

They did not stay long enough for him to find out.

PANSY

FACED WITH THE MENACING TEETH of the bloodthirsty killer and the anesthetizing boredom of her prison cage, Pansy chose to end it all. Why would she do any different? This empty life had nothing left to offer.

She spent her days waiting for Connie to come home, only to be shunted aside for the television. She spent her nights waiting for a few minutes of morning freedom, followed by another grueling stretch of staring through bars. They never did anything fun anymore. Rarely was she allowed out of the apartment because Connie's two biggest fears in the world were that Pansy would *get loose* and *get eaten by something*—in that order.

There was that one time that Mr. Jeff took her to a package store, tucked away in his jacket pocket. Pansy had loved every minute of that adventure, even though the store had no packages that she could see—only brightly colored bottles. But when Connie found out what Mr. Jeff had done, they had an argument that involved lots of shouting and a slammed door.

Pansy never saw Mr. Jeff again. She missed him. Probably not as much as Connie did, but what's done is done. He would not come back.

After that day, life had slowly withered into an unappetizing buffet of loneliness. Ten minutes of couch time in the morning, an uneventful dinner of bland grubs and iceberg lettuce, and staring at the idiot box until ten when Connie tucked her back into her cage, said "Good morning!" and left her in gloomy isolation for another eight long hours.

Pansy hated what her life had become. There was no spontaneity anymore. Days blended into each other until they became meaningless. Food had no taste. Colors washed away. Nothing promised excitement. No one came to visit.

She wanted more. She wanted tastes, bitter and sweet. She wanted the smell of grass and flowers. She wanted wind to ruffle her fur and rain to soak her to the skin. She wanted heart-stopping adventure, bone-chilling fear, and nausea-inducing romance. And if she could not have those, she wanted *out*.

So when faced with a choice between the gaping, slavering maw of a ferocious predator and the soul-sucking loneliness of her prison cage, Pansy grasped the opportunity with both forepaws and threw herself at destiny.

But the predator had not consumed her. In fact, he had been rather considerate in the way he moved his head to catch her as she flung herself into oblivion.

Now, perched on top of this magnificent beast's head like a jaunty marsupial cap, she felt a certain sense of calm. If the hunter chose to eat her, so be it. She was not afraid anymore. There was nothing left to fear. She had seen death, and it had not taken her. She would not spend her waning hours of life cowering from unnamed evils. She intended to seize this day and shake the ever-loving bejeezus out of it before she died.

THE MORNING SHIFT

BRAD WANTED TO GO BACK to the portal last night but when he checked the employee lot at closing, Karen's car was gone. Dennison's was still parked two stalls down though so he changed gears. It might be a good time to have that little chat with Mr. Funny Man, maybe put him straight. He wasted twenty minutes in search of Dennison before he realized that he was gone too. Dammit. They probably left together.

After his shift, he went straight to Karen's house but her car wasn't there. It wasn't anywhere in a four-block radius. He'd driven past Dennison's house too but her car wasn't there either. After an hour of fruitless searching, he finally went home, disgusted with himself and determined to do better in the morning.

Now, with a few hours of sleep behind him, he was calmer. His thoughts were clearer. He was confident he would find her. There was no need for urgency.

Three of the cars parked along the curb in front of Karen's new apartment building were unfamiliar to Brad. He noted the plate numbers down of a scrap of paper to run a plate check later but even if they were a dead end, he wasn't concerned. In fact, he was feeling rather optimistic about the day. This was his day. The world was going to change for him today, he just knew it.

He checked the time on his dashboard and smiled as he headed towards the freeway entrance. The morning crew didn't clock in until eight on Saturdays. It was only ten past six. He had plenty of time.

The stall door was locked, just as he'd left it last night. Brad thought about locking the whole bathroom but decided against it. It was

Saturday. The Bunny Bus from Maple Acres Retirement Villa would be here at nine a.m. and if the bathroom was closed, they would have a senior riot on their hands.

He crawled underneath the door and began searching for the portal. A minute later, he still couldn't find the damn spot. Another minute and he started to panic. He fell all over the tile, running his hand along the grout. He was about to give in to his urge to kick the shit out of the door when his thumb brushed over a crack that pulsed with energy. He stared at it, gritting his teeth, willing the portal to open back up.

The crack looked more like a spot of black. Then the spot fell away at the edges making it wider and wider until he could see nothing. *His* nothing. The nothing no one else had ever seen. He'd found it.

Next came the white spot. Brad knew the white spot was key. He concentrated on it until it grew large enough for him to see faint scribbles within, corners and lines that resolved themselves into tantalizing shapes like puppets behind a screen. He focused on the shapes, pushing his mind farther and farther out into the void.

Brad knew how this should work. There should be zaps of energy and wind and swirly blue magical crap. But it didn't happen like that. There were no sparkles or electrical shocks of any kind. It was neither mystical nor magical. Yes, there was a tiny glow, but it hadn't lasted more than a second. It felt almost pedestrian, like the Universe picked up its coat and scooted over one seat to allow another bit of reality to sit down. And suddenly, the shapes behind the screen reorganized themselves into a scene. It was almost anticlimactic in its likeness to his own reality, especially since the new reality looked a lot like the beer aisle at the Safeway.

He stepped forward. Where he expected his hand to meet with the tiled bathroom wall, it met with nothing. An overwhelming urge to sneeze caught him, but he stifled it. Instead, he pushed his arm through the wall. Or at least he tried to. There was nothing to push against. His arm just hung in the air as though inviting the rest of his body to step through and help itself to a beer from the refrigerated case. The air felt cool.

The watch on his wrist caught his attention and Brad smiled. He didn't own a watch like that. He liked it, though. It had a big face with lots of dials. It was shiny, too. Wear a watch like that, and people would definitely think twice about messing with you.

That's when he made the mistake of looking at the edge of the hole. Instantaneously, it filled his mind. It shrank down to nothing, with his arm still in it! He jumped back in anticipation of blood or pain or maybe ectoplasmic goo, but nothing like that happened. His arm was still attached. The fancy watch was gone, replaced by his crappy digital telling him it was 7:02.

Brad found the crack again by running his hand across the wall until his fingers tingled. This time it yawned open without delay. The beer cooler was back. He could even hear someone saying something over an intercom.

"Produce, Line Two, please."

SPY DIRT

DIABO FELL FROM THE BOX to the strange hard ground. It was the color that ground should be, but there was nothing ground-like about it. For one thing, it had no tiny rocks or small plants over which he had to step. It was smooth—perhaps they had this kind of ground in larger villages? Diabo knew enough about villagers to stay alert. They would try to kill him without a second glance.

The ground was much cooler on his abdomen than he anticipated which made him mince along the floor until he came up against the trunk of a tree so large it appeared to be flat. He tried to climb the tree in order to get a better look around, but found that its bark was too smooth and straight to get a foothold. At length, he eased his abdomen onto the cold floor and gave way to his thoughts.

A set of boots stomped the ground next to him, and Diabo concluded that he must be in one of the bananito's nests. Every other human nest he'd been in had felt much smaller and warmer by comparison, though. Perhaps he had found their queen?

The floor here shook with slow-moving wheels and deafening footfalls. There were many humans nearby. For a moment, the imagined panic of ten humans flying in terror overrode the empty hole in his middle, and Diabo relaxed his stance. If he did this correctly, it could become the most *excelente* game of *os Gritos* ever.

A set of smaller feet that squeaked as they walked approached him. Diabo was still weak with hunger, but he recognized an opportunity when he saw one. The squeaky shoes tripped closer to him. This was a hatchling—he could tell by its higher-pitched sounds and the fact that it smelled strongly of milk. If he could crawl up one of the hatchling's feet, he could pretend to bite it. Then, when the mother saw him, she would surely let out a shriek strong enough to curdle human blood.

The squeaky shoe came closer. Diabo marshaled all his strength and jumped. He landed square on the top of its foot. But when the drooling, bumbling hatchling saw him, Diabo began to doubt the wisdom of his plan.

"Spy dirt!" it said and followed this declaration with a bouncing sound Diabo sometimes heard the bananitos make when they were all together and smiling. He did not understand why they made this sound but found that he often had better results if he struck in the middle of it.

Diabo planted his back four legs on the hatchling's foot and waved his front legs menacingly.

"SPY DIRT DANCING!" it shouted and made the bouncing sound again. "Mama! SPY DIRT DANCING!"

At this exclamation, the mother turned her attention to the hatchling. Diabo waved his leg spines at her.

"Oh, icky!" she said in a depressingly mid-ranged shout. Diabo was discouraged for only a second before remembering his fangs. He menaced the child with his waving feet and slavering fangs. Surely, as soon as the mother saw the blood-red hairs on his chelicerae, her screaming would start in earnest.

"Sweetie, what did mommy say about wolf spiders? You have *got* to stop picking them up. They could be poisonous or something."

With a practiced sweep of her toe, the mother kicked Diabo from the hatchling's foot. He tumbled into a ball and landed with a *whump* underneath another one of the strange flat-trunked trees.

Diabo had no idea what just happened. He had never been defeated before. Worse than that, he had never been *mocked* before. He did not like it, *at all*.

He missed his tree. It was a glorious tree with warm, sandy hidey-holes near the roots and moist, green hidey-holes near the top. The tree which he currently sat beneath had neither of these things. It was cold and smooth and hummed occasionally. Lit from the inside by two weak suns, this tree bore colorful *cerveja* fruit, which Diabo only recognized because the bananitos sometimes ate them with their midday meal. Until now, he hadn't realized they grew on trees.

Diabo thought about his tree and grew maudlin. He was having a difficult time accepting the defeat. It occurred to him that perhaps the mother had not understood the threat. He could not imagine why this would be so. Every human within a week's trek from his tree knew and feared Diabo.

He had threatened to kill her hatchling! But she did not fear him. He had tried to pierce her hide with his leg spines, but she wore a protective coating of rubber, and he could gain no purchase. Instead of screaming and running away, she kicked him like a dog. Like *um vira-lata!*

Then she called him a *wolf* spider.

Diabo did not know what a wolf spider was, but clearly, it was an inferior being. The human woman had treated a wolf spider as one might treat a cowardly dog, with kicks and disdain. Diabo understood and even appreciated that treatment—so long as it was directed at the weaker, more deserving creatures. But Diabo was the strongest! He was the deadliest! The woman *must* have been mistaken.

He kept his lateral eyes trained on the open area of the human nest and used his middle eyes to look up to the cerveja tree. It glowed intermittently from within from the light of two cold, white suns. Diabo had never seen more than one sun before and never one that could turn on and off as rapidly these two did. When they blinked on, the light they gave off barely registered in the chromagraphic scale.

At length, he found a seam running up the trunk of the cerveja tree that he could exploit. He would climb to the top and orient himself within this human nest. If he climbed high enough, maybe he could find where they kept the real sun. Then he could find his jungle. Heartened by this idea, Diabo set about trying to find purchase on the cerveja tree's slippery-smooth trunk.

He'd only just crested the lower part when his lateral eyes warned him of impending danger. A human approached. He scrunched his legs into a jumping stance in case the human meant to do him harm, but the cerveja tree was very cold, and he was very hungry. He could not get his frozen joints to work well. The most he could do was try to get out of the way.

The human came closer. With all eight of his eyes, Diabo watched him lift a leg and aim a kick in his direction. His joints may be sluggish, but his instincts were not. He coiled his legs and leapt, clearing the metallic bark and landing in a nest of cerveja fruit a split second before the foot came crashing into the spot he'd just occupied. The tree's suns blinked back on.

"I hate wolf spiders," the human said and walked away at a leisurely pace.

In the cold belly of the cerveja tree, Diabo did what wandering spiders do best: He hid inside a bunch of fruit and let the anger wash over him. If one more of these humans called him *wolf spider*, he was going to bite the *merda* out of them until they were dead.

SHE SAID SHE MIGHT COME OVER

MAYBE I'LL STOP BY after my shift?

Jake read the message and tried to put his heart back into his chest. Why was that a question? Did she think he didn't want her to stop by? He typed his response and hit send. *I'll be here!* He didn't want seem needy. Did he sound needy? Did that imply that he would be sitting at home waiting for her? He had no idea.

Jake argued with himself all the way to the store entirely overlooking the fact that the text had come in last night. Up ahead, the lights of the grocery store shone on through the grey Seattle afternoon.

She might stop by. After her shift.

The Eighty-Five Cent Lady stood in front of the grocery store entrance, smelling like lemon vodka and old shoes. She'd been panhandling this stretch of Broadway for years. Jake didn't give her money any more. Occasionally he bought her sandwiches and coffee. It helped to keep her from getting interested in his coat pockets. He didn't mind panhandlers, but the Eighty-Five Cent Lady could teach pickpocketing to a rat. She would gladly relieve you of the Devil's Finest Con (as she called it). All you had to do was show her where you kept your wallet. No one walked away from her a sinner.

"Hey man, you got eighty-five cents?"

"Sorry." Jake jammed his hands in his pockets, looked at the ground, and sidestepped into the store.

He cut through the floral department to the bakery, still arguing with himself. His brain overflowed with so many logical reasons for Kix to cancel that he felt nauseous. He focused on his grocery list.

Last week Sacha made everyone pulled-pork sandwiches for the metrics meeting. At first Jake had teased him for being a terrible Jew, but then he ate the sandwich and had to apologize. He'd had no idea regular people could make food taste like that. Sacha just laughed and told him it was easy.

Facing an afternoon of compiling code and anxiety, Jake thought he might try making some of those sandwiches himself. He even looked up a recipe before he left for the store but now he couldn't remember if Kix ate pork or not. Bacon was pork, wasn't it?

In the thirteen years that he had been shopping in this store, Jake had never once talked to a butcher. He'd always assumed that they were like stockers for steaks and stuff—but when he finally broke down and admitted that he had no idea what a pig shoulder even *looked* like, the butcher-guy came out from his little meat room all smiles and lemme-help-yas. Not only did he find Jake the right cut of meat, he also suggested a few things to add to the recipe and pointed him in the direction of the Mexican food aisle. Who would have guessed butchers were so nice?

The imported foods section was exactly where the butcher-guy said it would be. Everything went smoothly until he got to the dried chilies. Ancho? Guajillo? Serrano? Arbol? What the hell? The butcher only said *chilies*, he never said there were different *kinds*. Crap. What if one was super-duper spicy and Kix hated it? He didn't want to make some sort of death-wish pork sandwich.

Toward the end of the aisle, a woman with two young kids came strolling around the corner. The kids argued loudly over a box of sugary cereal while she studied the end cap of baking supplies as though her sanity depended on it. Judging by the way the kids fired questions at her, Jake thought it probably did. If she was tuning all *that* out, she probably wouldn't notice if he just...

He grabbed a small packet of chili powder off the shelf and tried to tear it open as quietly as he could. Unfortunately, whoever sealed that particular bag of chili powder must have been preparing for the zombie apocalypse because the damn thing refused to open. Jake pulled and pulled on the plastic packaging, but it would not give. He snuck another peek at the sugar cereal kids to make sure they weren't watching. Their mother was still in a Zen-like shopping trance, entirely calm in the middle of the sugar-induced storm around her. He gave the plastic bag one more half-hearted try.

Suddenly, like all jackass packaging everywhere, the bag gave way. It ripped in half, sending a quarter-ounce cloud of chipotle pepper powder into the air.

Jake gasped. It was the wrong thing to do. Fire and spice filled his head. He sneezed violently as he waved his hands in the air to clear it. The sugar cereal kids broke out in laughter.

"That guy is going to die, Mom. Look!" said the older kid.

"Not today, dear. Put it back," said the mom.

Jake's eyes began to flood with tears. He shook his head to clear them but only succeeded in making himself dizzy. He clamped his eyes shut and sneezed again. Overhead, he could hear the zip-zap noise of the fluorescent lighting as it flickered. The kids had stopped laughing.

He stayed motionless and breathed as shallowly as he could until the dust cloud settled. *Screw this*, he thought. *I need some stupid chilies, not a chemical peel.* Through squinted eyes, he grabbed one of everything and dumped them into his basket. He would figure it out when he got home.

The beer aisle was empty save for a large rectangular hulk sitting on the floor and a female-shaped blob near the coolers. The floor hulk was probably a pallet of something. Jake's eyes watered too much to make out any detail on the female-blob, only that she had blonde hair and judging from the location of her blurry silhouette, was interested in domestic beer.

"Hey, you okay?"

Jake jumped. Behind him stood a gigantic blue duck. He rubbed his eyes with the insides of his wrists. The picture resolved into a tall guy wearing a bright blue coat and ball cap. Below the cap, all Jake could see was a chin so chiseled he could sharpen a knife on it.

"You look like you could use some help, Cuz," said the guy. As he did so, he turned his head slightly giving Jake the impression that he was also talking to the female-blob near the beer case.

"Um...thanks but I'm fine. I just got some chili in my eye."

"I saved a girl from being mugged once in Chengdu and got a face full of *la jiao jiang* for my troubles, so I know what it's like. Sit down, Brah, I got you."

Before he could protest again, Ball Cap marched him over to the hulking thing. It turned out to be a pallet of Mountain Dew. Or maybe it was Sprite. Whatever it was, it was green. Jake sat down and wiped the tears from his eyes with the inside of his coat.

"Nah, nah, don't rub your eyes. You need to flush them with something," said Ball Cap. But Jake's eyes were beginning to clear, and his lungs weren't as spicy as before. The situation began to resolve itself around him, and what he saw made him angry.

The blonde blob had given up her search for beer and wandered over to watch. She was beautiful, dressed up for the evening and very probably the reason for this whole Good Samaritan charade. Jake wasn't about to be someone's stooge, least of all this asshole's.

"Look, I'm fine." He tried to stand up, but the guy pushed him back down by the shoulders.

"Just sit down, Brah, you're all jacked up. Excuse me, *Miss*? Maybe you could help us? Please could you hand us a bottle of that water behind you?" He laughed a hearty laugh of goodwill and fabulous intent. Behind him, the blonde woman giggled.

"Certainly," she said.

Jake wanted to punch Ball Cap in the nose. Instead he scrunched his eyes closed to squeeze the rest of the tears from them. When he opened them again the guy had removed his hat and was right up in his face, trying to look in his eyes. Jake jerked his head backward.

"Tilt your head sideways, Brah, I'll pour the water for you." The blonde woman now stood behind Ball Cap, looking worried.

"I'm fine," Jake said. The powdered chili stung his eyes, but he no longer cared. He stood up, forcing Ball Cap back a step. Jake ignored him. He walked over to the beer case and grabbed the nearest six-pack of something and kept walking. Behind him, the blonde woman giggled again.

"I guess you can't help everyone," Jake heard Ball Cap say. Then he turned the corner and walked to the farthest register, so he wouldn't have to hear any more.

IN THROUGH THE FRONT DOOR

WHO DID THAT GUY think he was? How dare he use Jake to pick up women? He splashed down the sidewalk, half angry, half anxious, until he turned down his block.

Ahead of him on the sidewalk, a vaguely woman-shaped person struggled to anchor herself against a rocket-powered dog. It pulled her along, oblivious to the rain, the mud, the puddles and the occasional scream of "*I said leave it!*"

As he neared the poor woman, he recognized her. She lived in the house across the street. She looked up at him as he walked past. Jake nodded.

"Hey!" she said. She looked ready to say more but her dog had other plans. The leash jerked sideways causing the woman to stumble into Jake who lost his balance and fell sideways into a rhododendron. The handles of his paper grocery sack tore away, launching most of his foodstuffs into the air. The six pack of beer he'd been holding hit the ground sideways with a muffled crack.

"Oh crap, *sorry!*" said the woman. She followed that statement closely with a slightly angrier "*Oh crap!*" as the leash flew from her hands and the dog, free at least, tore across the lawn and into a laurel hedge on the far side. She shouted apologies one more time and dove after her rocket-dog.

"Don't worry about it," he said to no one as he dug himself out of the soggy rhododendron. Dried chilies littered the ground. A small puddle of porter had formed around one of the beer bottles although the rest seemed to be intact. He gathered up the remaining bottles and shoved them back into the cardboard holder.

The pork shoulder had proven surprisingly aerodynamic. Jake found it in the neighbor's yard covered in mud and pine needles where the packaging had torn away.

"You have got to be kidding me," he said. Then he sighed. Maybe this was the Universe telling him he should order a pizza. At least he'd get to see Kix.

Jake rounded up his muddy groceries. Shoving everything but the beer back into the torn paper sack, he marched up to the front entrance of the house. Usually he went around the side to the back entrance but he was not in the mood for any more crap. He would use the secret entrance.

The secret entrance to the basement apartment made most people jealous that they didn't get to live in such a cool house, but Jake and Carl rarely used it. For one thing, the stairwell was super narrow, and although there were a few glass bricks set in the outside wall to light the space during the day, there was only one anemic light bulb to see by night. Jake thought it made everything look creepy. Add to that the fact that the knob on the door at the bottom of the stairs always jammed if you turned it too fast, and the key often got stuck in the lock on account of it being one of the first deadbolts Jake had ever installed himself, and it was usually easier to just go around.

"Al. Tess." He nodded at the stone horses that flanked the front door. They did not nod back. The key pad booped as Jake entered the code, and he let himself into the building.

The grand stairway dominated the entrance to Horsey House— an elegant concoction of oak and brass inlay that, when properly polished, glittered in the sun like a glass slipper. Unfortunately, when polished, the stairs were also slicker than snot; which is why Jake only polished them when Gloria did her yearly building inspection. He marched around to the side where the secret bookshelf entrance was, but his hands were too full of wet groceries and muddy beer to reach the book that opened the secret door. When he shifted the bag around so he could reach it, the pork roast slipped from the sack and fell right on top of his foot.

"Oh, that is *it*," said Jake and set down the beer. He picked up the pork roast and marched over to the row of mailboxes with his groceries. Using his master key, he opened Sacha's mailbox and stuffed the pork roast in. Then he threw in the chilies and whatever else would fit, and slammed the door shut before anything fell out.

"Special delivery," he said and tossed the wet sack into the waste basket reserved for junk mail.

Merow.

Jake turned around to see Toesy staring down through the second floor railing at him, whiskers pointed forward with joyous salutation or approval, it was hard to tell sometimes.

"Hey Toesy! What are you up to?"

Mrrrp, said Toesy and ducked away from the railing.

Jake didn't move. He knew little chirrups like that meant Toesy had something he wanted to share. Usually, it was half a rat, but Jake always stuck around to see what it was because one time, it was a whole gopher. It took him an hour to shoo the thing out of the house. Afterward, it became a common sight to find Toesy sitting in the sunshine, communing with mounds of dirt. Jake pretended not to see that part.

"What have you got *this* time?" he said, mostly to himself though because being snarky to a cat was useless. He waited a few seconds until Toesy's head reappeared near the top of the stairs.

At first, it looked to Jake as though Toesy was wearing a tiny coonskin cap, like a feline Daniel Boone. But when he stepped closer, he thought maybe it was just a really furry eye patch. Certainly *something* was on the cat's head. Something with a tail. Then the tail twitched, and he realized the hat-patch was alive.

"What, er...*who* are you wearing?" said Jake.

Merrr, said Toesy, and a tiny head, fashioned mostly out of eyeballs and fuzz, popped up.

Ark, said the eyeballs and fuzz.

"What the hell is that?" said Jake.

Ark, said the eyeballs and fuzz again. Toesy looked pleased. Or maybe worried. Again, it was sometimes hard to tell with him.

"Okay." Said Jake. Toesy blinked in recognition of him, but said no more.

"Well it was nice to meet you...tiny thing. I'll be downstairs if you guys need anything."

Mrrrp, said Toesy.

Jake nodded smartly and headed for the bookshelf behind the grand staircase. He reached up, tugged on a battered edition of *Moby-Dick* then stepped aside as the entire bookshelf swung outward. He turned back to Toesy and said, "You're welcome to join me, but I understand if you have, uh, plans" before disappearing.

*   *   *

Thanatos, Dark Lord of the Underworld, did not know what to do. Jake the Holy Man was upset, but the only upsetting thing Toesy had seen was the Holy Man himself. He was not all there.

Or rather, he *was* there—just not all the time. He flickered in and out like a guttering candle flame. Toesy had seen this kind of thing before, mostly in the fragrant people that lived in street alleys and empty basements. He used to be scared of the fragrant people, as some of them were not put off at the thought of roasted feline. But since his deification, they respected him more. They found Toesy to be a generous Dark Lord. He always had a rat or two to share.

But the Holy Man had never flickered before. That was worrisome.

Ark ark, said Pansy.

You saw that, too?

Ark, said Pansy.

You are very observant then. Not everyone can see the travelers. But he is a Holy Man, and I have heard that Holy Men can travel.

Toesy bowed his head. He had known the Holy Man for many months now, not once suspecting he had this power. It did not feel right.

All the same, we will be vigilant tonight and see what we see.

Ark? said Pansy.

Because I am afraid that this Holy Man may be traveling to places he should not go.

Ark, said Pansy.

Ark indeed, said Toesy.

THE END STALL

BRAD COULDN'T LOOK AWAY. The entire scene had played out so perfectly. James Dennison sitting on a pallet of soda, crying his little eyes out. When the snot bubbled out of his nose, Brad almost lost it. Dennison finally ran away with his tail between his legs.

He was still reeling in the glory of the moment when the blonde woman walked over. She looked directly at him and smiled.

"Are you a doctor?" she said.

"Oh gosh, no! I've never been that dedicated to workin' hard. I just make movies." He stuck out his hand. "My name is Thad."

As far as pickup lines went, Brad had seen few better. The girl nearly fell over her shoes trying to introduce herself.

"I'm Tracy," she said.

He followed the conversation. It was...easy. The blonde wrote down a number and handed it to him—or rather, the other him. *He said his name was Thad.* When she finally walked away, Thad turned to watch her go.

He flirted shamelessly with the cashier as he paid for his groceries. Outside, rain fell in fat cold drops that Brad could almost feel hit him, and he was relieved when he heard the *beep-beep* of a car-door remote. Thad walked south along the busy road and found his car, half a block down.

It was a late model Jeep—that much Brad could tell—but it wasn't a model he knew. The person on the other end of this reality portal or whatever it was unlocked the Jeep and put the bag of groceries in the back seat. Then he climbed into the front seat and started the car. Brad wondered if he should say anything to announce his presence? Could he even announce his presence? Maybe this was all a dream. If it was a dream, how was it so detailed? But philosophical thoughts of dreaming, lucid or not, were completely thrown from his train of thought as soon as the person at the other end of the reality divide tried to pull out into traffic. Reflected in the rearview mirror was a nearly identical version of himself.

He watched, dumbfounded as his other self checked for oncoming traffic. When Thad looked away from the mirror, Brad could no longer see his reflection so he stared at the hands. Those were his hands. But not his hands. They were his other self's hands. It was too dark to see how identical they might be, so he looked out the window at the street sliding by and saw that it was familiar and not familiar at the same time. More trees and shorter buildings, but Brad knew the neighborhood. He'd lived here. Well, not *here* here. Back in his world.

The situation was so absurd, Brad half expected them to turn left toward his apartment building, but they didn't. They turned right down a quiet street and from there onto an even quieter street, until they finally came to a stop in front of an old house that looked as though it had been sectioned off into apartments. He knew the house. This was Karen's house.

Karen, he said, though not out loud and certainly not to anyone but himself. He hadn't considered that anyone would be listening.

"Hello?"

Brad was startled. He didn't know how to respond. Should he speak? Was he supposed to think really hard? He didn't know, so he thought about saying, "Hello."

"Who is this? What are you doing in my head?"

"I'm Brad, and I'm in your head because I think we might be related somehow. I think I might be you—but in a different place."

"Dude, that doesn't make any sense. Is this because of those mushrooms? I knew I shouldn't have eaten those. You can't trust Cuban mushrooms."

"I don't know anything about mushrooms."

"Then why are you here?"

"I don't know. I found this spot. It was like a portal. It opened up, and here I am, like I'm supposed to be here or something. You're in my head. Or we're in each other's heads. I can see you and where you are. I live in a different world, though."

"Like where, like Mars? Are you using mental telepathy from Mars?"

"No, I think I'm from a different reality. I know that guy you were talking to in the grocery store. I know this town. I know this house. I know who lives here."

"I live here."

"You do? Who lives upstairs?"

"You mean Kix?"

"What's her name?"

"Kix. It's short for Katarina."

"In my world, she's Karen."

"What do you want with her?" said the other him. Brad felt the defensiveness around the words.

"Easy there, big guy. I think we're on the same team."

"Not if you're horning in on Kix, we're not. Get your own."

"Look, I don't even know how I got here, and I'm not horning in on anything. I don't need to, anyway. In my world, she moved out of this neighborhood three months ago. I helped her move. We've been dating ever since."

"I call bullshit on that."

"I take it you're not having the same luck here, then?"

"Hell no! She's so frigid her nipples are probably blue."

"I can fix that for you. How well do you know cars?"

ALTERNATOR PROBLEMS

KIX WOKE UP IN THE EARLY AFTERNOON disturbed by her dream. It wasn't a bad dream, it just had fewer clothes in it than normal. It certainly had more Jake than she was expecting. The content hadn't disturbed her nearly as much as how *real* it all felt.

She rolled out of bed, irrationally irritated with Jake. Dammit, how dare he have awesome dream-sex with her without permission? They weren't even like that. Although it's possible he was like that with someone else.

Dammit twice.

Her shift didn't start for two hours which meant that she could stay in bed for an hour, surfing the internet or she could get moving. Kix chose to get moving. Later, she would call Jake and figure out what was going on. Or maybe she wouldn't. She wasn't ready to forgive him just yet, which was awkward because she didn't know if she needed to.

Outside, the rain was picking up again. Or still. It never stopped long enough to start *again*. Kix had never experienced passive-aggressive rain until she moved to Seattle. It definitely took some getting used to.

She scoured her apartment for something to wear but the only truly clean things she could find were her pantsuit and that god-awful blue dress. Another, less-picky sweep turned up a clean-ish pair of jeans and an old Sleater-Kinney t-shirt that smelled faintly of garlic. These she threw on. Everything else she tossed in a pile and began to sort.

After everything was bundled, Kix sat near the front door, keys in hand ready to bolt as soon as the latest torrent of rain subsided.

When the roar on the roof dialed back to a low chatter Kix yanked her hood over her head and ran. Front door, stairs, around the house, car—from door to door, she only had thirty-eight seconds of rain. Of course, this was her third winter here, and she was getting pretty good at it.

The clock on her dash had fogged over, so Kix pulled out her phone. She had about forty minutes to get to work—plenty of time to get her laundry going. This day may have started out weird but she was beginning to feel optimistic. Maybe things wouldn't turn out so bad after all.

She jammed the key into the ignition and turned. Nothing happened. She turned the key again. Still nothing happened. Kix leaned forward and wiped the condensation from the clock face. There were no numbers. She reached up and flipped the dome light. It remained dark.

"*Come on,*" she said. The feeling of optimism still lingered, albeit faintly, so she tried the key one more time. One more time, nothing happened.

"For reals? What the hell, Maxine?"

Kix tried the key a fourth time, but she knew it wouldn't work. Maxine's alternator had been dicey lately. It was probably dead now, along with her battery. *Dammit.*

"Okay, fine. Be that way," she said and stuck her tongue out at the steering wheel. If she left right away, she could probably catch the next bus to the laundromat. Pizza Joe's was two blocks from there, and Marco would let her use his Monte Carlo for deliveries. She didn't like driving the Monte Carlo. It always smelled weird, like one of those pine tree air fresheners got beaten up by a head of feral garlic or something. It also meant spending tomorrow getting a new battery, but maybe this was a good thing. Maybe she didn't want to be free tomorrow. Maybe she wanted to have something else to do instead of waiting for her stupid phone to ring. Outside, the rain poured down. Maybe she would do her laundry tomorrow, too.

But the moist interior of the car was warming with her body heat, and the smell of pizza sauce became unmistakable. Even if it was just undies and t-shirts, she needed to get some laundry done. The clock on her phone said she had five minutes to get to the bus stop.

"Hey there!"

Kix let out a surprised squeak and turned around. Thad stood in the window, rainwater dripping from his hood. He smiled and made roll-down-the-window circles with his hand. The last thing she wanted right now was Thad's attention. She rolled the window down.

"You need some help?"

"Hey, Thad, that's okay, I—"

Kix almost told him she was going to take the bus but thought better of it. Thad saw her at a bus stop once. He parked his Suburban right in the middle of the bus lane to offer her a ride and stayed there so long badgering her about getting in his car that her bus pulled up behind him. The bus driver wouldn't open the doors until he moved out of the way and she had to get in his stupid car just to get him to move. She'd watched the bus drive off without her and had to listen to Thad talk about how generous he was all the way home.

Kix sighed. She saw two options on how to deal with this. They both included Thad. She chose the option that didn't mean getting into his car.

"Actually, if you could give me a jump, that would be awesome." Thad's smile went crooked and his eyes lit up. She probably shouldn't have phrased it that way.

"No problem, little lady," he said. "Lemme just pull my rig around." He winked.

Kix tried to smile but failed miserably. She wanted to use her time to figure out what to do with this day, not spend it with someone who thought sexual innuendo was charming. Rain came down through the window so she rolled it up, but not all the way though because she didn't want Thad sneaking up on her again.

He walked to his car and Kix pieced together a plan. If she could get Maxine running, she could drive to work and park in the back. From there she could walk to the Laundromat. If she did it all just right, she might still be able to get some laundry started before her shift. Maybe the day wasn't completely lost.

Thad drove up the street from the opposite direction. Street side parking was packed so he pulled his Suburban alongside Maxine and cut the engine. Then he jumped out of his truck like he was doing the world a favor by parking in the middle of the road.

"Okay, pop the hood," he said and walked around to the front of Kix's car.

She took a deep breath and tried to feel grateful for the help as she pulled the hood-release lever.

With the hood propped up between them, she couldn't see Thad as he clamped the cable to her battery. But when he came around to clamp the cables to the Suburban's battery, she realized he'd parked so close to her door that he had to stand right next to her window. She tried to ignore him, but he stood about eight inches away.

"You going to work then?"

"Uh, yep," she said.

"You know when you didn't show up to the party, I thought you were working late again."

"I was working late."

"You came home at five, Kix. Don't tell me you were working that late."

"What is it to you? I was at a friend's house."

"No you weren't. If you were at a friend's house, you would have stayed until breakfast. But you didn't. You came home. So I guess no after party nookie for you, huh?"

"That's none of your business Thad."

"You weren't at a guy's house then?"

"I really don't want to talk about this."

"I'm just concerned for you is all Kix. I don't want to see you fall for a guy that's not that into you."

It took quite a bit of self-control for her not to reach through the window and throttle Thad. Why was he being such a dick? A better question would be, why was she surprised?

"First of all, this is still none of your business. And secondly, you don't even know him."

"I don't need to know him. I'm right. You want to know why?"

"Oh, please enlighten me."

Thad squatted down so that he was at eye level with Kix.

"If you were at my house that late, I would have done everything in my power to make you stay," he said.

He stayed low, near the window like he expected her to respond. But Kix didn't know what to say. A small part of her agreed with him and she didn't like that.

She closed her eyes, took a deep breath and exhaled slowly. Then she opened her eyes and looked at Thad squarely. "Can you start your engine please?"

"Hey, don't be mad. I'm just trying to look out for my girl."

"I am not your girl Thad. You don't have a girl. You'll sleep with anything that moves. Please let's just get this over with."

Something in Thad's eyes changed. The smile on his face froze, and he stared at her without emotion.

"You bet," he said. But he didn't leave. He stared at her through the window, making the space tight and uncomfortable.

"You know, I'm nice to you all the time. I invite you to my parties. I help you with your car. The least you could do is be nice back."

"*What?*"

"You always have to be such a *bitch* about everything."

She wanted to tell him off but there was a sliver of anger in his voice that she didn't recognize.

Thad glared at her for another second then stepped from the window. Kix rolled it up immediately. The SUV growled to life beside her and she reflexively hit the door-lock button.

It took three frantic tries, but Maxine's engine finally turned over. Kix concentrated on keeping the engine running as Thad removed the cables and closed the hood of his Suburban. When he snapped Maxine's hood back in place, he turned back to her window and stared at her. She rolled it down an inch but no more.

"You even gonna thank me?" he said.

"Thank you for the help."

"Guess I'll talk to you *never* then," he said, his jaw tight and angry. He marched back to his Suburban and revved the engine so loud, Kix thought he was going to drive straight into her. Without even looking, he lunged backward into the street then popped into gear and squealed away leaving a fishtail of rain water in his wake.

Kix didn't look to see where he was going, just that he went. She left before he decided to come back for any reason.

*   *   *

"Nicely done. Word for word. I liked that."

"What are you talking about? Did you even hear what she said? She said I would sleep with anything."

Brad could feel Thad's ego getting bruised. It was ridiculous. He had actually been hurt by what she said. *What a fool*, he thought—but not so loud that so Thad would hear.

"It's not your fault she can't recognize leadership skills, Thad. Don't beat yourself up about it. Trust me, she's going to change her mind in a little bit, anyway. That was just to prime the pump, if you will."

Siiiillllnix. A mosquito buzzed loudly near his ear.

"Do you hear that?" said Brad.

"Hear what?" said Thad. He sat quiet for a moment, listening, but the Universe remained silent.

"Nothing. Never mind," said Brad and immediately changed the subject. "She's mad right now because you're right, and she doesn't like it. The next time you talk to her, you have to show her you're just trying to help."

"How?"

"Give something up. Tell her something you're afraid of. It doesn't really matter what, make it up if you have to. You just need to sound honest."

Siillniiiix.

The mosquito turned up its volume, drawing Brad's attention. It wasn't a buzz, as he'd thought. It sounded more like the tinny voice from an old-time radio.

Radio.

"Islenix!"

And just like that, Brad was back. Locked inside the bathroom and staring again at the tiled wall.

"God *dammit* Islenix, where are you?"

The excitement of his success boiled away into anger. Brad tore the radio from his hip and shouted into it.

"*I'm here.*"

"Where the hell have you been? This is the second time I haven't been able to get you on the radio. I've been calling you for twenty minutes."

Before he replied, Brad made himself slow down, get his breathing under control. It wouldn't do to get angry at Paul. An idea struck him.

"Sorry, Paul, this radio must not have charged fully last night. The range on it is shot. I'm down here by the food court."

"Bullshit. Stop dinking around, and get up to the office. I got something here I need you to take a look at."

"Can you give me five minutes? I got a request for help, and I want to follow up on it."

Paul didn't answer right away. After a few seconds, he clicked on and sighed. "Fine, follow up your request—but then get your ass up here."

Brad ran his hand across the wall. He did not see the divide, but when he brushed his thumb over a crack in the grout it zapped him with static electricity. It was there, and it was his. He would find it again easily.

The *Out of Order* sign still hung on the door but it no longer felt like enough. He found some duct tape underneath the sink and ran a line of it down each side of the door, sealing it shut. If someone really wanted to be a punk they could get in, but Brad would be back soon. It should be safe enough until he returned.

He walked out of the men's room feeling confident. Dennison had been there. And Karen was there too, somewhere. Finding the portal could not have been coincidence. There was a reason that he, of all people, found it. And as he walked down the long, tiled hallway, Brad began forming ideas about what that reason was.

"SO, DO YOU *LIKE HER* LIKE HER?"

SAM COOKE SANG ABOUT *Another Saturday Night* while Deli sat on the arm of the couch, swinging her legs in time with the beat. She peppered Jake with all sorts of questions that he really wanted to answer but didn't because Deli was friends with Kix and he didn't want it getting back to her that he would kiss and tell.

"I thought that part was obvious," said Jake.

"Yeah, you're right. If it makes you feel any better, I'm pretty sure she likes you back."

"Really?" He tried not sounding hopeful. The smile on Deli's face widened.

"Well, I'm not *for sure* for sure, but I know she thinks you're funny. And she always asks what you guys are up to."

"Really? Like, how often?"

"Oh honestly, Jake, what are you, fourteen? I don't know statistics on stuff like that. She thinks you're funny, and she talks about you a lot, but not all the time because there is more to life than gossip and boys."

"Like what?" He hadn't meant to say that part. Deli rolled her eyes at him. She was really good at that.

"Freestyle kicking stances for starters. *And* there's a tourney coming up in Wenatchee that we're thinking about going to. It's small, but that's good. You have a much better chance of meeting talented people that way. I hear Marylyn Daniels is going to be there this year."

"Who's Marylyn Daniels?"

"Stop trying to change the subject, and tell me what happened last night."

"She came over, that's all. She came over and brought a pizza for that wave function experiment I was talking about last week."

"Oh my God. You two are such geeks," Deli smiled. "So did you win her heart through scientific research?"

"I think I won something."

"*What*? Tell me what you mean, *right now.*"

"I don't mean anything."

"Tell me. Tell me. *Tell me.*" Deli spoke louder and louder until she was nearly shouting. Jake put his hands up in surrender because he really did want to tell her and also because Deli could be super loud when she put her mind to it, and his head was pounding.

"She watched a movie while I ran calculations on the pizza she brought."

"What did you do after that?"

"Um…"

"I knew it! You totally had sex, didn't you?"

Jake did not say anything. He did not blink. Nor did he smile. Deli got irritated with his lack of reaction and punched him in the arm.

"Ow," said Jake.

"Tell me the truth," said Deli.

"Okay, yes."

Deli grinned lasciviously, then punched him in the arm again for good measure.

"See? I told you she likes you," she said.

"Maybe?" he said. But the question he'd been thinking about— the one that started out as a small nothing and morphed into a huge deal over the last few hours—sat on his tongue and refused to let any other words out until it was asked.

"Do you know who Brad is?"

There, he'd said it. He wasn't going to, but he did and now there was no taking it back.

"You mean *Thad*? The documentary guy?"

"The what?"

"You're talking about the guy that lives downstairs from her right? He films people doing extreme sports. He calls them *thrill documentaries.*"

"Thrill documentaries?"

"Yeah, you ever see that movie of those guys base jumping off the Burj Khalifa in wing suits?"

"He made that?" Jake suddenly felt a little woozy.

"Yup. He has a huge following."

"Did they ever uh…date?"

"He's her *neighbor*, Jake."

Deli looked at him as though she were imparting some sort of arcane wisdom, but Jake had no earthly idea what she meant. Did Kix want to date him and choose not to because he lived downstairs? Did she move downstairs because they were dating? Why wouldn't she tell Deli? Jake thought girls told each other all sorts of stuff like that.

He was about to ask her to explain when Carl walked out of his bedroom adjusting his tie. His black suit was spotless, as was the white shirt he wore under his jacket. Tilted across his brow sat the fedora from last night.

"How we doing?" said Carl. Deli hopped up from the couch.

"Ready when you are."

Carl took one step in Deli's direction and stopped. He turned around and ducked back to his room. A second later, he reemerged from his room with a pair of dark glasses.

"Let's get to the gig," he said, snapping the sunglasses in place.

"What gig?" Jake only asked because the word *gig* implied some sort of musical talent, of which Carl had exactly none.

"It's ladies' night," he said.

Deli smiled at him and shook her head. "We're taking his mom out to dinner for her sixtieth birthday."

Carl took Deli by the hand and led her across the room. He opened the door, let Deli walk ahead of him, then spun around on his heel and tipped his hat at Jake before walking out.

Well, thought Jake. *That was certainly weird.*

IN THE SECURITY OFFICE

"WHAT DO YOU MEAN *FIRED*?"

"I mean you can't work here anymore." Paul had been standing when Brad walked in. Now he crossed his arms over his chest and leaned against his desk.

"Because of a stupid piece of paper?"

"It ain't a stupid piece of paper, Brad. It's a court order."

Brad stared at Paul, half disbelieving.

"Look, I'm sorry, man. For what it's worth, I only found out ten minutes ago. Gayle told me. She says you gotta go."

"I thought Gayle was out this week."

"She is. I just got off the phone with her."

"How'd *she* know?"

"She's the boss, Brad." Paul uncrossed his arms. "Look, you're a good security man, but I gotta side with her on this one."

"But I didn't even *do* anything, Paul. I didn't even *see* Karen yesterday. Danielle wouldn't let me, so I left. Ask that slimeball Dennison if you don't believe me. She never talked to me once."

"I talked to him. He says you were shouting threats into the store."

"He's lying, Paul. You know he's lying. He's trying to get me fired." Paul had to understand. He knew what Dennison was doing. He could see for himself what a low life he was.

"I'm sorry Brad. I know you've had a tough time, but I can't ignore this. I have to ask you for your keys."

"I can't believe this," he said. "You're actually firing me?"

"It's out of my hands, Brad. It's corporate policy."

"But I didn't *do* anything. Look at the security footage. You'll see I haven't done anything."

Paul shook his head. He had a pinched and painful look on his face.

"Can I at least get my stuff?" said Brad.

Paul stared at the ground for a long time. Finally he sighed and said, "I'm not supposed to let you out of my sight. I have to walk you over there and then accompany you out of the building."

"For Christ's sake, Paul, I just want to empty my locker. The break room is next door. You'll *hear* me." He reached in his pocket and extracted a complicated knot of keys held together by several small carabineers. He unhooked one of the carabineers from the mass and threw it onto the desk behind Paul. "Here's my keys for the building. Now I can't even get into my own locker without using the combination like a schmuck."

Paul sighed heavily and shook his head some more. "Fine," said Paul. "Go get your stuff." Brad walked across the hall immediately.

He pulled his key knot out of his pocket again and extracted another carabineer, much like the one he'd thrown onto Paul's desk. In fact it was so alike as to be almost identical. The keys in Brad's hands were much shinier, though.

In the breakroom, Brad headed straight for a locker covered with bumper stickers. On one of the stickers, the name *Gerry* was written in black marker. Brad used one of his shiny keys to open it. He opened a few more lockers in quick succession before returning to the office a moment later with a ball cap and a coat.

"Thanks man, I appreciate you being so decent." Brad stuck out his hand. Paul gave him a quizzical look at first but returned the handshake.

"I'm sorry this happened," said Paul.

"Yeah, me too," said Brad. "Please tell Gayle I'm sorry. If she looks at the footage, she'll see the truth. Anyway, I'll see ya around." Then he turned and walked out of the office.

Paul, who had looked uncomfortable throughout the whole conversation, relaxed as he followed Brad down the hall. Probably because he thought the hard part was over, and that Brad would soon be gone.

EIGHTEEN MINUTES INTO
HER TEN-MINUTE BREAK

PAUL STOOD AT THE FRONT ENTRANCE of the mall and watched Brad drive off the property. He then went inside. He did not see Brad circle the block. Nor did he see Brad turn into the back parking lot of the Chicken Coop restaurant. He wouldn't have been able to anyway, not unless he'd been standing there at the time. The security feed in the back lot hadn't been functioning properly since that power outage in February. No one bothered to fix it either because the owner of the Chicken Coop was a total hard-ass who wouldn't even give mall security free sodas if they ate there. They never ate there.

Before he got out of the car, Brad put on Gerry's jacket and the ball cap he'd found in its pocket. *Thank you Gerry*, thought Brad, *for being a stupid baseball fan.*

He needed to get back to the bathroom before word got around that he'd been fired. He could count on Paul not to make his business known unless he had to, but Gayle was probably drafting an interdepartmental email right now. He thought about her smug smile as she typed. She'd hated him from day one. She must be enjoying this.

He walked into the Chicken Coop smiling at the hostess and pointing at the bar. The hostess, a perky twenty-something, smiled and nodded to show she understood. He walked into the bar slowly enough for her to lose interest, then out through the other side, toward the gigantic fiberglass rooster holding a hamburger and giving everyone in the mall a big thumbs-up. The bartender looked up at him as he left so he patted his stomach and gave her a big thumbs-up like the rooster. She smiled and went back to stocking glasses.

The long, tiled hallway that led to the bathroom had two security feeds trained on it. The first feed was Camera Fourteen, near the entrance. Brad avoided this camera by waiting for a group of senior citizens to walk past the entrance. He slipped down the hallway as they obscured the feed.

The second camera was the reason he'd stolen Gerry's ball cap.

As he passed the doorway to the Family Lounge, Brad stopped. It was strict policy that the cleaning crew not use their phones in public, but he could hear Velda Prinz chatting away on her cell. That wasn't unusual. As soon as she thought no one was looking, Velda was talking with one of her daughters. It was like she couldn't function if she didn't know how badly her snotty grandkids had crapped themselves at preschool.

He took off Gerry's jacket and hat and walked across the room to the soda machine.

"Look sharp, Velda, Gayle is around." He said it with a smile on his face, knowing it would strike fear into the elderly woman's heart.

"Hold on a second, baby," she said into the phone. She covered the receiver and spoke to Brad next. "What do you mean Gayle is here? She's supposed to be gone until Thursday."

"I just saw her in the security office."

Velda sat up straight. "Rachel, baby, I gotta go. Gayle the Whale is back early. I'll call you when I get home. Tell Isabella that her grandma loves her very much!"

"Thanks for the heads-up, Brad."

"Yeah, I thought since you're supposed to be on probation, you might want to know. Hey, how's your head doing from yesterday? Still in pain?"

"You're so sweet for asking. Yes, it still hurts quite a bit. What's going on with the bathroom? Did they fix the gas leak?"

"Turned out not to be a gas leak. Some punks from the head shop across the street came in and vandalized everything. The tile is so messed up Maintenance had to close the stall."

"Is that why it's all taped up? I tried to peek in, but I couldn't see anything. Then of course Rachel called, and I had to answer."

"Yeah, it's pretty bad. That's why Gayle is here. She wants to see it; see if it's bad enough to take legal action. You know how she is."

"Wait, Gayle is coming *here*?"

"She's on her way. You have about five minutes."

"You know, the food court is a terrible mess. I better go see to it. Thanks again for the heads-up, Brad. You're always so helpful."

"Just don't tell anyone I said anything okay? I don't need her after me too."

"Not a soul," said Velda.

She made lip-zipping motions with her hand and wheeled her cleaning cart out of the men's room at top speed. She would not be back for the rest of her shift.

PAST THREE OF THE CLOCK

THEY STARTED DELIVERY at four p.m. Sundays, even though phone orders before five were a rarity. Today, however, the clouds gathered into angry knots, and a chill wind ran through the streets. It was a day for staying inside and watching movies. It was a day for ordering pizza.

A burst of cold air followed Kix in the front door. It hit Marco across the face and blew his hair askew. Marco closed his eyes in contempt and sneezed at it. The cold air died away, ashamed of itself for being so forward.

"Miss Kix!" Marco said, his watery eyes bright with warning. "Already it is past three of the clock."

"Hi, Marco," she said. "I'm fine, thanks. How are you?"

She smiled wide, knowing that Marco would not catch the sarcasm. Marco was sarcasm-deaf, which is like tone-deaf but less useful.

"I am waiting for you *five minutes* is how I am."

"Sorry. I think Maxine's alternator is acting up. I had to get a jump earlier. My battery is probably dead. Can I borrow your car for tonight? I swear I'll get her a new battery tomorrow."

"Is not garage here, Miss Kix. You need good car. Can't be driving shit heaps."

The complaints trailed behind him as Marco disappeared into the back office. He reappeared twenty seconds later, still complaining but also jingling a set of keys.

"Already we have deliveries. Take my car. I look at Maxine." Kix caught the keys with one hand. She grabbed the warming bag and headed toward the back door. Marco made to follow her when the phone rang again. He stopped and raised a finger in the air at her.

"Do not be gone long. We have more orders!" He snuffled and puffed, but his scowl had gone soft at the corners and she knew he really didn't mind.

"I'll be as quick as I can, but the traffic out there is pretty horrible."

Marco's eyebrows went up half an inch but slid back down after the phone rang again.

"And do not change my radio!" he said.

"I never do that. That's Eric." She blew him a kiss and headed out the back door. Behind her, Marco rubbed his nose with a handkerchief and started grumbling again.

"*Stupid name for car.*"

She totally changed his radio.

PRAISE FOR MAMA AYAHUASCA

THE GROUND SMELLED LIKE CERVEJA where the over-ripe fruit had broken open. Diabo did not mind the smell, but it reminded him of his hunger and that made him tetchy. He climbed out of the shrubbery into which he'd fallen and followed his instincts. They led him to the scent tracks almost immediately.

He was not familiar with many of animal smells associated with this particular track. When he did finally pick up on one he recognized, he did *not* sigh in disappointment because wandering spiders do not sigh in disappointment. Wandering spiders take things as they come even if those things are rats.

He followed the scent track, assuming it would lead him toward the human nest. Rat tracks could always be counted on to lead back toward human nests. But to his surprise, the track stayed far away from this particular nest. The markings were spaced farther apart as well, indicating that any rat travelling on this path must have been doing so at a very high rate of speed.

He followed the trail until he came upon a large wooden barrier. Diabo had seen these before. They were meant to keep wild pigs out. His mood improved at the sight of it. Was he nearing his jungle back home?

It took less than five seconds for him to scale the pig fence. At the top of it, Diabo used all of his eyes to survey his surroundings. There were no pigs, which was a shame. Nothing squeals in fear quite like a surprised pig. But that did not matter at the moment. What mattered was the tree.

It was a lot of tree to behold. Not at all like the magnificent banana trees back home. This tree was slick and shiny; its leaves were sinister with spikes. Diabo would bet a week's worth of victims that those spikes were razor sharp. It was the most glorious tree he had ever seen.

He thanked Mama Ayahuasca and all her spirit children for leading him to the tree which so clearly had been meant for him. He thanked them for the rat, too, although in truth, he had eaten cockroaches with better flavor. Especially those ones that live off rotten bananas. Those were delicious.

Again, Diabo did not sigh. He was lonely and lost, for sure, but Mama Ayahuasca helped him find the glorious tree and provided him with sustenance. She never turned her back on her children. He was honor bound make the best of it, indigestion and all.

The trunk of the tree was not spikey. It had a pebbly bark that provided many footholds. Diabo began to climb. Soon, he was at the top of the tree.

Scrambling out among the spiny leaves, Diabo turned his attention to the night around him. There were human nests larger than he'd ever seen. They were everywhere! All of them had their own suns, shining out from inside. Diabo was no brainless cockroach—he knew the bananitos kept artificial suns, but he had never seen so many in his entire life. And the wheeled machines! All lined up, one after another, as though the humans made wild pig fences from them.

Diabo surveyed his new kingdom and rejoiced. Once again, Mama Ayahuasca proved how well she knew him. She had not simply given him a tree; she had given him an entire bananito *hive*.

THE FOUND SOCK

KIX TOSSED THE EMPTY WARMING BAG on the counter and plucked the next delivery ticket from the magnetic line. She checked it against the boxes Marco had lined up on the table.

"Your keys are on counter, Miss Kix." Marco said. He jimmied the peel handle back and forth as he shuffled pizzas around the oven.

"Did you look at Maxine?"

"Yes."

"Well, what do you suppose is wrong with her?"

"Nothing. She is fine."

Marco pulled a pizza from the oven and brought it over to the table. Kix reached over and grabbed the correct box without even looking.

"What do you mean fine? Did you do that thing with the flange?"

"No need. I fixed that last time. She is not running badly."

Wham. Kix smacked the pizza cutter down through thickest part of the crust. It was a trick she'd learned from Marco. *You have to sneak up and attack. Show who is boss.*

"Huh," she said. Her car had definitely not started this morning. "What about the battery?"

"Is good battery. Started right away. Enough chit-chatting. We have orders up."

She finished packing up the pizzas and checked the addresses. The first delivery ticket was on the same street as the Found Sock. Kix upgraded their order to include an extra-large side salad and two free sodas on account of them being outstandingly loyal customers. It had nothing at all to do with the unwashed laundry sitting in the back of her suddenly working car.

*   *   *

The Found Sock was Kix's Laundromat of choice. It had cement walls plastered together with spider webs and dryer lint. Only five of the washers worked, and the magazine area always smelled like cat pee, but it was only two streets over from Pizza Joe's, and that made it ideal.

She didn't bother moving her car after the last delivery; she just grabbed her laundry and humped it down the sidewalk like some sort of smelly-sock Santa. That's probably why she didn't see Thad walk in.

"Hey, Kix! What are you doing here?"

Kix looked up from shoving her unmentionables into a washer and saw Thad standing just inside the door.

"Um…" she said, because some questions were too stupid to answer right away. "My laundry? What are *you* doing here?"

"I was walking by, and I saw you getting out of your car. Look, can I talk with you for a minute? I think I need to apologize."

"…" said Kix.

"You know, for earlier."

Kix still didn't say anything.

"I was being a jerk," he said. Kix stared at him, until she realized he was serious.

"What do you want me to say, Thad? It's *not* okay. You *were* being a jerk."

"I know, and I'm sorry. I'm not sure why I did that." For a moment, Thad studied the air next to her left ear. Then he breathed deeply, as though he'd made some sort of decision.

"That's not true. I guess it bothered me that you didn't want to come to my party. I was really hoping you'd be there. To tell you the truth, my friends can be boring sometimes. I was hoping you would show up and be interesting. You're always interesting. That's the part I like best about you. I'm sorry I was a jerk. Please, can you forgive me?"

After analyzing all of the words he'd just said, she realized that most of them were not about sex. Kix hadn't expected that. She tilted her head sideways and squinted at Thad, but he still looked like the same douchebag. He was right, though. His friends could be terribly boring.

"What about Dr. Catwoman? I though she *couldn't get enough of the Thad*." she said.

"She doesn't like dogs. How do you hang with someone who doesn't like dogs? That's weird."

"Tell me again what you came here for?"

"To apologize. I'm really sorry I was a jerk to you earlier. Can I make it up to you somehow?"

"Like how? And don't you dare ask me out."

Thad gave a small but good-natured laugh. "I promise I won't. You're dating someone anyway, right?"

"*Still* none of your business," she said.

"Look, I just want to go back to being friends. I swear. I'm sorry for what happened. It was stupid. I just want to be able to say hi to you in the afternoons. Maybe ask about your day. No one ever asks about my day. I get lonely for friends sometimes. Don't you ever get lonely for people around?"

"Not really, no." she said, but it was a lie. She'd been in Seattle for almost three years and only now was she finally starting to click with people. That first year had been rough.

"Come on, friends?" he said.

"If you go back to being a jackass, I'm going back to ignoring you."

"Deal."

"I'm not kidding, Thad. I've gotten pretty good at ignoring you. It won't take much."

"I got it. *I promise*. I wouldn't mess with you, anyway. You'd probably kick my ass."

Kix laughed. She couldn't help it. Thad was being strangely honest with her, and he had a sense of humor. Who knew?

"I have to get back to work."

"You going out tonight?"

"I don't know. Maybe," she said and pointedly did not look at her phone.

"Well, I'm around if you're bored. After last night, my liver wants to stay in and watch movies and eat popcorn. You're welcome to join me if you like."

"Thank you for the offer, but I still have to work." She smiled a genuine smile. Thad smiled back, a big goofy smile that made him look like a teenager.

"You should give some thought to that bodu kura documentary. I could definitely get you some sponsors." He shot her with his cool-guy finger guns and walked out the front door.

Kix didn't say anything. Behind her, the door jingled closed, and she pulled her phone from her back pocket. No one had tried to get in touch with her since she last checked.

When she returned to the kitchen, she found Marco running the ovens. He had definitely noticed her absence, but since he had twelve pies in rotation, he couldn't leave the mat to lecture her. She readied the next delivery and left within five minutes.

JUMP

VELDA LEFT HER MOP AND BUCKET in the middle of the lounge area. Brad didn't want it to draw any attention on the security feeds so he wheeled it with him into the bathroom. He untaped the stall door and wheeled the mop and bucket in. There was enough room to stash it away in the corner where it would be out of sight from anyone unless they knelt down to look.

He left the *Out of Order* sign on the door and resealed the tape on the outside. Once that was done, he ducked under the door and sealed it from the inside as well.

After his security measures were in place, he spent two minutes searching for the portal and another two minutes trying to open it up. When the colored lights started resolving in front of the white spot, he had a difficult time making sense of them. He couldn't feel Thad anywhere on the other side.

Brad began to panic. What if he couldn't find Thad again? What if the portal only led him to that one area? He couldn't stand there all day looking for him, he had to make a move.

Brad concentrated on the street in front of Thad's house. The street had been very similar to his own world. He imagined the sidewalk, and the grass. Once he had it all set in his mind, Brad shoved every ounce of willpower he had at it; through the portal. This resulted in Thad's body being at that exact spot, whether it wanted to or not.

"Whoa, what was that?"

"Sorry about that," said Brad. "I panicked."

"Holy *crap*, Brah," said Thad. "I was just up on Broadway! Can you do that again? Only this time, aim for the end of the block."

They jumped back and forth down the street until it became easy. Thad suggested trying a spot farther away, maybe back to Broadway but Brad couldn't picture Broadway in his mind well enough, so they settled on the inside of Thad's car, which was still parked at the grocery store. It worked.

"That was amazing!" said Thad. Brad had to admit this was true.

"Hey, since we're up here, let's go talk with Karen."

"Kix, you mean."

"Oh yeah, sorry, Kix. We need to go talk with her again before too long. She works around here, right?"

"No need, Brah. I saw her earlier and totally apologized for everything."

"You *what*?"

"I was honest, like you said. I told her about how I was stoked for her to be at the party. And you know what? You were totally right! She didn't blow me off at all."

"You should have waited for me to come back before you talked to her."

"Sorry, Cuz, no time. I saw her walking toward the Laundromat, and I knew I had my chance. Am I right?" Brad could feel Thad throwing his hand up in the air for a high five.

"No, *not* right."

"Lighten up. I did it like you said to. Everything went fine, just like you said it would. She talked to me. I told her to come over after work if she wasn't busy. She looked like she was into it."

Brad listened to the recap of his conversation and seethed. Thad better not have screwed this up. He changed the subject in order to distract his anger for a moment.

"You remember that guy you ran into at the grocery store this morning? The one with the chili powder?"

"Sure. Why?"

Brad ignored the question. "Does Kar—Kix ever talk about a guy named James?"

"Not that I know of."

"It might not be James. It might be John or Jake or Jack."

"Oh yeah! I think she knows a Jack."

"Where does she know him from?"

"No, not Jack. I'm pretty sure it's Jake."

"It doesn't matter what the guy's name is. Where does she know him from?"

"I think they work together or something."

"Of course they do," said Brad but Thad was too confused to ask why. "Where does she work?"

"Oh, uh…Pizza Joe's. She's a delivery driver."

"Delivery drivers work solo though, don't they?"

"I don't understand where you're going with all this."

"You know the guy in the grocery store?"

"I do *now*."

"He's going to be a problem if we don't do something about him."

"That guy?" Thad looked in the rearview mirror and shook his head slowly from side to side. "But that guy was a loser."

"He may be a loser, but trust me. He's got his hooks in her somehow. And if we don't do something, he's going to win. We need to pay him a little visit." Anger flashed in his mind at the thought of James Dennison and Karen together.

"Whoa, what do you mean *pay him a visit*? Like, beat him up or something? I am not going to assault anyone, Brah. I ain't like that. I got sponsors."

"Relax, we're just gonna go talk with him. Make sure he understands what's at stake if he makes a move on Karen."

"You mean *Kix*. Her name is Kix. It's short for Katarina."

"That's what I said."

"No, you said *Karen*. But this isn't Karen, this is Kix. *Get it straight.*"

"Okay, *Thaddeus*, try picturing *Katarina* sucking that greasy guy's dick." Brad could feel Thad shudder mentally at the thought. "Because if she goes over there tonight, I guarantee you that's exactly what's gonna happen. Do you want that to happen?"

There was a long moment of silence in which Brad could feel Thad trying to piece together the situation. It was slow going.

"You're sure it's *that* guy?" he said at last.

"How do we get to the pizza place?"

"I don't know about this. I got sponsors, man. What if he calls the cops?"

Cops didn't worry Brad. Not here at least. There weren't any stupid court papers here. No, the problem here was *Thad*. If he didn't calm down, he was going to screw everything up.

"Don't worry, we're not going to hurt him at all. We just need him to back off a little. Give our girl some space." said Brad.

"I don't know, Brah. That seems a little pushy."

"In my world, all I did was explain things to him. I didn't get mad. He was cool with it. I'm sure this guy will understand."

"Really?"

"Oh yes, absolutely. I've done it before."

"Okay. But, I don't want to hurt anybody," said Thad. His defenses were still up but Brad could feel him beginning to relax.

"I don't either," said Brad. "Trust me. I can smooth things over with him. Just let me take care of this."

"Well okay but ..."

Brad didn't for questions. He jumped forward, into the void.

At first the noise was incredible. Thoughts, feelings, emotions, even smells crowded him as he jammed his consciousness into Thad's. For a moment, Brad remembered Thad's memories. He knew Thad's secrets, and he saw Thad's desires. He tried to keep his mind neat and orderly, in case Thad could do the same to him.

Unfortunately, Thad couldn't do the same. Before he understood exactly what was going on, Brad was inside his mind, pushing Thad's consciousness back through the portal, back toward the empty tiled walls and the empty shell of Brad standing in the Ashwood Super Mall men's bathroom.

"Hey, what just happened there, Brah?" he said across the reality divide.

But Brad was no longer listening.

SOME PHONE CALLS

RAIN FELL IN STEADY PITTER-PATS on the roof of the car, washing away the fading daylight while Kix sat at the red light trying to decide what to do. She hadn't heard from Jake all day. That shouldn't be upsetting, but today, for some reason, it really was. She wanted to know what was going on, and the only way she knew how to do that was by talking with him.

Maybe she should call him. She didn't want to seem desperate, but the more she thought about the voices she'd heard this morning, the more she wanted an answer. At this point, Kix didn't even care if there was another woman in Jake's room—she just wanted to *know*. She felt like she was going crazy.

She'd already delivered the last pizza and was making her way back to the restaurant when an SUV the size of Nebraska pulled away from the curb directly in front of the Found Sock. Kix had lived on Capitol Hill long enough recognize a nod from the parking gods when she saw one. Instead of turning left, she gunned it through the intersection and parked immediately.

She didn't like to lie to Marco, but she'd been gone long enough that he was likely to notice. After she set the parking brake she dialed work. No reason Marco had to know about her laundry stops.

"Hey, Marco, sorry this delivery is taking so long. Can you read me back the address on that last order? Eric must have typed the house number in wrong."

"Hello, my dear! I was hoping you would call. How are you?"

Kix frowned and held the phone from her ear to make sure she dialed correctly. It was Pizza Joe's, and the voice sounded incredibly like Marco. He must be tripped out on cold meds again.

"Marco?" said Kix. "Are you okay?"

"Of course I am okay! I am more than okay. You are going to party tonight, yes?"

"What? I just need the address again—"

"Ah, you are always a funny one. Your friend called here."

"Jake?" she asked, hoping that it was but knowing it wasn't.

"No, no, no! The tiny one who beats people up."

"Deli?"

"Yes, she could not get your cell phone so she called here."

"Really?" That was weird. Kix had her cell phone turned up all day. Not because she was waiting for a phone call or anything, because she wasn't.

"She says do not forget to bring chips for party."

"What party?"

"Have fun tonight my dear, and don't wake Papa up when you get home."

"Uh…" said Kix. "Marco, have you been at the cold meds again?"

"Do not worry about Papa! I have a bit of the heartburn, but I am okay. Eric is here. You know how he takes care of me. Go enjoy your party!" he said then hung up without another word.

Kix disconnected the call, frowning. Did that just happen? Even in a pseudoephedrine haze, Kix refused to believe Marco would encourage her to attend a party, especially during work hours. Was he running a fever? Maybe she should go check on him.

After she folded her laundry, of course.

* * *

Marco waited a moment more before hanging up the phone. Sweat trickled down his forehead. He did not wipe it away.

They stood facing each other in Marco's tiny office. In his hand the crazy man held a stapler that had, until very recently, been innocently weighing down papers on the desk.

"Was my daughter," he said and gave the fatherliest of chuckles he could.

"Bullshit. You just told her to go somewhere. Where?"

"Was my *daughter*," said Marco.

The man moved frighteningly fast. The stapler came down on his nose. Marco fell to his knees, clutching at his face.

"You will not get away with this," he said through his fingers.

"And you're going to learn how just how much I hate liars," said the man. Then he kicked Marco in the stomach.

It hurt. But Marco hadn't gotten this far in the pizza business by giving in to punks like this. He stood up and spun himself around at the same time, kicking out with his foot in the direction of the man's leg. It was a clumsy move, the move of a man well into his sixties. But even though his knees couldn't aim properly anymore, the blow should at least have knocked the man off balance. Instead, Marco's foot never connected with anything. The man had disappeared.

"I'm gonna ask you one more time, old man, and you better not fucking lie to me. *Where is Karen going*?"

Marco turned around slowly to see the crazy man now standing behind his desk. In his hand, he held a baseball bat. He recognized it as the one he kept under the front counter for emergencies.

FRIEND OR FOE?

A PIRATE, DRESSED IN SATIN PANTS and an impressively large hat, stepped through the breezeway. Toesy felt Pansy shy away from him.

Do not be alarmed my friend. He is not a real pirate. Real pirates would not wear such ridiculous pants.

Ark, said Pansy.

Miss Julie seems to be having a party this evening. She would grant us admittance if you care to attend. I often do. Sometimes she serves smoked salmon.

Ark, ark. Said Pansy.

I understand your reluctance. I am not keen on shiny pirates either. Let us continue with the tour then, shall we? Toesy said and headed down the stairs.

He'd been showing her all his favorite spots in the house. So far they'd seen the window seat with the comfy pillow, the extra-large heater vent and the hidden closet on the third floor. Toesy thought next he might show her the Holy Man's napping couch by way of the secret entrance. Going outside in this weather would most likely not be appreciated. He sat on his haunches, about to stretch up and grab the book that opened the secret door when he heard the front door buzz. More pirates? Toesy sneaked toward the entry way, keeping low to the ground.

The front doors of Horsey House were framed with many leaded windows that looked in upon the grand staircase. In its heyday, they must have been beautiful, but most were now warped and bulging with age, distorting everything outside into unrecognizable shapes. Toesy could not get a good look at whoever stood on the front stoop. He could *hear* well enough, though, and currently he was listening to

Mr. Sacha speak through the squawking box on the front stoop.

"Hello?"

"Yeah," said the person at the front door. "I have a package delivery for..." Here he mumbled something incoherent.

"Nice try, asshole." Mr. Sacha clicked off.

A loud bang at the bottom of the door made both Pansy and Toesy jump. This strange person had kicked it! The door frame held, but Toesy was offended all the same.

He curled into a shadow at the corner of the room, waiting to see what else this villain might do. Upon his brow, he felt a tiny rage building and knew he was not the only one angry at this Kicker of Doors. But the villain did not kick again. Instead, he buzzed the intercom to another apartment.

"Hey!" A female voice this time, high and cheery. Toesy could hear lively conversation in the background.

"Hey!" said the stranger, matching the excitement with a soprano of his own. "Sorry I'm late!"

"Uh, okay. Come on up!" said the girl.

The door buzzed. Toesy melted into the shadows. *My friend, you must keep still.*

There was no responding *Ark!* Instead, a tiny claw poked him in the ear in such a way as to convey irritation at the pokee's presumption that the poker could not have guessed this for themselves.

The man bullied the door open and walked into the entryway. Someone had optimistically placed a swatch of industrial grey carpeting in front of the door, but it sat crumpled to the side, waiting for some kind citizen to smooth it out. He stepped over the hump of mat and continued toward the grand staircase, not seeing the unlikely duo of cat and sugar glider standing silently in the corner. But that was no surprise. No one could stay as still as Toesy.

He wore a blue puffy jacket made from some sort of slick material that kept the rain off. His trousers, however, were simple cotton. They turned deep brown where the rain soaked up to his calves. The bill of his baseball cap was so wet it looked black. The man searched around the entryway until he spied the mailboxes on the wall opposite Toesy. He stomped over to them, slipping on the tiles in his wet sneakers.

"Yau, Calabi, Denny." He scanned the entryway and Toesy

slipped further into the shadows to keep from being seen.

"Where is she?" said the Kicker of Doors. Then, without so much as a blink, he disappeared. *Pop*! And reappeared near the base of the grand staircase.

A small claw poked Toesy in the ear.

This is dark sorcery indeed, he said. *He is no mere Kicker of Doors. This is a Boundary Walker.*

The responding *Ark!* was more enthusiastic than fearful. Toesy was glad about that.

They followed him silently, marking the path the man took up the stairs. Human Boundary Walkers were rare. At least the sane ones were.

In the middle of the staircase, the villain disappeared. Toesy froze. A moment later the man reappeared in front of the mailboxes then, just as suddenly, he was back in the middle of the staircase, three steps away from a Toesy hiding in shadow.

Cats, of course, are natural Boundary Walkers. They key is not being entirely sane at the outset. But even cats refrain from tempting the infinite so carelessly. They know that in order to step into an alternate reality, you need only imagine it but therein lies the risk. If you are not sure where you are headed, anything imaginable can happen.

Toesy was sure of where he was and he knew exactly where he wanted to go. It would be much easier to follow this scoundrel in a different dimension but Toesy could not assume that Pansy was up to the task. The infinite realms can be extremely disorienting, sometimes for days. Long-term psychosis can develop. Also, it may cause slight stomach upset. He did not want to risk making Pansy uncomfortable.

My friend, I would not take you beyond what you know, but if you can trust me, this villain will be easier to catch if we risk a very short walkabout.

Ark! said Pansy.

In that case…please do not worry about what you see. It is all false. And it is all true. You cannot make sense of it until—

He was going to say *until we have arrived and you we see what we see,* but the small claw poked him in the ear again. It was followed by a tiny sigh of impatience.

I guess just hold on tight then.

Pansy responded by grabbing a tuft of hair from the back of Toesy's head and leaning forward.

Ark, Ark, ARK! she said and pointed toward the future.

*   *   *

Most humans are insensitive to the stretch of reality and therefore do not witness anything unusual when it bends or weaves. Some individuals, however, *are* sensitive to the plasticity of the world. Fortunately, the Universe likes to be tidy about these things and even those sensitive to interdimensional shifts of reality do not notice much beyond a small physical reaction. Many of these people have a similar reaction to bright sunlight; it makes them sneeze.

In this case, anyone watching Thanatos at that moment would have experienced a tightening in the sinuses around their eyes, then a sudden, overwhelming urge to sneeze. Upon opening their eyes, reality would no longer contain a cat wearing a sugar glider hat and would therefore think no more of it.

Reality is funny that way.

APARTMENT 2A

EVER SINCE SACHA MOVED out of the Dungeon they'd been at war. Not a mean war, just…war. It started when the kid with the *Legalize It!* button had asked them to sign his petition. *Of course* Sacha had signed it. His uncle Mike owned a chain of convenience stores throughout the city. Legal weed would probably double his profits in the Cheetos and beer departments.

He put Jake's address down on the mailing list because he thought it would be funny. Jake thought the ensuing marijuana-themed junk mail wasn't as funny as Sacha did and retaliated by signing him up for a year's subscription to *Siempre Mujer*, which, as far as Sacha could tell, was a magazine for dynamic, Spanish-speaking women.

At first he'd been confused. Then he was annoyed. *Then* he realized that Spanish-speaking women were kind of hot. They also, it turned out, knew some excellent recipes.

Jake and Carl were up to something. How stupid did they think he was? First the pork shoulder in his mailbox and now a package delivery? No one delivers packages on Saturday evening.

He wiped his hands on his apron and sat down at the computer and texted Jake.

I'm not falling for the "package delivery" BS, dude.

He pressed *Send* and headed back to the kitchen. By the time he heard the knock at the door, he was elbow-deep in jalapeño peppers.

Come on Jake, he thought. *You got better game than this.*

He peeled off his dish gloves and headed for the front door. On the other side of the peephole stood a man wearing a dark ball cap and bouncing on his heels. Sacha rolled his eyes, unlatched the safety chain, and opened the door with a flourish.

"Can I help you?"

"Uh," said the guy. "I don't know. I'm lost. I thought this Delilah Peltman's apartment?"

Sacha grinned. He was totally not going to fall for this.

"You've got the wrong floor, Bud, sorry."

"You know her?"

"Of course I do. And her last name is *Pelham*. Can I ask what you need her for?" Sacha did not sneer. It was hard.

"I leant her my bike helmet. I'm just here to pick it up. You don't know where I can find her, do you?"

Deli on a motorcycle? With *this* guy? Sacha could not imagine it. This had to be part of the prank. Oh wait, maybe he was supposed to *think* it was a motorcycle and really it's a ten-speed or something dinky. Whatever it was, this was definitely a prank.

"Yeah, sure," said Sacha. "She lives in 3B." His smile broad, and friendly. The ball-capped guy got out a pen and clicked it open. Sacha leaned in as he wrote.

"*B* as in *best of luck!*"

"Thank you," said the guy.

"Anytime," said Sacha. "You have a good night now."

He tipped a forefinger in salute before closing the door on the guy. Deli had his helmet? How stupid did Jake think he was?

Now he just had to figure what they were up to. Was he supposed to walk that guy upstairs? Like hell he would. Last time Jake and Carl tricked him into leaving, those assholes snuck into his apartment and replaced all his condiments with Jell-O. He wasn't leaving his apartment this time. Sacha slipped the security chain back in the lock, congratulated himself on a plan well foiled, and went back to chopping peppers.

A VERY CONFUSING
ALTERCATION

DELI WAS GLAD that Carl's mom had been called away from dinner early. Margaret Sanderson was a wonderful woman, but she needed to get a dog or two, or maybe a goat. *Anything* really, so long as it kept her mind off of grandchildren. Ugh. Deli wasn't sure she even *liked* kids— she certainly wasn't about to make her own any time soon.

Things with Carl were going pretty well, though, and she really wouldn't mind seeing where they went from here. Well, maybe not exactly *here* because currently Deli was standing in front of a sink full of dirty dishes. She and Carl had gone their separate ways this evening after the Ad Department suggested that they go out for beers. Since his girlfriend dumped him, the Ad Department had been kind of a downer. Deli had already endured most of a meal under duress today so she declined the offer; opting instead to stay home and clean her apartment. The bathroom was beginning to get a little grungy, and there was definitely something growing in the sink.

A knock at the door derailed her train of thought. Was Carl back already? She thought of the Ad Department and sighed. That poor guy. Even Carl couldn't stand to be around him right now, and Carl was the nicest person she knew.

Deli snuck across the kitchen to the door, intending to scare him by ripping the door open just as he got it unlocked. Deli loved surprising Carl. If she caught him off guard at the right moment he screamed this high-pitched *Wha*! that never failed to crack her up.

Tiptoeing the last five steps to the door, Deli stretched up to look through the peephole. She held her breath so that Carl wouldn't hear her but the person standing in the hallway wasn't Carl. She couldn't tell who it was at first. Then his head twitched to the side and she recognized him. Standing in her door way, soaked from ball cap to sneakers, was Kix's neighbor. Why would he be here? She opened the door to find out.

"Hello?" she said.

"Where is Kix?" he said.

"Why? Has something happened? Is she okay?"

"Are you alone?"

"Excuse me?"

"Where is she?" he said and craned his neck to see around her on the left.

"Hey," she said. And jumped in his way. "What are you doing? Is something wrong with Kix?"

"I know she's here."

"Why would she be here? She's probably at work."

"Don't lie to me, Danielle. *Tell me where the hell she is.*" He got up in her face and shouted at her.

"Or *what*? Are you threatening me?"

"*You are going to regret every single word you've said this evening if you don't tell me where she is right now.*"

Deli didn't regret anything. In fact, the way he grunted after she punched him in the mouth made her kind of happy. At least he shut up.

"You shouldn't have done that."

"Or what? You're going to beat me up? Don't you *dare* come to my house and threaten me. You have two seconds to get out of here before I kick your ass down the hall."

* * *

Up until this point, Toesy had been watching quietly from shadowy doorstep of apartment 3C, but this Boundary Walker enraged him. His mistress might not mind this villain, but Toesy took great offense. He would not tolerate these kinds of shenanigans. The fire in his belly flared to life, and he flexed all twenty-four of his claws.

My friend, you may want to stand aside for this.

Instead of jumping down, Pansy threw herself flat against the back of Toesy's head and dug her paws into the depth of his fur.

Are you certain?

Ark! she said and began a disjointed, warbling song that was halfway between purring and growling. Toesy flexed his claws again, this time with more flourish. He suddenly found himself glad for the chance to prove his strength.

The man threw a fist at his mistress. She stepped to the side. His fist missed her cheek and plowed into the wooden doorframe. Although it made her jump, Deli did not yell. She did not scream. She did not even raise her voice.

"Are you kidding me?" she said and immediately started bouncing from foot to foot. "You know what I do for a living, right?"

Toesy was immensely proud of his mistress—she could go up against a Tibetan mastiff and win. But this was no dog fight. This was a Boundary Walker. She would need all the help she could get if she intended to win.

He launched himself into the air, ripping the tension in half with a demigod-like growl. On top of his head, Pansy bellowed out her own squeaky-toy war cry. Together, they flew at the man, claws outstretched, in hopes of snagging some of his softer parts.

The man grunted like an elephant as the massive cat/marsupial complex hit his shoulder. Upon impact, Pansy jumped from Toesy's neck to the man's shoulder and busied herself trying reach the man's earlobe so she could bite it off. Toesy stuck fast to the man's shoulder, using his front paws to hold on while his back claws tried to jackrabbit his coat into tiny pieces.

"What the *fuck*? Get off me!" His left arm flew up and tore the hat from his head throwing it to the floor. But Pansy had predicted the movement and jumped back to Toesy before she got clobbered. Toesy continued trying to claw his way through the man's jacket. He was gaining ground.

His mistress took advantage of their furry blitzkrieg by aiming a kick to the man's groin. It was a hard kick, strong enough to incapacitate or possibly even infertilize a weaker man. Unfortunately, her foot never connected. It *should* have, but the moment it was supposed to hit, the world slipped a little, and the man disappeared. He reappeared in the same instant, ten feet down the hall, grinning.

Toesy, who was master of his own reality, stayed where he was—five feet in the air, no longer attached to the man's shoulder. Together, he and Pansy fell to the floor with a solid thud because gravity doesn't give a crap about interdimensional tomfoolery. It works whether you want it to or not.

*   *   *

Deli shook her head, trying to clear the confusion away. Her body was definitely not in the last place she left it and it took a second to figure out where she went. Unfortunately for her, Thad knew exactly where she was and headed there directly. Before she could get her bearings, he grabbed her by the throat. Her arms flew up to her neck, trying to loosen his grip. Black dots swam across her eyes.

*   *   *

In his life, Toesy had never felt so much like murdering a human person before, and that was including the crazy berserker woman that tried to kill him last summer. Seeing his mistress struggle for air as this man held her by the throat angered him so greatly that he no longer sounded like a cat. He became a tectonic nightmare, an earthquake of granite and claws.

He lunged for the man's outstretched arm, hitting with enough impact to break his hold. Toesy then grabbed his sleeve and held tightly as Pansy scampered past him to the wall. She climbed high enough to get the speed she needed and leapt.

Her aim was impeccable. Unfortunately, so were the man's reflexes. Just as her hind claws struck him in the eyeball, he jerked his head to the side and swatted at her with the arm not currently wearing a murderous cat.

The sharp squeak stabbed at Toesy's heart, and he concentrated on finding a way through the man's sleeve. When another squeak, not nearly as strong but very angry, came from the far wall, Toesy rejoiced. Pansy was safe. Now there were only three in this weird fight.

*   *   *

Deli had been too busy sucking in air to see Pansy attack Thad's face, so she was understandably confused when he suddenly threw a squirrel at her. She ducked. The squirrel in question hit the wall right behind her and sank to the floor. She did not see where it landed. She was too busy going ape-shit all over Thad for throwing a squirrel at her.

The world slipped again. Again Deli stood in the wrong spot, facing the stairway and kicking nothing's ass.

"Stop doing that," she said as she looked around for him. People shouldn't be able to disappear like that. That is impossible. But Deli was a realist. Even if what she saw didn't make sense, she trusted her eyes to see it. And right now, her eyes were telling her that she should watch her back because this maniac was jumping around without any regard for the forces of nature.

"Why? You scared?" He said, out of breath.

"No, I'm not scared of cheaters. You couldn't take me in a fair fight, that's for damn sure. I don't know what you're doing, but you have to do it to win, don't you?"

"Maybe you're right." he said and smiled. "Maybe I can't fight you, Danielle, You're a tough girl. But I still need you to do me a favor."

Deli looked confused. "Did you just call me Danielle?"

For the third time that evening, she watched Thad disappear. He reappeared right next to her, balanced at the top of the stairs.

"Tell Jake to stay away from her," he said. "*Or I'll find him.*"

Then he grabbed Deli in a big bear hug and leapt off the top stair. Mid-flight, he wobbled and disappeared. Deli was not so lucky. She wobbled as well but instead of disappearing entirely as Thad had done, she reappeared immediately, two inches closer to the floor. That dampened her velocity only slightly before gravity once again proved it could be a jackass.

SPACE HOLE?

THAD WASN'T SURE what had happened. The orangey scent of aerosol bathroom freshener hit him squarely in the nose, and he sneezed...maybe. He was getting really confused about where his body was. He thought he was in it but now he wasn't so sure. Hadn't he just been standing in front of a woman's door? Where had that space hole come from?

He recognized the woman eventually but only after he'd found himself in this new place. Thad didn't know where he was, but it looked and smelled a lot like the men's room in a department store.

In fact, he'd been so astounded to find himself in a different place that he made the mistake of looking away from that hole in space and it closed up. He panicked for a moment, thinking for sure he was lost, but soon after that it had widened again, catching his attention before he was yanked back and forth across realities several times in a row, and somehow there was a squirrel involved. He tried to get his bearings, but everything happened so fast that it was impossible to tell what was going on. The last time he returned, he'd fallen face-first onto the floor. Thad rubbed his nose and stared at the tiled wall. Where was he? Why was he in a bathroom? Where had that squirrel come from?

In front of him the wall suddenly fell away and a huge dark chasm appeared out of nothing. Thad stared into it, stunned to see the colors swirling around suddenly solidify into a scene. It felt familiar, a world he knew. *His* world.

"Hey, Brad, where am I? That was Kix's friend, wasn't it? What happened back there?"

"A little bit of good luck for us, Buddy. Don't worry about it. Let's go."

"Should we go back there and see if she's all right?"

"No way! She tried to kill you, man. She pushed you down the stairs, don't you remember? Who is that chick? Why does she hate you so much?"

"I don't know her, really. Just that she's one of Kix's friends."

Brad stumbled on the last stair and landed on his ankle wrong. Thad felt a bolt of pain shoot up his leg, but it was muffled and indistinct. He knew it was there, but it wasn't hurting as much as it should. There was so much wrong with this. Pain or no pain, Thad wanted to get back into his own body. This was weirding him out.

"Hey, let's trade back now."

"Trade back what?"

"Bodies. Where am I?"

"You're completely safe. Don't worry. We can switch back any time you like. Right now, if you *want*. I mean, I don't know if the police are on their way or not, but we can deal with that later. No big deal."

A police siren started wailing in the distance. Thad's mind flooded with panic.

"No, don't. Let's just get out of here."

"You sure? I mean, we gotta drive, and I don't know if it's a good idea to be jumping back and forth through that."

The siren got louder, drowning everything else out.

"Nah, let's just get out of here, man."

"You said it, Boss. I'll take care of this—just sit tight."

A COMPLAINT

NICK WAS A PRACTICAL MAN. He believed in practical things like toothpaste and stamps and the value of a well-balanced account ledger. He did not believe that animals had souls. Neither did they make friends. And they *certainly* did not have the ability to high five those friends with their tails. That wouldn't even *be* a high five. That would be more like a high one. An *impossible* high one.

He sat on the couch, rocking back and forth, trying to forget what had happened. It took him a while, and even then he only succeeded in forgetting the smug look on Pansy's face as they walked off. He could not forget that she'd been stolen by a gigantic, fierce-looking cat.

There might still be a way to salvage this situation. If he found Pansy, maybe Connie would focus on the fact that he had *saved* her instead of lost her. He had to hope.

Nick stood up, brushed off imaginary fur from his slacks, and made his way back to the kitchen where Connie kept emergency phone numbers. Surely the building superintendent would know to whom the cat belonged.

* * *

"Jake Denny."

"Mr. Denny, are you the superintendent for this building?"

Jake exhaled. He didn't recognize the voice, although that wasn't unusual. He was hoping it would be Kix.

"I just talked to Julie about the noise. She's turning the music down."

"I'm not calling in a noise complaint, Mr. Denny. I'm trying to get Connie's sugar bear back."

"Connie from 2C?"

"Yes, my name is Nicholas Miller. I'm watching Pansy—that's the sugar bear in question, while Connie is at a convention in Portland."

"Sorry…what is a sugar bear?"

"Sugar glider, sugar bear—two names for the same thing, Mr. Denny."

Jake sighed. He didn't have the energy to get into an argument with a snotty thesaurus right now. "Did it get loose or something? Because Connie's got a two-hundred-dollar pet-damage deposit I'm holding in escrow. Any damages beyond that, and we'll have to bill her directly."

"There's been no damage to anything as of yet, Mr. Denny. I'm trying to figure out who owns the gigantic beast of a cat that somehow got into this apartment and stole Pansy away."

That explained the tiny fur hat Toesy had been wearing. Jake inhaled slowly and tried playing dumb. "Can you describe what the cat looked like, Mr. Miller?"

"It was gigantic. And ugly."

"Sure, but what color was it?"

Don't say grey.

"It was grey. With stripes. Abnormal amounts of whiskers if you ask me. Also, he seemed unusually good with the hinge on the cage."

"I think I might know the cat you're talking about, Mr. Miller. If it's him, he probably won't do any damage. I don't think I've ever seen him kill a fly." Jake did not add that the reason for this is because flies aren't meaty enough.

"He had better not, or whoever owns him is going to have a hefty lawsuit on their hands."

"I'll try to track him down, okay?"

"Make sure you do. I need that sugar bear by this evening—"

Jake hung up before the man finished his thought. After that idiot in the grocery store, he wasn't in the mood to hear any more self-important bullshit. He'd come home in a rotten mood, and everything had gone downhill from there.

When Carl had suggested he join him and the Ad Department for *brewskies* Jake nearly tore his head off. He felt bad about that now, but Carl wouldn't shut it with the stupid eighties banter and the joke was getting old. Plus, this was the seventh time the Ad Department and his girlfriend had broken up. How do you console a guy who won't stop making himself miserable?

Jake wasn't about to leave the house, anyway. If Kix was going to stop by later, he wanted to be here. But the more he thought about this morning, the more he doubted she would. He walked back to his desk and picked up his cell phone. No messages waited for him.

The clock on his phone read 6:04 p.m. Kix had been at work now for three hours. He kept trying to imagine what she was doing. Not since high school had he found himself this distracted.

A loud thud rocked the ceiling and his hands automatically went up over his head. After the surprise wore off, Jake jumped up to go investigate. It sounded like someone had driven a car into the building.

Outside the wind picked up. In addition to the rain, fat splotches of sleet now pounded at the windows. He decided to take the secret hallway again. As cold and creepy as it was, it was better than walking through slush.

He emerged from the secret staircase without precaution of any kind. The grand entrance was soggy. Someone had tracked mud all over the tiles. Toesy was nowhere to be found.

"Toes-man? Are you here?" Jake poked around the breezeway but saw nothing out of place, nothing that could have created such a loud bang.

"Toesy? Can you hear me? I need some help."

After a minute of searching, Toesy was still nowhere to be found. Jake headed up to Deli's apartment.

* * *

In fact, Toesy *was* there and he could hear Jake just fine. Pansy could as well. They just didn't know what to do about it.

Thankfully, Pansy had not been seriously hurt. They stood in the shallow doorway to apartment 2A, unable to approach Deli because of the wobbly reality surrounding her.

She was breathing, they could see that much, but otherwise she did not move. Toesy wanted to go to her, to make sure she was alive, but even standing this close made him slightly nauseated. Pansy must be sick enough to eat grass.

Toesy was no physicist, but that was of little consequence. One need not know intricate mathematical formulas in order to understand that something was deeply wrong here. Watching the room shift and fade from one reality to the next was not a normal thing. The world wasn't supposed to work that way. No one would be able to get anything done.

Footsteps announcing the Holy Man drew near. They watched him climb the last three steps to the second floor. When he walked into the hallway, his face was scrunched up in confusion. Toesy wanted him to run to his mistress and pick her up, but the Holy Man did not do that. Instead, he stared down in confusion, almost as though he could not decide what he was seeing. What happened next was very curious indeed.

Toesy felt a shift—not a great shift, just enough of a shift to stop reality from wheeling around. The Holy Man stared at his mistress, crumpled on the floor, then world settled down. The nausea in Toesy's stomach dissolved. His mistress faded back in, as though someone had turned the volume and brightness back up on her. The Holy Man's brow unknit itself from confusion and turned sharply to fear. Toesy felt a kick in his heart as the reality of the moment took over.

"Oh Jesus, *Deli! What happened?*"

HE DID *WHAT?*

DELI LAY ON HER SIDE, blinking her eyes. A gash across her cheek bled with enthusiasm, and her arm looked as though it had the world's worst rug burn.

"Are you okay? What happened?"

"He pushed me down the stairs."

She stuck an arm beneath her body and started to push herself up to sitting. Halfway there, a sharp look of pain flashed across her face and she crumpled back to the floor.

"Don't move. I think you may have broken something. Can you feel your legs?"

"Shut up, Jake. I'm fine. Help me sit up." Jake knew better than to argue. He stretched out an arm.

"Who did this?"

"Your buddy."

"Who?"

"Kix's neighbor."

Jake's eyes went wide.

"I didn't recognize him at first. I thought he was Carl trying to sneak in."

All the blood drained from Jake's face. The arm he'd been holding out to Deli for support went limp. "Um…" he said. "Why was he here?"

"That's a great question. I'm glad you asked it. I'd love to answer that in detail, but just for the moment let's pretend that my foot has gone completely numb. *Now, will you please help me sit up?*"

"Gah! Sorry."

Jake considered picking her up entirely, but he wasn't sure if he should. What if he dropped her? She would kill him.

"We need an ambulance."

"No," said Deli.

"But you just said you can't feel your foot. That's not right, Deli. You should be able to feel your foot."

"Oh, I do. Trust me. It hurts like hell. I just can't seem to feel it enough to move it."

"It may be *broken*."

"There's no *maybe* about it. It's definitely broken."

She held on to his arm and rolled herself over onto her back. As soon as she was settled, Jake pulled the phone from his back pocket.

"Who are you calling?"

"Nine-one-one. You need to get to a hospital."

"Don't do that. Call Carl."

"But—your *foot*," said Jake

"Is broken, I know. But I'm not *dying*, so can you please call Carl? I don't need the National Guard, I just need some x-rays."

"But—your *foot*," said Jake.

"*Jake*." Deli clapped her hands at him, and he jumped. "Have you ever had to ride to the hospital in an ambulance? I have. Do you know how much that costs? They charge you like, a million dollars for it. No thank you. Just call Carl. I want to get some x-rays, and then I want to figure out what the hell just happened."

"What *did* happen?"

"*Will you call Carl?*"

He snapped to attention and dialed Carl's number before the edge in Deli's voice got any sharper.

"Hey, Carl, where are you?" Jake's eyebrows leaned toward each other. "*Joliet*? Is that in Ballard? Never mind look, you have to get back here quick. Deli's hurt, and she needs you to come drive her to the hospital."

Jake shook his head slightly back and forth. "Uh, sure. I guess you could call it that," he said. "Just get here quick, okay? Come in through the front. We're on the second floor."

He disconnected the call and looked at Deli. "Carl hasn't found religion at all has he?"

"What are you talking about?"

"Nothing, never mind. He should be here in a few minutes. I think he was dropping the Ad Department off when I called. You need anything from your apartment? Like a wallet or anything?"

"Yes, grab my backpack and a hoodie, will you? They should be on the chair next to the bookshelf."

Jake made sure Deli was comfortable before running to her apartment for stuff. Considering that everything she owned seemed to be on the chair next to her bookshelf, it took him a while to find her hoodie. When he returned, there were elephants running up the stairs. Or at least one elephant. Jake guessed that the elephant's name was probably Carl.

Seconds later, Carl appeared in a flapping ball of elbows and knees. The skinny tie he wore flew over his shoulder as he crested the last of the stairs two at a time. Five feet from Deli, he fell to his knees and skidded across the hardwood floor, coming to a perfectly choreographed stop. *Dammit, how did he do that?*

"Oh sweet darlin', I thought you were dead."

"Uh...okay. It's nice to see you, too. Can you drive me to the emergency room? My foot is broken."

"I'd do anything for you, baby. You're some kind of wonderful," said Carl. He slid one arm under Deli's neck and another under her thighs and picked her up slowly. Deli winced.

"I still think we should call an ambulance," said Jake.

"Shut up and help me get to the car, Jake. We're not done talking," she said.

SACHA'S APARTMENT

SACHA KNOCKED ON THE WALL and turned the volume up on his headphones. Julie's parties weren't usually that loud, but he thought it was rude that she never invited him to any of them, so whenever he could hear anything over his headphones, he knocked on the wall. Sometimes she knocked back.

He'd been sitting at the table, chopping onions and analyzing the situation for more than ten minutes. The onions were well beyond minced, and he still couldn't figure out what Jake's plan had been. Maybe that guy really was just here for the helmet. But that made no sense. Deli didn't have people over. Especially people she didn't know well. Why wouldn't she tell that guy to go to her gym instead?

The more he thought about it, the more Sacha worried that he might have read the situation wrong. He washed his hands before picking up his phone (that was a lesson he didn't need to learn twice) and noted immediately that his earlier message had failed to send. He hit *Resend*. Again, it failed to send. Sacha grew suspicious.

He dialed Jake's number. It never even rang, just dropped him into voice mail. He was either on the phone or ignoring calls. Sacha hung up and called the Gloria phone instead. After eight rings, the answering machine finally picked up.

"Hey, ladies, you need to come up with more original ideas. Did you think I was gonna fall for all that motor cycle helmet BS? You best prepare yourselves because I'm gonna bring the pain to you now, bitches!"

He let the last word linger long enough to get the point across then he disconnected the line. There. Now he felt better.

Jake always thought he was so smart about stuff. Well, this time, Sacha would prove he was smarter. He topped off the roast with chicken stock, stuck it in the oven, then plopped down on his futon to bask in the warm glow one gets when they foil their best friends' practical joke plans. He decided to celebrate by watching one of his favorite movies. In the meantime, he rooted in the refrigerator for something to eat. He was getting kind of hungry, and the roast wouldn't be done for two hours.

CARL'S CAR

GETTING INTO CARL'S CAR had proved a little harder than just setting Deli down. To make her comfortable, Jake had to climb in the backseat so she could rest her leg on his lap while Carl drove twenty miles an hour through the back roads of Capitol Hill, avoiding all the potholes and making sure not to stop too suddenly. Deli insisted on going to Northwest Hospital. ("Parking is only seven dollars.") It was a painfully slow ride to the freeway entrance.

Luckily, Jake had thought to grab a baggie of ice out of the freezer before they left. He held it lightly against Deli's ankle while she did some sort of circular breathing thing to take the pain away. Jake didn't know if it worked though because on each exhale she went into pretty intricate detail about how she was going to beat Thad to a bloody pulp when she saw him next. It only frightened him mildly.

"He shouldn't have been able to do some of the things he did, Jake. At one point, he pushed me all the way down the hall—but I didn't feel it. It was like one second he was in front of me and the next, I was ten feet away. But I didn't move. It was all *Matrix*-y and shit."

"What happened exactly?"

Deli recounted the fight.

"He threw *what* at you?"

"It looked like a squirrel, but it had big eyeballs and racing stripes."

"Could it have been a sugar glider?"

"One of those little rain forest things? I suppose so, but where would Thad get a sugar glider and why would he throw it at me?"

Jake didn't know how to answer that without sounding seriously crazy so he shrugged his shoulders and changed the subject.

"Did you see where he went after you landed?"

"No, he disappeared."

"Did you at least *hear* which way he went?"

"No, you misunderstand. He didn't land. He completely disappeared. *Whoosh*! Gone."

"In midair?"

"That's what I'm saying."

"That's impossible."

"I know that, but it still happened. I haven't even told you the best part yet."

"There's more?"

"Oh yeah. He told me to tell you that you better leave Kix alone or he's coming for you."

"*What*?"

Jake shouted so loud it lifted Carl from his oldies-station-induced trance. He turned his head toward the backseat. "How y'all doin' tonight?" he said.

"And that's the other thing we need to talk about. *Why* is Carl talking like that?"

Jake cringed. He had been hoping Deli wouldn't notice that part. "I don't know. It seems like a lot of weird things are happening right now." He looked out the window into the soggy darkness, but Deli wasn't about to let him off so easily.

"Jake." She grabbed the sleeve of his coat and pulled herself closer to him. He tried to pull away, but she had the leverage thing down pretty well. "The *last* time a bunch of weird things happened, you turned my cat into some sort of immortal feline hell-hound."

The bottom fell out Jake's his stomach, and his free arm shot into the air reflexively.

"I didn't do anything, I swear!"

"My cat has *thumbs*, Jake."

"Okay, I don't *think* I did anything."

Deli responded by turning as much as she could toward Carl in the front seat. His fingers and elbows bopped in time with the oldies station as he concentrated on safe driving and the Motown beat.

"Hey, Carl," she said.

His sunglasses focused on the rearview mirror.

"What are your thoughts on"—she took a deep breath in and shouted the last word to the front seat—"*War!*"

"Good God!" said Carl in a conversational tone. "What is it good for?"

This he followed with a high-pitched warbling sound that may have been slightly musical. "*Absolutely nothing.*"

Deli rolled her eyes from Carl back to Jake.

"You may have a point," said Jake.

"Say it again!" shouted Carl.

"You *think*?" said Deli.

SACHA'S APARTMENT

ON THE TELEVISION, George Clooney discussed criminal plans with Brad Pitt. Sacha tried to watch, but the motorcycle helmet still haunted him. Did Jake really think he could be so obvious? Clooney would never be that obvious. No, Clooney would have turned that shit around and pranked those guys while they *thought* they were pranking him—an uber-prank, with Clooney in the middle like some sort of prank savant.

Suddenly, the veil lifted from Sacha's eyes, and he knew what it was he must do. He must be like Clooney. He must become the prank savant. If only he hadn't left that message like a noob. Master pranksters did not tip off their quarry that they were about to get pranked.

Dammit. Had Jake already heard it?

Probably not. If Jake had heard the message, he would certainly have called to hassle him. If he hadn't heard it, then it might be possible to erase the message before he did.

Sacha headed to his bedroom, or rather, the northeast corner of his apartment. There weren't any walls per se, but he'd marked it off from the kitchen area with a clever arrangement of milk crate bookshelves and ten years' worth of single-issue *Hellblazer* comics. He dug through the laundry on his bed until he found some pants.

Leaving the television on, Sacha tiptoed to the front door. Now that he wanted to be unnoticed, he became acutely aware of the noises around him. He didn't hear anything out of the ordinary, but that didn't mean much. It could all be a ruse.

Down in the main entrance to the house, he pulled on the

tattered copy of *Moby-Dick* and slipped behind the bookcase before anyone could see. He made his way down the stairs. It was cold and creepy, but the secret entrance had something the other door did not—an even *more* secret spare key. Jake thought no one knew about it but Sacha knew. Sacha also knew that Jake was a dumbass who locked himself out all the time.

He fumbled around for a while until he found the loose brick that hid the spare key. As quietly as possible, he slid the key into the lock and twisted the dead bolt back. When it was unlocked Sacha turned the knob and opened the door just enough. He tried to ease the door knob back into place quietly so it wouldn't make any noise but it wouldn't ease. It was jammed again. *Dammit.*

Sacha jiggled the key back and forth in the lock a few times. In the past, that had been enough to get things moving again. Unfortunately, the spare key was not made of hand-forged steel. It was made of an inferior aluminum alloy which was not meant to deliver blunt force trauma often. It rebelled by snapping neatly off at the lock.

"Crap," said Sacha. He would have to leave it. He pocketed the broken half of the key and stepped into the linen closet where he sat quietly, trying to determine if anyone was home. The place seemed quiet enough to be empty. Most likely, Carl was upstairs with Deli, but Jake might be at his desk with his headphones on. He listened for sounds of typing, or a chair squeak but after a minute of nothing, he decided to risk it.

Sacha held his breath as he opened the cupboard door wide enough to step through. The apartment felt empty. He snuck down the hall toward the living room. No one sat on the couch. No one manned the computer terminals. The door to Jake's room stood ajar, and inside was nothing but empty darkness. It seemed unlikely that Jake would be asleep, since it wasn't even nine yet. Carl's door was shut but no light shone out from under his door, either. They must all be out.

Jackpot.

Sacha hurried over to the answering machine and hit the *Play All* button so he could scroll through the messages and delete the one he left. Gloria Denny's voice pierced the quiet of the apartment.

"Jake, I am coming to inspect the property on the twentieth of November. Make sure you have the—"

Sacha scrambled to hit the *Forward* button. He scrolled through the rest of the message without stopping until he came to the last one.

"Hey, ladies, you need to come up with more original—"

He smiled and hit *Delete.* Then he headed to the living room. Carl had a box of movie props sitting on the shelf and there was something in it that Sacha wanted to use.

NORTHWEST HOSPITAL

THE REST OF THE RIDE went as smoothly as possible considering, the fact that Carl wouldn't stop singing the blues and insisting they join in on the refrains. Jake went along with it only because it meant he didn't have to explain why they were being forced to sing along to the oldies station in Carl's head.

When they hit a pothole near the entrance to the hospital parking lot, Deli went white with pain. As soon as she caught her breath again, she used it to profane God and *that Jag-Hole Thad,* to everyone within earshot. She had quite an extensive vocabulary. Jake did not think the situation was funny in the least. All the same, he had to cough to stifle a giggle during the Mr. He's-Gonna-Get-a-Broken-Foot-Up-His-Ass-Next-Time-I-See-Him part.

Carl parked the car at the curb and jumped out to fetch a wheelchair. Jake wheeled Deli into triage. When they asked what happened, Deli's only response was that she tripped and fell down the stairs. Jake went along with it because he didn't know how to explain it either. Plus, he was still a little afraid of her.

A nurse wheeled her away as he filled out paperwork. By the time he found her again, Deli had gone ever so slightly cross-eyed with pain medication. She'd stopped swearing, though, so that was a plus. A large man in blue scrubs swished in through the sheets that made up the walls of Deli's room. He said something about radiology then whooshed out again, dragging Deli along with him. Jake did not protest. He had no idea where Carl had gone.

He knew from his own recent hospital experience that police officers usually had a presence in the ER, so he wandered out to the front entrance. To the left of the security doors sat a tiny desk. At the tiny desk sat a medium-sized officer with a super-sized gun at her hip.

Jake rarely did anything a street cop would consider illegal, but talking to police officers was still nerve-wracking. He always felt as if he was going to say the wrong thing and they would find out about something stupid he did in college.

He walked slowly toward the officer with no idea what to say. *Excuse me, ma'am, but my friend was attacked by a crazed documentarian who may be able to teleport?* Yeah, that wasn't going to go over well. Jake walked slower, unsure of how to broach the subject. Unsure about a lot of what had happened, if he were being honest.

He stared at the polyester knees of the officer as he approached, trying to think of words but when he finally looked up, she smiled like an elementary school teacher and Jake felt mildly less guilty.

"Hi, Officer…"

"Greene." She offered her hand, and Jake shook it.

"I saw your friend in admitting," she said. "Her boyfriend do that?"

"Who, *Carl*? God, no. He wouldn't last three seconds against Deli." Which, while never fully proven, was Sacha and Jake's best guesstimate.

"She certainly seemed angry with someone."

"She likes to swear," Jake said, trying to keep the conversation light. He didn't want to seem suspicious to Officer Greene, but he also needed some information about stalkers. Specifically, what are you supposed to do if you have one?

"Did you have a question Mister…?"

"Denny. I just—" At that moment the front doors slid apart, and in walked Carl, still wearing the fedora and sunglasses. If he came over, Officer Greene would probably arrest them on suspicion of being idiots or something.

"Actually, could you please excuse me? I think I found what I'm looking for." Jake turned abruptly and walked as fast as decency would allow, across the waiting area to Carl, who was towering over an admitting nurse.

"Hey, Carl. Did you get the car parked? That's great! Why don't you take your sunglasses off?" Jake didn't wait for Carl to respond before reaching up and ripping the glasses off his face.

"Hey, man, how low can you go?"

Jake stared blank-faced at Carl, then reached up and yanked his fedora off, too. "Pretty damn low while the police are here. You need to stop being weird for a minute. There's a cop over there watching at you."

"*They in our groove?*" Carl said in an urgent whisper that was less of a whisper and more of a hissing shout. Thank goodness no one had any idea what he was talking about.

"Yes, very probably in our groove and up our tail feathers if you don't keep it on the down low, so stop talking and let me handle this. Come on." Jake carried the hat and glasses as he led Carl back to the ER. Carl loped along behind him, mumbling. When they reached Officer Greene's desk, she smiled again.

"How you gentlemen doing this evening?"

"It's a hard rain out there, ma'am." Carl said with a sigh. "A hard rain."

Officer Greene squinted at Carl and smiled. "You family?"

"No, ma'am. I grew up in an orphanage, ma'am."

Jake elbowed Carl in the ribs to get him to shut up. "This is her fiancé. They're getting married next month."

"An orphanage, huh?"

"Yes, ma'am. St Mary Catherine's School for the Coordinationally Challenged. It's out in Sequim. You ever been to Sequim, ma'am?"

"No I haven't Mister...I didn't catch your name?"

"Carlton Leif Sanderson."

"Well, Mr. Sanderson, it seems your girlfriend was in a little bit of trouble."

Jake could see the concentration on her face as she memorized Carl's full name. "Don't you want to go see how your fiancé is doing, *Carlton*?"

"It does seem so, ma'am," said Carl, shaking his head. Jake watched him closely. His head shaking had a rhythmic quality about it that he did not trust.

"My baby is makin' me blue. She hurts too-oo." The delivery of his words came very close to resembling a tune, so Jake stepped on Carl's foot as hard as he could under the pretense of leaning in to talk with the officer. Wherever Carl's mind had gone, at least it got the message. He shut up immediately.

"Is it okay if he goes in to see Deli?"

Officer Greene looked Carl up and down, clearly unimpressed but apparently not so unimpressed that she wanted to further their conversation. She gave Carl one more once-over and signaled to a woman sitting behind the bullet-proof glass of the nursing station wearing a serious expression that clashed with her cheery pink scrubs. Pink Scrubs buzzed the door. Jake opened it immediately.

"Thank you," he said. Then he grabbed Carl's sleeve and dragged him down the hallway to Room Five as fast as unimpressive decency would allow.

FOUND

THE CEILING OVER THE GRAND STAIRWAY of Horsey House had been designed as a light well, open all the way to the roof, in a dramatic effort to increase the light in an already dim house. It was the perfect spot to sit with one's head through the bannister uprights in order to keep watch over all of the floors at once. Indeed it had been on that very spot that Toesy had greeted the Holy Man earlier in the evening.

Since the Holy Man had accompanied Toesy's mistress to the hospital, he and Pansy had kept a steady watch over the house, particularly the area where the Boundary Walker had been. They kept to the shadows mostly, serious and determined. Toesy had been so focused on catching the evil Kicker of Doors that his concentration had wavered in other aspects. This, he decided later, had been his only mistake.

"There you are, you *brute!*"

The man stood in the hallway on the other side of the grand staircase. He could see them clearly but would have to run around the perimeter of the second floor to get at them. Toesy did not worry. They had plenty of time to escape if they needed.

"You give me back that sugar bear *right this instant.*"

On his back, Toesy felt Pansy's tiny paws stiffen with fear. He found this curious. Why should she be afraid of this man? He was not tall. He held no weapons. The shoes on his feet would not carry him far, especially in this weather. Even his pants were a non-threatening wool-blend. Still, Pansy's miniature body trembled.

Ark. Aaarrrkk. She rumbled, low and angry. Toesy translated this roughly as, *There is no way in Satan's pajamas I am going back in that cage.*

Pansy pressed a claw gently into his right ear. Toesy looked out of the corner of his eye; the grand staircase was close. He began to inch toward it.

Downstairs the front entryway buzzed. The sound of it spurred the two opponents into action. Toesy ran toward the stairs. The man ran at them. They were half way down when the front door opened and Sacha walked through it chewing on a stale crust of pizza. He saw Toesy and nodded.

"Hey Toesy!" Sacha said. Toesy stopped running immediately as did the man. "How's it hangin' man?"

Toesy sat down on his haunches. Sacha looked at him and cocked his head.

"Have you got a squirrel on your head?"

Toesy stood up straighter.

"Well I guess it's better than that gopher." Said Sacha and took a step up the stairs.

"Don't move!" screamed the man from the second floor. Sacha kept walking.

"I said don't move!"

"Take it easy, man," he said. "What's your problem?"

"Is that your cat? Because if it eats my sugar bear, I am going to sue you." The man stood in the hallway now, closer to the stairs. His anger shone brilliant and pink through his blond hair.

"Why are you so uptight about a squirrel?'

"It isn't a squirrel. It is a *sugar bear*, and it belongs to my girlfriend, Connie."

"What in the world is a sugar—wait, Connie? The hot chick with the dark curly hair?"

"Yes."

"She's *your* girlfriend?" The end of Sacha's sentence shot up in surprise.

"*Yes, she is,*" said the man, because he didn't know what else to say.

Ark! said Pansy because she hated liars.

Sacha didn't say anything else. He was too surprised.

"Now, can you catch that cat, or do I have to call Animal Control?" He'd said it like a threat—and Pansy certainly heard one—but Sacha merely smirked.

"You're kidding, right?"

"Certainly not! Connie is going to be back very late this evening and if that sugar bear isn't in its cage by then, I am going to take action."

"I don't think he's going to eat your squirrel, man. I think they're friends."

"*It is not a squirrel*, it's a sugar bear. They are indigenous to Australia, Tasmania and—"

"*Okay*," Sacha said putting his hands in the air. "You don't have to get all *Linnaean* with the biology. I'll solve this for you right now. Hey, Thanatos." He turned to Toesy, who was still inching his way down the stairs. Toesy stopped inching and looked up. Pansy stared without blinking. She did that a lot.

"You gonna eat that fancy squirrel?" Sacha said.

Toesy shook his head.

Sacha took another bite of his pizza crust and laughed. "See? That was easy."

"*How can you say that*? You are talking to a cat. It doesn't understand what you're saying. It's a *cat* for Pete's sake."

Toesy's ears went flat. Sacha squinted at the prissy man. "I'm guessing you haven't met Toesy yet, have you?"

"I've never seen that horrible thing in my life before this evening. It looks illegal, if you ask me."

"I *didn't* ask you," said Sacha. "He'll bring your damn squirrel back."

"Sugar bear."

"*Whatthefuckever*. He'll bring it back."

"He'd better, because if he doesn't, I am calling Animal Control."

Sacha started up the stairs. "Yeah, you let me know how that works out for you."

The man huffed out a fussy huff and stormed back to Connie's apartment. As soon as he was out of earshot, Sacha turned back to Toesy.

"He's not really dating Connie, is he?"

Pansy *arked!* so loudly that Toesy's ears twitched.

"Yeah, I didn't think so. You both on guard tonight?"

MMmmrRRRRRR, said Toesy.

"Right, well, you should probably not use the secret entrance for a while, okay? Wait until Jake or Carl use it first." Toesy cocked his head to one side but said nothing. Pansy stared at Sacha. Sacha tried not to look guilty.

"It's just a little payback, for all the Jell-O."

Toesy would not normally interfere with their unending battle of booby traps, but he did not want any shenanigans compromising security. He cocked his head further to the side and stared at Sacha. Long ago he discovered that if you stared at a human long enough, they eventually told you everything you wanted to know.

"Toes-man, don't give me that. They put it in everything they could! The apple juice wasn't so bad, but the soy sauce? That was just gross. And I don't even know how they made the glass cleaner do that. Just stay out of the back hallway, and you'll be fine." Sacha continued up the staircase. "Have fun on your date."

He gave Toesy a thumbs-up as he passed and hurried back to his apartment. Pansy *ark*ed! in surprise. Toesy stood straighter on his hind legs. His whiskers quivered, but other than that, he stayed motionless, trying to regain his composure.

FLIGHT

"IF YOU THINK I TRUST YOU like that idiot does, you are highly mistaken." The voice came from above. Leaning over the second-floor banister, Nick grinned at Toesy like some sort of evil monkey overlord. He held a soft-looking box in his hands. Before Toesy had time to react, it sailed through the air and landed to his right with an overstuffed thud.

A couch cushion? The man was throwing couch cushions at them? That was *not* nice.

Ark! said Pansy. Toesy agreed.

"Pansy, I *order* you to get up here this very instant, or I am telling Connie you ran away. Oh, why am I even talking to you? You're a stupid animal. You can't understand anything I say."

Toesy became agitated. He did not want people talking to his friends like that.

Let us go before trouble befalls this man.

Ark! said Pansy and doubled her grip on Toesy's fur, pinching his neck. Toesy did not mind.

But the man had already moved to the top of the stairs. He stood there, another couch cushion at the ready, his cheeks flush with crazy.

"You are in so much trouble when I catch you. You are going back in that cage, and I am not giving you your bedtime treats. Do you understand me?" He let out a maniacal laugh.

"No, of course you don't understand me! I don't know why anyone would have a pet like you. You're stupid and tiny, and you can't even stay in your cage. When Connie gets home, I'm telling her to get rid of you."

Toesy flexed his hind leg muscles ready to run.

"In fact," said the man, brandishing a lemon-colored bolster. "I could just save her the trouble right now."

The man raised the cushion to aim. Toesy leaned sideways to jump out of the way but changed his mind when he realized that behind the cushion-wielding maniac, the door to Connie's apartment stood wide open.

LAWYERS CAN'T SOLVE EVERYTHING

NICK TRIED CALLING ANIMAL CONTROL, but as soon as he recited the address, they hung up on him. Now they wouldn't answer the phone. He had to take this into his own hands. That cat was destroying his chances with Connie. What else could he do?

He descended to the middle of the stairs with every intention of doing bodily harm to the dratted thing. But Nick was an accountant, not a ball player. He had horrible aim. He'd have to get closer in order to hit it with the pillow. Hopefully, he could get close enough that he could kick it as well. Maybe that would knock Pansy off its head.

Beyond this thought, Nick stopped thinking. This is because his brain had a difficult time explaining why Pansy had been riding on the cat's head like she was riding a horse. There is no reason she would be riding on the cat's head, because she was an animal. And animals did not ride other animals like horses unless those other animals were *actual* horses. They certainly wouldn't be holding on to the fur of those other animals like a tiny set of reins because frankly, everything about that is confusing. It goes against all of nature. Therefore, Pansy was *not* riding the cat like a horse. She was being held captive by an animal that intended to eat her. Nick didn't care what that stupid hippy told him. The cat was clearly a menace.

He raised the pillow above his head, keeping a firm eye on his victims below. There was no place for the cat to run. Did it think it was getting out the door? Not on his watch. He stepped down four more stairs and let fly.

As the bolster flew for its mark, the cat took off. Before Nick realized in which direction it was headed, it was five stairs up and gaining. He dropped to his knees like a goalie, intent on saving the net. He'd seen enough hockey games to know how it was done. Unfortunately for Nick, hockey was less dangerous than Thanatos. The cat ran up to and over him, substituting Nick's wool-blend-covered knee and then his left shoulder for the stairs.

Pain shot down Nick's back where the cat dug in and power-jumped to the second-floor landing. Then a loud bang startled him.

"You horrible cat!"

There was a huge hole in his pants and probably one in his shirt. He felt the uncomfortable tickle of something dripping down his back and realized he was bleeding.

That blasted cat was going to pay for all of this. Nick would see to it. And if Pansy was in cahoots with him (which she absolutely was not because animals could not be in cahoots with anything), *she* would pay for it, too. He would not have a bunch of idiot pets making a fool out of him.

He pulled his cell phone from his trouser pocket and scrolled through his contacts until he found the name of his lawyer. He was about to hit *Send* when he noted the time on the clock above the main menu. If he called now, he would have to pay on-call rates. He scrolled through to his new to-do app and entered:

Call Terkle in morning Re: Cat.

He slipped his phone back in this pocket. Whoever owned that cat was going to be in for a huge punitive surprise. He would get Connie a sugar bear even if it meant making someone else buy a new one.

He rounded up his fluffy ammunition and headed back to Connie's apartment, not at all noticing that the door he'd left wide open was now closed.

NEVER ANGER A CAT WITH THUMBS

THEY STOOD JUST INSIDE the door. Toesy was not tall enough to reach the peephole, but he didn't need to. The man galumphed down the hallway like a mastiff chasing cows: slow and kind of stupid. Toesy could hear him bumbling toward the door.

Ark! said Pansy. She followed that with a sharp clicking sound. The footsteps outside closed in. Toesy could smell the man's soap through the crack in the door.

"Oh drat it," said the man outside. Three pillowy thuds landed on the ground. Toesy wedged himself against the door, ready to hold it shut so Pansy could flee.

Ark, ark! said Pansy and ran, a fuzzy bolt of striped lightning, up to the deadbolt latch.

My friend, that is a brilliant idea!

He reached up to the door knob and grabbed the deadbolt. The lock slid into place with a solid *thunk* and was immediately followed by a loud, wooden one, as the man outside walked straight into the door he thought he was opening.

"What the?" said the man. The door knob began to shake violently.

Holding her arms out to create wings, Pansy kicked off the door knob and glided to the floor. Toesy had never seen an animal fly like that before. He was very impressed. He would have said as much, but she gave him a stern look and *ark*ed very quietly.

On the other side of the door, the man was shouting. "I know you did not lock this door! There is a good reason that this door is locked, and it is not you! Do you hear me? It is *not you*." He punctuated his sentence by kicking the door very hard. Toesy growled. That made two door kickers this evening, and he did not like it.

Pansy gave another quiet *ark* and headed down the hallway. Toesy stopped growling and followed.

The back bedroom was thick with darkness. The blackout curtains kept light from the street from penetrating into the room. The smell of wood chips and urine filled his head and made his heart heavy. This poor creature spent her days and nights in this gloomy cell. He could not imagine a life so cloistered. Toesy vowed then and there, that she would never go back to living as a prisoner, even if it meant stealing her away forever.

Back down the hallway, the furtive jingling of keys told him they had little time.

Ark! said Pansy from somewhere above him in the curtains. Toesy searched with his ears. She *ark*ed three more times before he could find her.

Yes, I see what you mean!

Toesy tunneled under the heavy curtain. It was colder on the other side but dry. The window sash, made of heavy wood, held four aging panes of glass. There was a stylized hinge on one side, meaning that it would open outward like a door when it was unlocked. He found the latch and tried turning it. It would not move. Perhaps it was already unlocked? Toesy pushed on the nearest pane of glass, but it did not budge. He moved down the sill to the farther pane and pushed. It still did not budge.

The keys stopped jingling. Toesy did not panic. He tried another windowpane. When it, too, did not move, he thought about panicking, but only a little bit.

Across the apartment, they heard a metallic *snick* as the deadbolt slid open. The sound of music from the party down the hall grew louder as the door opened. Pansy began to chitter. She jumped up to take refuge, once again, on top of Toesy's head. He did not mind. It felt natural that she should do this.

He moved to the last pane of glass in the upper right corner, stood on his hind legs and punched out at the glass. The window frame did not move, but the glass inside the pane cracked. That was good. Toesy could work with that.

"*Where* are you?" The edge in the man's voice was sharp. Toesy could tell the man was at his limit. When his mistress sounded like that, it meant someone was about to get lectured.

As quietly as he could, he centered himself on the wobbly pane of glass and gripped the sill with his hind legs. Thanks to Steve, and his kareto-titanium claws it took little effort.

"I know you're in here somewhere, you little rat. You had better be back in that cage when I find you, or else there is going to be *big trouble.*"

His voice got louder and louder as the man walked down the hall toward the back bedroom. They were almost out of time. Toesy whipped his head back with just enough force to drop Pansy onto his back.

"And if I find *you* there, Mr. Cat..." On the other side of the blackout curtain, the door opened, and the man's voice thundered into the room. "You are going to know what the underside of my shoe feels like!"

But Thanatos, Dark Lord of the Underworld, was no schlub. His reflexes were honed to a point so sharp they could draw blood. Quite frequently, they did. Before the man stopped bellowing, Toesy's head shot forward into the glass. It broke into several large pieces, most of which fell forward into the dark abyss of a gigantic holly tree.

Go, he said.

Pansy did not move.

"What was that?" said the man.

You must go NOW, said Toesy. He reared his head back again, preparing to launch his friend into the holly if necessary. *I will find you.*

Pansy scampered up and over Toesy's head, toward the broken glass of the window. Light suddenly filtered in from underneath the blackout curtain. She stretched herself outward, as Toesy leaned in. Then, to his great surprise, she bit him again on the nose. This time with gentle affection.

Ark, she said and disappeared into the night.

"AHA!"

The pain in his tail as he was being dragged backward was nothing to the pain this man would feel when Toesy finished with him. Unfortunately, Toesy never got a chance to start. As soon as he turned to attack the crazy man, some sort of cloth got in the way. It covered his head and paws.

"You horrible beast! What have you done with Pansy?"

Toesy growled and tried backing up.

"Oh, you're not getting away that easy." He struggled wildly until he felt the cloth tighten around him and he was lifted off the floor.

Toesy grew very still. He knew this helpless feeling—this terrible weightlessness. He'd been only a kitten the last time, but some things you do not forget.

He was in a bag.

This man, this fussy excuse of a human, had better be far away when he got out of it.

KIX FOUND A STICKY NOTE
ON THE DRYER

SORRY IF I'M IMPOSING, but I came back this way about an hour after I saw you, and your laundry was done. I figured you might not have a lot of time in between deliveries, so I took it back to the house. I'll run it up as soon as you're home. I promise not to stay.

—Thad

Kix read the note three times, reminding herself each time that Thad was not trying to be a jerk even though he was basically holding all her clean underwear hostage. Knowing he did it because he was trying to be friendly somehow made it worse. If that guy didn't leave her alone this evening, she was going to go ballistic.

"Can I have my clothes?" Kix stood at the sliding glass door on the back porch. Rain dripped from the eaves onto the crown of her head.

"Hey! Yes, of course. Let me get them—they're right here." He ducked around the corner and returned with a new looking laundry basket holding all of her clothes, neatly folded.

"I'll carry it up for you if you like."

"That's okay, Thad. I'll take it." Kix held out her arms to take the basket, but Thad stepped forward and slid the door closed behind him.

"Don't be ridiculous. It's raining too hard out here to fight about it. Let's go." He started up the stairs before Kix had a chance to protest again. She followed him, too tired to argue.

The landing outside her front door wasn't very large. Two people and a basket full of clean laundry filled up all the available space. Thad leaned to the side so she could squeeze pass. It was uncomfortably tight. When she finally stood right in front of her door, Kix turned to take the basket from him.

"Just open the door," he said with a smile. Kix hesitated. "I'm only going to set it down for you. I promise."

He wouldn't move so she didn't really have much choice. Kix opened the front door and took one step inside. There she stayed put. Thad walked all the way over to her bed and set the basket down. Then he turned to her nightstand and switched the lamp on.

"There you are," he said.

"Thank you, Thad. I'll return your basket tomorrow." Kix hadn't budged. She held the door open, hoping he would get the idea to leave.

"Oh, don't worry about it. I bought you a new one."

"I didn't ask for you to do that. I'll return it tomorrow."

"It's not a big deal. It's just a basket. Keep it." He waved her concern away with a flick of his hand. Kix continued holding the door.

"Thank you. I will return it tomorrow. Right now, I need to get back to work."

"You *do*? I thought you were off for the evening."

Kix looked at him curiously, increasingly glad the door stood open. "Why would you think that?" She said.

"Well, because you're home. Why would you come home in the middle of your shift just to take your laundry upstairs?"

The pleasant we're-just-friends tone was still in his voice, but Kix no longer trusted it. "I'm on the closing shift. I won't get back until late, and I need my clothes for tomorrow. I didn't want to wake you."

His face fell from smiling to neutral. "Well, that *is* considerate. You're such a good friend, being considerate like that."

"Thad, I need to leave. Marco is expecting me back at work."

"Of course," he said but made no move toward the door. Instead he crossed his arms. "I like that you're direct. People should speak their mind more often instead of lying all the time. I think liars are the worst type of people, don't you?"

Kix stared at him and ignored his question. After an awkward moment of silence, he walked toward the front door.

"I would hate it if I ever found out *you* were a liar, Kix."

"Thad, can you please go? I have to get back to work." She

stepped out onto the landing and stood to the side so he could get by. She started to close the door.

"You see, that's exactly what I mean. You're lying right now, aren't you?" he said from the top of the stairs. Kix was so stunned by his nerve that she stopped locking her door and turned around to tell him off. How dare he?

But when she turned around, he wasn't there. She peered down the stairs, but he wasn't there either. Where did he go?

Without warning, her head was yanked backward. Instead of standing on the stairs as she assumed he was, he was somehow standing behind her, in her apartment.

"I'm not stupid. I know what you're doing," he said. Kix tried to scream, but the surprise of it all took the words from her throat. She fought to keep her balance.

"It's shit like this, Karen. You can't be trusted at all."

He pulled her into the apartment and slammed the door. She tried standing up straight but he yanked her hair sideways and it was all she could do to keep from falling over.

"I know what you've been up to, Karen. You aren't fooling anyone." He dragged her by to her tiny kitchen table. "You better start telling me the truth or you are going to regret it."

THE OTHER SIDE OF BRAD

THAD HAD BEEN LEANING against the bathroom counter for about ten minutes. He'd climbed under the door, out to the sinks after he'd lost sight of the weird space hole thing that sucked him over here. Besides *a bathroom*, Thad was not at all sure where here was.

Suddenly, a pulse of energy, like a sharp zap of electricity, came from behind and zapped Thad in the shoulder. A second zap hit him from somewhere near the end stall and Thad realized it had to be the space hole. It must still be open! If he could find it again, maybe he could get back to his old body.

He checked the other stalls to make sure he was alone before ducking back under the stall door.

Energy, sharp and angry, radiated outward from the wall like a beacon. Thad ran his hands along the crumbling tiles until he found the source: a bit of cracked grout, throbbing with energy. He leaned over and studied it closely, not at all sure what to do.

As he stared, the crack began to twist itself into circle. The center fell away and it widened into a dark spot. Soon a white dot formed in the middle and inside of that, a bunch of colors swirled around. Then, as if nothing had happened, he was back in his world, standing next to Kix, holding something soft. Thad was so pleased to be back, he spoke without thinking.

"Hey, Brad, we need to trade back. I have no idea what I'm supposed to be doing over here. What is going on?" he said.

"You shouldn't be here," said Brad but Thad wasn't paying much attention; he was focused in on Kix. She looked like she was in pain.

"What are you doing, Brad?"

"Just taking care of something. Don't worry about it."

But the words he heard in his head were contrary to the feeling of rage within, a fullness of anger threatening to implode. Thad looked down to see what was in his hand and suddenly, the look in Kix's eye made sense.

"What are you doing? *Get out of here,*" he said to Brad.

Acting on impulse, Thad pushed every ounce of himself forward, back into his own body, back into his own mind. He concentrated on loosening the grip Brad had on Kix's hair. He found words again.

"I've got him, Kix! Go."

She untangled her hair from his fingers and spun around, delivering a roundhouse kick directly to the softest parts she could reach.

Thad fell forward, into his own reality and into the pain shooting from his left testicle to his stomach. He came very close to barfing.

"Don't you ever touch me again," she said.

"I won't. I promise. *But he's still here,*" he said, dry heaving onto the porch. *"You have to leave."*

Kix looked into his eyes. She looked more surprised than mad. Or maybe she was about to murder him. Thad really couldn't tell.

"What are you waiting for? Go."

Kix ran.

BACK FROM RADIOLOGY

WHEN THE SCRAWNY GUY wheeled Deli back into the room, he'd been accompanied by a doctor who couldn't have been more than ten years of age. She patiently explained to Carl that although it was a clean break, they needed to operate in order to set it properly. She carefully outlined how Deli would have to spend the night at the hospital and that a pre-op nurse would be around soon to prep her for surgery. Carl responded to everything she said by nodding his head and saying, *"Right on!"*

That had been ten minutes ago. Jake was now huddled in the corner reading a three-month-old copy of *Us Weekly* and trying not to listen to Carl passing off the lyrics to "I'll Be There" as conversation. Deli was too drugged up to notice.

A tiny nurse squeaked up to the room in efficient shoes. She stopped outside the curtain that served as a door and read off a chart. Jake stepped out to talk with her.

"Miss? Is there any chance Deli will get into surgery soon?"

Her brow creased. She read the chart in her hand. "Ms. Pelham is scheduled for the next OR. Are you the fiancé?"

"No, uh, I'm her brother."

"Sure," she said though she looked less than convinced. "But we can only have one of you back here. If you and the fiancé want to duke it out to see who gets to wait in the lobby, we can make sure the loser gets updates." Jake tried not to look too happy.

"Thank you. I have to go make some phone calls anyway," he said this in a way that implied calling other family members and alerting them to the situation was definitely on his agenda. The nurse gave him an efficient smile and turned to the computer station near the wall.

Jake hadn't lied. He *did* have calls to make. Technically it was only *one* call but he'd made it five times now and Kix still wasn't answering. Maybe she didn't answer her phone while she was making deliveries. It was almost eight thirty. She was probably still at work. Hopefully probably. Maybe. He'd seen her get off sometimes as early as nine. Jake really wanted to be home by nine.

He was a little worried about leaving Deli alone with Carl until he realized that, if anything weird happened, they were already at the hospital. He just hoped that weird thing wouldn't be Carl.

Jake needed to get going if he was going to catch a bus. He ducked back under the privacy curtain.

"The nurse is here to prep Deli for surgery," Jake said. "She says they can only have one of us back here though, so…"

Carl looked up from Deli. He smiled his big, goofy smile. "Let it go, man. You get to the gig." Jake was ninety-eight percent certain this meant he was free to go home.

"You sure? I don't want to abandon you guys here, but I think there's something wrong with my cell phone. Kix said she might come over this evening. I don't know if she's there or not because she's not answering. I just want to make sure she's okay."

"Yeah, yeah, yeah," said Carl with enthusiasm. Then he threw his car keys at him and made *shoo-shoo* motions with his other hand.

"I can't take your car, Carl. How are you going to get Deli home?" He threw the keys back, and Carl caught them without flinching.

Jake walked over to Deli and leaned in. "Hey, are you okay with me leaving you two alone? He's still in a, uh…a grand funk."

Deli had uncrossed her eyes as he spoke and struggled to focus. She pointed a finger in his general direction.

"It's okay, Jake. I figured it out. It's that thing. You know. The thing on Thursdays with you and Carl. About your *hair*," she said and made twirly circles in the air next to her ear.

"Okay, you know what? I'm gonna go ahead and go. The eight-forty bus should be here soon. If I start now, I'm pretty sure I'll make it in time." Jake stood up and walked across the room.

"Reach out," said Carl and held up his hand, thumb and pinky stretched apart, the universal sign for *call me*. Deli shook her head and waggled her finger at the blood pressure monitor.

"I'm over here," said Jake. Deli turned and waggled her finger at Jake.

"Don't pretend like you don't know what I'm talking about. You *know* what I'm talking about. On *Thursdays*. It's your wig, Jake. Don't believe what you think, it's your *wig*," said Deli. She'd gone cross-eyed again, and Jake had to bite his tongue in order to keep himself from laughing.

"It's *fuzzy*," said Deli. She nodded to prove her point. Then nodded again for good measure.

"Yeah. I gotta go catch the bus now. I'll call to check on you guys later. We'll talk about my hair then, okay?"

"No, it's *fizzy*," Deli said. She hadn't stopped nodding her head yet. Jake gave a little wave and walked out. He did not look at Officer Greene when he walked past.

It's a shame he wasn't paying more attention because Deli was right about the wig.

ON AUTOPILOT

IT WAS VERY IMPORTANT TO KIX that she did not freak out about what just happened because freaking out would mean losing control of herself. She did not want to lose control of herself right now. She wanted to figure out what happened and what she needed to do to make it not happen again.

She should have called the police from the driveway, but she was afraid Thad might find her if she stayed there, so she headed directly for the station. Hopefully Sergeant Ellis would be there. Sergeant Ellis had been on duty the evening Jake had been shot. He was a good guy. He would listen.

Traffic was at a standstill. Kix drove south in the slowest escape ever; the previous twenty minutes replaying in her head over and over. First surprise, then pain, then paralyzing fear. Her cheeks flushed, and her ears burned. It felt so unjust to be embarrassed by it. She'd done nothing wrong. But for one horrible moment, she'd been unable to defend herself. It was terrifying and humiliating, and she kept reliving it. The worst part was that she hadn't even seen it coming.

At the next red light, Kix took a deep breath and made a conscious effort to stop berating herself and start trying to piece together what happened in a rational way so she could tell the sergeant. Thad took her laundry. When she went to get it back, he followed her upstairs. He was holding her basket of clean clothes. He set the clothes on her bed. He walked past her out the door...then somehow, he was back inside her apartment again? How did he get back inside without her seeing him?

However he did it, she knew he'd intended to beat her senseless. She could feel the anger coming off him in waves. But then he stopped being angry, almost like he woke up from it or something. Instead of sleepwalking he sleep-attacked her? That was stupid.

Her thoughts bounced back and forth between the attack and the look in Thad's eyes when he told her to run. When she was finally able to wrest her attention back to the road, she discovered she'd been on autopilot for the last fifteen minutes. Instead of the police station, she'd driven back to work.

"What the? Argg...*everything* about this night is messed up," she said to no one in particular. She swore a few more times and pulled into the back parking lot. Marco's office felt safer right now than driving across town anyway. She would call from here. Sergeant Ellis would still listen.

The spot behind the Dumpster was strictly off limits to anyone who wanted to remain in Marco's good graces but Kix had an excellent excuse, and Marco could kiss her ass if he didn't think so. She killed the motor and stepped out into the alleyway. Her body was finally coming down from the adrenaline high, leaving her feeling weak and empty. But even as she cursed the aftereffects of panic, Kix's instincts flared back to life. As she approached the back door, something felt wrong. She stopped and listened.

There wasn't enough noise. Usually, after the dinner rush, Marco was in the dish room, shouting at the dishwasher. He liked shouting at the dishwasher; it made him happy, and it kept him from shouting at the customers. But she'd listened carefully for over a minute and didn't hear any profanity at all. Was sleeping off the cold meds?

Kix went back to her car and grabbed the empty warming bag from her last delivery. The noise of the car door made her flinch in the strange quiet. With the warming bag slung over her shoulder to obscure her face, she let herself in the back door. Instead of going straight to the kitchen she took an immediate left down the back hallway towards Marco's office.

Pizza Joe's only bathroom was across the hall from the office. Kix did a quick check to make sure no one was there before she stepped into Marco's office and closed the door behind her.

ASHWOOD SUPER MALL

THAD MANAGED TO PUSH HIM OUT but Brad wasn't worried. Thad was weak and stupid. Weak people look for reasons to believe in lies. Stupid people look to others for answers.

Brad was neither weak nor stupid. He knew who he was and what he wanted. He wanted Thad's reality and he knew how to get it.

"Thad, can you hear me? What's going on?"

"Stay the hell away from me. Get out of my head and don't ever come back."

Brad felt Thad redouble his effort to block him out of his consciousness. He played along.

"Thad, what is going on?" he said. "What just happened? Something came in here. Something just got inside of me. Did you feel that?"

"I'm not listening to you. You're a damn psycho. Stay away from me. Get out of my head and never come back."

Brad let Thad push him all the way back to the Ashwood Super Mall bathroom before answering. He felt the handicap stall solidifying around him. There was the toilet, the toilet paper holder, the mop and bucket.

"Thad, I swear it wasn't me. Something else was here. Didn't you feel it? Thad. Please help me."

"You, sick *bastard*. I don't believe a word your saying. Get—"

"Wait, did you hear that?" said Brad.

With his heel, Brad nudged the mop bucket toward the toilet. As the bucket rolled away, the mop resting within it began to fall forward.

"He's here," said Brad. "Oh God he's—"

The mop smashed into the back of Brad's head. It rocked him forward. Brad steadied his footing and concentrated on the pain until he felt Thad's attention peak slightly. Then he closed his eyes and stepped away from the interdimensional portal, severing their already tenuous connection.

AURORA AVENUE

THE RAIN HAD SOFTENED while they were in the ER, less assaulting but still very wet. Jake shrugged into the collar of his jacket and kept his head down, avoiding people whenever possible. He wasn't trying to be rude. Anyone walking this particular stretch of busy road was probably in the *business* of walking this particular stretch of road until God or one of Seattle's Finest happened to notice. Jake didn't want any trouble. He just wanted to get home.

The eight-forty bus pulled up to the curb in time for Jake to see his connecting bus drive away. He cursed. He hadn't had such a horrible night since he got shot. Everything was going wrong. Carl speaking in tongues, Deli getting attacked by the jackass who might have actually meant to kill him. Even Toesy was out to get him. What did he mean by kidnapping a sugar glider anyway?

Jake was not a superstitious man but he had noticed a certain pattern to his life so far. When things started to go right, they always ended up going wrong somehow—usually in spectacular fashion.

It would be the same with Kix. She left as soon as she could this morning and hadn't called him all day. She wasn't going to come over. She probably didn't even have to work. He wondered what made her lie about it. Was he being too clingy? He kicked the curb and swore again. This time not so loud. Then he turned up Pike Street and walked for a solid five minutes without changing his mind.

Halfway up the hill, a twenty-four-hour coffee shop lit up the sidewalk. An ostentation of hipsters in skintight pants and two-hundred-dollar haircuts headed straight for it, desperate for atmosphere or an audience—it was always hard to tell with those guys. The alpha hipster stepped up to open the door at the exact same time a woman stepped out. They nearly collided.

She reacted first by stepping to the side and holding the door with her foot. Even from down the block, Jake could see the woman knew how to play the Seattle game well. As the filed past, they checked their phones or studied the ground, looking anywhere but at her. She, in turn, ignored them by running her fingers through her hair to smooth it down. Then she dusted imaginary lint from the front of her overcoat.

They were almost inside when she stepped away from the door, cutting the last hipster off from his flock. His friends within ignored him by staring apathetically at the menu board. The woman said something, and the hipster turned to answer, effectively blocking Jake's view of the exchange. It was none of his business anyway. He walked on.

Jake was less than ten feet away when the kid started to dance. No, he wasn't dancing. He was trying to get a hand into the front pocket of his pants. He laughed to himself and looked at the woman, expecting to exchange a get-a-load-of-this-guy,-eh? look with her.

Instead, he looked directly into the eyes of the Eighty-Five-Cent Lady, holding her cup out and smiling with most of her teeth. When she saw Jake she scowled.

"What are you doing here?" She said.

Jake was so startled, he tripped. The omega-hipster, hand successfully wedged halfway into his front pocket, used the diversion to grab the door and dive for the safety of the coffee shop. His friends still weren't paying attention.

Jake righted himself. He wasn't sure if he should be offended or confused. He chose to be diplomatic, in case he was wrong.

"I live here," he said.

"Not *here*, you ponce." Eighty-Five-Cent stared into Jake's eyes. He stared back. He hadn't realized how blue her eyes were until now. They looked like sky and mountains and little yodeling girls named Heidi.

"I meant *here*," she said and dropped her gaze. Jake felt the weight of it fall and hit the ground. He looked down.

Between his feet, the sidewalk had buckled where a tree root had grown up. No wonder he'd tripped. He contemplated the buckle in the sidewalk until his eyes fell upon a set of dainty ankles, standing in the exact same place Eighty-Five-Cent had been standing not half a second ago.

Jake looked up.

There stood the blonde woman in the white overcoat, buttons too large to be anything but designer. She stared at him with her Alpine eyes, clear blue and cold.

"You aren't supposed to be *here*," said the new and improved Eighty-Five-Cent Lady. Her lips were glossy red, her teeth shining and perfect.

Jake blinked.

He blinked again.

Then he threw up.

ANOTHER CONVERSATION, THIS ONE NOT SO QUIET.

KIX HAD THE PHONE in her hand, ready to dial, when she heard footsteps tromping down the hall. She hung up quickly. When the door knob began to turn, she jumped behind the door and waited, ready to kick whoever came around the corner.

"This is ridiculous. I am losing customers from this crazy man! I do not have time for this."

Marco walked into the room without looking in her direction. He kept his back to the door and started searching the filing cabinet on the far wall. Blindly, he reached behind with a foot and nudged the door closed. Kix thought she ought to draw attention to herself before she scared the pants off of him, but when the door clicked shut, he turned and faced her directly. Kix gasped.

Marco's lower lip was purple and swollen. A gash on his cheek sported a superhero-themed bandage. The bruise behind it looked red and angry, but not nearly as red and angry as Marco.

"My dear, you should not be here," he said. Then he took her by the shoulders and gave her the only hug she'd ever seen him give anyone, ever. It was very short, and it made tears well up in her eyes.

"I am glad to see you," he said.

"How did you know I was here?" said Kix, wiping her nose on her sleeve.

"I know what happens in my own restaurant. You are in danger. Are you hurt?" Kix had never seen him so upset before. His brow looked ready to knit a sweater.

She stared at his swollen cheek. "Not as hurt as you are, Marco. What happened here?"

"*Mangusta*," he said and spat on the floor. "Waiting for me by the Dumpster. I thought he was bum at first, but he asked could he come in to talk with you. I said no, you are working on deliveries. He says okay, can he come in to leave you note. I told him no, I do not run dating service." Marco made go-away movements with his hands.

"I thought he went. He did not follow me inside. But when I walked into office, there he stood." Marco pointed to the spot Kix was currently standing in. "I told him get out, he is not welcome here. Then the phone rang, so I answered. I thought he would leave. He did not."

"Is that when I called? Is that why you were so nice to me earlier?"

Marco shrugged. "What could I say? Hello, my dear Kix? Please don't come back to work, there is crazy man here? I made up party, hopefully for you to go there instead. He got very angry at that. Said I was warning you."

"What happened then?"

"He threatened me, many times. Do not call police. Do not call anyone. Do not leave restaurant. Do not close restaurant. He would find you. And for all of these things, he would kill you. Then he did this."

Marco pointed to his superhero bandage. Kix winced.

"Marco, are you sure you're okay? You don't need to go to the ER or something?"

He looked offended that she would even ask. "Of course I am okay. And now that you are safe, he will *not* be."

Marco plucked a key ring from a nail board full of key rings and bent over the file drawer of his desk. He unlocked the drawer and rummaged around. When he sat back up again he held a strangely shaped bundle wrapped in a blue rag. It hit the desk top with a heavy thud. The cloth fell from the bundle easily, revealing two handguns.

"Take this." He put the smaller gun in her hand. It weighed more than she thought it would.

"Marco! Where did you get these?"

"Jaquish."

"What is Jaquish?"

"Not what, *who*. He is my brother."

"You have a *brother*?" Kix said, handing the gun back to him. "Wait, is he really your brother? You're not connected are you? Please say no. I don't want you to be part of the mafia."

"*Cowards*." Marco turned his head and spat on the ground again. He took the gun in his hand and enunciated all his words by shaking it. "I am not mafia. This is for if they come *back*." He puffed out a great big breath and steamed slightly from the ears, although Kix might have imagined that part. He certainly looked past his boiling point.

"Wow, okay. I don't really know about *that* but I'm pretty sure Thad isn't a mafia hit-man or anything. I think he's just a regular psychopath. And I'm not even sure *he's* the bad guy. I think there might be another bad guy."

"He tried to kill you, my dear. That is *bad* guy."

"I *agree*. But I didn't overpower him. He was choking me, then he just…stopped. Like he woke up. Then he yelled at me to run. He said, *I've got him. Go!* I don't know how to explain that. Something weird is going on. He was not himself. To be honest, it felt like he was in trouble."

Marco immediately made the sign of the cross and spat on the ground again.

"Yes," he said and held the gun very steady in his hand as he offered it to her again. "He *is* in trouble."

"Marco, you can't shoot him."

"I am not aiming for kill shot. I am aiming much lower down."

"Yeah, I'm kinda worried about how much you're smiling."

"I do not like you being threatened."

"I can see that. But you still can't go out there with guns blazing. Do you even have a permit for this thing? You're going to get yourself in trouble."

"I told you. I am not the one in trouble."

This wasn't a fight she could win. Kix decided to change her tactic.

"What did he want?"

"Who?"

"Thad."

"Is that his name? I will remember that," he said, then he seemed to remember himself. "He brought a warning for James. Said he was not to visit you anymore. He was very angry."

"James who?"

"The one who orders light garlic on his pizza."

"You mean *Jake*?"

"Yes, Jake! The one who is in love with you."

"No," she said, her voice very flat. She met his stare and did not back down. "He isn't."

Marco looked at her intently for a few more seconds, then shrugged his shoulders and gave her a capitulating nod. He leaned over and opened the bottom file drawer. There was a heavy *clink* followed by a smaller *tink,* and he soon resurfaced with a dark green bottle and two small glasses. He opened the bottle and poured each of them a shot of whatever was inside. It was such a deep purple it almost looked black.

"Good for colds," he said. "And dealing with men who order light garlic. Drink."

He saluted her briefly before pouring the entire glass of mystery liqueur down his throat. He followed that with a distinctly bovine grunt. When it was her turn, Kix threw the shot to the back of her throat and swallowed it before her sinuses had a chance to protest. Marco was right, it was good for dealing with nonsense. Every stray thought that had been worried about Thad was now focused on the fact that her nose hairs were being singed off.

"Has Thad," she said after her lips stopped trying to melt, "come back at all?"

"Twice," said Marco. "First time was very quick. I was on phone taking orders. I told him, people call. They want pizza. But he did not like it. He cut the land line. The second time he came for the delivery book. Said he would check for himself. Then he..."

Marco looked down to the desk. Through his thinning black hair, Kix could see his scalp turn red. He shook his head a few times before looking back up to her.

"Then he was not being there anymore."

"What do you mean *not being there anymore*?"

"He was no longer standing where you are standing."

"You mean he disappeared?"

"No. He was very suddenly *not being there* any longer."

Kix thought about how Thad had gotten past her on the landing.

Like he'd disappeared from one spot and reappeared in another. That would certainly explain what happened.

"I think he did the same thing to me. He was standing behind me, then suddenly he was in front of me, like he could teleport or something."

"No. This makes no sense." Marco said, much more to himself than her. "People *cannot* teleport."

"It makes about as much sense as anything else does right now. Did he do anything else weird?"

"Is all weird to me, Miss Kix. Every part of it." Marco stared at the handgun on the table and seethed.

"Yes. It is. Look, I need to go check something out before I call the cops. Keep doing what you're doing. If Thad comes here, pretend you haven't seen me, okay? Just do business as usual."

"Where are you going?" Marco stood up and leaned slightly toward the door. "You must be careful."

"Marco, even hopped up on cold meds, I trust your gut. If you think weird things are happening, then it's a safe bet that something is wrong. Like, *really* wrong. I need to find—"

"Go to police. They will help you."

"I will. But if Thad really can teleport—"

"He *cannot*."

"I know that, but if he *can*, then I think I we're going to need more than the police. I've got to find Jake."

"The one who is in love—"

"Nope, just shut up about that."

"Fine. Take this," he said and pushed the gun into her hand again.

"I can't take that. I don't even know how to use it."

"Is very simple. Just pull back here, aim at bad guy, then pull this part." He demonstrated what to do with efficient hand motions. "Already I have put bullets in."

"What do you think I'm gonna do, shoot Thad?"

"Yes! You are getting picture now. Shoot him if you see him. But take safety off first." He pointed to a little button on the side of the gun marked *safety*.

Kix had no intention of shooting Thad but she took the gun anyway because stoved-up Marco didn't need *two* loaded weapons at his disposal. She tried tucking it into her back pocket, but it was really heavy and almost fell out, so she stuck it in her coat pocket instead.

She slipped out the back door and headed to Maxine. Folding herself into the front seat, she fidgeted with where to put the gun. It was too heavy to rest in her waistband, too bulky to sit in her lap, too large and too scary just to toss on the seat. The glove compartment was full, so she tucked it underneath the passenger seat and pushed a bunch of books in behind it to keep it from sliding around too much. Tomorrow she would return it to Marco, after he had calmed down. Until then, no one would know she had it. Kix kept the lights off as she drove through the alleyway.

Just as she turned out onto the street, a dark car pulled away from the curb. She watched it in her rear view mirror as she rolled up to the stop sign. It had those annoying blue headlights so she couldn't see who was behind the wheel. For half a second, she got the creepy feeling that it was going follow her but then it turned in the opposite direction and drove off. Kix sighed in relief.

The car with the annoying blue headlights wasn't following her because it didn't have to. The driver already knew where she was going.

SHE CALLED DELI
FROM THE RED LIGHT

BUT COULDN'T GET AN ANSWER. She tried three more times with no additional luck. What was going on with the phones tonight? Was there some sort of solar flare no one knew about? Carl's phone rang four times before he answered it, but at least he answered.

"Hey now!" said Carl.

"Hey, Carl, is Deli there? I can't get through on her phone."

"My head is spinnin'," he said. Kix heard a beeping noise in the background. It did not sound like music.

"Okay, sure. I'm just checking in to see what you're up to. Have you seen Jake at all?"

"And we're takin' it higher," Carl said. At that point, a voice in the background shushed him. This was followed by a loud thud and some shuffling noises, then Deli's voice came on the line.

"Kix, is that you? I'm here, room eleventy-twelve or something," she said. "I don't know. It doesn't matter anyway 'cause it's the wrong *here*. Carl is here and he's wrong, too. That's probably Jakeses fault. Not my leg. That's Mitzleplik's fault." In the background, Kix heard a shout, followed by something that sounded like an anemic rooster.

"Deli, what's going on? Are you drunk? Where are you?"

"I fell pushed the stairs. My leg is broken, but Carl is brokener."

"*What?* Did you get into an accident? Do you need me to come get you?"

"No. it wasn't an accident. It was Miztleplik. Stay away from him. Tell Jake to fix it. He'll listen to you. He loves you. He told me you guys are all sexy time and everything. Make him fix Carl."

"*He did what*? Deli, where *are* you guys?"

"We're at the radio station. A pink lady made me wear that heavy blanket thing." Behind her slurred speech, Kix heard an official-sounding voice announcing the need for Dr. Schwartz to attend radiology at once.

"*Radiology*?"

"Bingo! Thass it!"

"You really broke your leg?"

"Not me, *Mitzleplik*. Make him stop. Tell Jake. His wig is wizzy. He'll know."

"His wig is fizzy?"

"No, *wizzy*. With a *wuh*."

"Yeah yeah yeah!" crowed the rooster in the background.

"Is Carl *singing*?"

"Jake did that, too. Make him fix Carl," said Deli. Kix tried pressing for a few more answers, but nothing else Deli said made any sense, so she said good-bye and disconnected the call. They were in a hospital. Kix had to assume they were safe.

This wasn't about her being clingy any longer. Things were getting downright strange. She took a deep breath and dialed Jake's cell phone. It was busy.

Who gets a busy signal anymore? Hadn't busy signals gone extinct with fax machines and pay phones?

Someone calling from a blocked phone number might, said a little voice in her head.

Shut up, she said back. *You don't know.*

Hey, you're the one who asked, the little voice said.

He wouldn't do that, would he? She waited a moment, but the little voice had no more to say, so she dialed his number again. It was still busy.

She drove through the backroads towards Jake's place, fighting her instinct to dump the whole business. She did not need any of this drama. If Jake didn't want to talk with her, then so be it. He could be an ass for all she cared. She could just go home, get her jammies on and watch Michelle Yeoh movies until she fell asleep.

Except she couldn't, could she? For all she knew, Thad was still there. A quick Internet search produced a number that Kix thought might be the Gloria Phone. It felt a little stalkerish to be calling him there, but she no longer cared. At least she could leave a message.

"You've reached 206-555-5309. I'm not available right now, but if you leave a message, I'll get back to you."

"Hey, it's me," she said. "Sorry to call you here but I can't reach your cell, and none of my texts are going through. I just talked with Deli in the hospital. She said to tell you that you need to fix Carl and also that she doesn't like your Halloween costume for some reason. She says your wig is too wizzy. Those are her words by the way. I don't know what that means. Jake, can you please call me when you get this? There is something fundamentally weird going on."

Kix knew he had her cell phone number, but she recited it anyway, then disconnected the call. She dialed Jake's cell phone one last time, in case he picked up. It was still busy.

WELL, THERE'S YOUR PROBLEM, RIGHT THERE

IT SEEMED LIKE A REASONABLE IDEA at the time. Nick hadn't wanted to kill the cat—merely incapacitate it until he could get someone from Animal Control to come pick it up in the morning.

He'd tried walking a few feet, but when he moved forward the pillowcase swung toward his leg. There followed a very painful minute of trying to keep hold of the bag while also stanching the blood flow from his shin. Now he held on to the pillowcase as if his life depended on it. A small part of his mind thought that maybe it did.

Nick tried to ignore the increasing pain in his back by listing the defendants in a rapidly expanding lawsuit he had planned. Certainly the landlord and whoever owned this cat. He momentarily considered adding Connie to the list, but his better judgment won out there. It might make things weird between them if he sued her.

The pillowcase stopped struggling for one blessed moment, and Nick was glad for the rest on his back. But just as soon as it stopped struggling, it started again and the cotton, slick with sweat, began to slip through his fingers. He scrambled to get a better grip. The cat hit the floor and twisted, but Nick already had the pillowcase in his hand again. He wrenched it a few inches off the ground so the blasted animal couldn't gain any traction. When he had the cat contained again, he noticed that he now stood a little closer to the doorway. This gave him an idea.

Nick dropped his arm, letting the cat hit the floor. Then, he picked it up immediately while also taking a step forward. He repeated the process, bouncing the struggling cat onto the floor and back up before it could get oriented. He worked his way out of the back bedroom, trying desperately to come up with an idea that would free him.

Halfway down the hall, Nick finally found his opportunity.

PIZZA

JAKE WOBBLED UP THE SIDEWALK to Horsey House trying to figure out exactly what had happened back at the coffee shop. He was here, and then he was *there*, and then he was sick. Eighty-Five-Cent looked more like Ten Grand, but the more he thought about that, the more he felt like he was going to throw up again, so he took the long way around to the back, just in case he did. There were four stairs down to the Dungeon's front door. He only stumbled down three of them.

Inside, the queasy feeling deepened. It didn't help that the apartment had gone all clammy and cold. For half a second, Jake thought that Thad had broken in and he started to freak out. Then he realized the door to the linen closet had popped open. Sometimes it did that and the cold air from the secret stairway seeped into the apartment.

He walked to the hallway and closed the door, all the while trying to think about something other than the Eighty-five Cent Lady. She wouldn't get out of his head. He bounced back and forth between both images of her like the worst game of table tennis he could imagine. How had there been two of her? She must have done something.

But why? She didn't care about him. She hated him. To be fair, Jake thought she might actually hate everyone, but back there, that was all for him. He hadn't even done anything wrong—he was just walking up the street. It wasn't his fault that he tripped into some weird dimension.

But the deep-set fear in him—the part of his mind that calculated the bad news first and played every scene of rejection he'd ever endured on an endless loop—*that* part of him knew differently. He *had* done something, hadn't he?

You pushed, it said.

And Jake knew it was true. The Eighty-Five-Cent Lady was absolutely right. Standing in his chilly living room, staring at the futon Kix had been lying on less that twenty-four hours before, Jake finally realized what it was that had been niggling in the back of his mind while he and Kix been busy.

"Sweet merciful crap, *please* tell me I didn't jack up space-time."

A TRICK OF THE EYE

BRAD LOOKED IN THE MIRROR. The deep red welt over his eye started to swell and he was sorry he hadn't thought of getting some ice. But timing was important, and he wouldn't have been able to get to the food court and back before the pills started to kick in. If all of this worked properly, it wouldn't matter anyway. He smiled and a fresh stream of blood poured from his nose. It would work properly. His plans always did.

He ducked under the stall door, tucked the mop and bucket farther back beside the toilet so they wouldn't be in the way, and concentrated on finding the crack in the grout.

The portal widened. Brad opened his mind to it keeping himself just out of reach of Thad's consciousness. It wasn't easy. He had to sort of cross his eyes a little bit, but the pills were helping.

"Thad." He tried to sound weak. "Thad? Are you there? I'm in trouble."

For a long while, there was no answer, and Brad considered repeating himself. But he didn't. Thad was predictable. That's why this would work.

"...I'm here," said Thad finally.

"I'm sorry, Thad. I know you think I hurt your friend on purpose, but I didn't. I promise. I found out who did, though."

"What do you mean?" Brad could feel Thad's attention turn toward him. He concentrated on the pain.

"He's here. He attacked me. I can't feel my body. Thad, I think I might be dead."

"What am I supposed to do about it?"

"I don't think you can do anything. It's my fault for going after him anyway. I just want you to know who did it. He might be after you too."

"Who is it?"

"I don't know his name. I'm trying to show you the picture in my head, but I feel like you're so far away that I can't reach you."

For a long minute, Thad stood resolute in his thoughts, firmly rooted in his own reality. But Brad could wait him out. Brad was good at waiting if it got him what he needed. After a while, he could feel Thad's resolve slipping.

"Brad, you still out there?" said Thad.

"I'm...trying to show you," said Brad. "Everything is getting...hazy."

It was the dramatic pause that did it. Thad was stupid for dramatic pauses. It also helped that the pills were starting to take effect and everything really *was* getting hazy.

"Hold on," said Thad. Brad could see familiar patterns forming around Thad's thoughts. The tiled wall of the Ashwood Super Mall men's room began to take shape. He was reaching out toward him, getting closer.

"Thank you, Thad," said Brad. "Can you see him now? That's the guy you need to watch out for. He killed me."

Thad finally saw the image and immediately became confused as Brad knew he would. The sleeping pills he'd stolen out of Velda's locker were claiming his consciousness at an alarming rate, and he had to concentrate harder on the image of his murderer. It was the same image from before: Brad looking into the men's room mirror, face bloody and bruised, the welt over his eye now an angry shade of purple.

"I don't get it," said Thad.

"Yeah, I didn't think you would," said Brad. Then he jumped.

DON'T JACK UP SPACE-TIME

THE MORE HE THOUGHT ABOUT IT, the more he freaked out. Jake had definitely messed with something. Of course he had—why else would Kix have slept with him?

For a moment, he decided it was Carl's fault. Hadn't he left Jake alone with his own thoughts as he sexed it up with his new girly-friend? If he had been there like a true friend, as girlfriendless as Jake, then none of this would have happened. Why couldn't Carl be just as hard up as he was?

But Carl was tall and smart and devilishly good-looking. *Dammit.* That handsome bastard never had problems with girls. Well, except the crazy one who tried to kill everybody, but that really wasn't Carl's fault.

Jake also had to admit that even as irritatingly handsome as he was, Carl was a hell of a guy. He would do anything you asked of him, and if he couldn't, he would find someone who could. *Double dammit.* It still didn't explain why he always had his pick of girls while Jake *literally* had to bend time and space just to convince one to sleep with him.

"I cannot have jacked up space-time. I don't even know *how* to jack up space-time."

Behind all these self-serving thoughts, he remembered Deli's speech in the car. He heard again her lecture about the last time everything went all wobbly. Imaginary Deli did not buy his lame excuses.

What did you think you were doing with that pizza, Jake, card tricks?

He winced. It was strange how much Imaginary Deli sounded

like his mom.

Fine, I might have bent space-time a little bit. What am I supposed to do, unbend it?

Yes, said Imaginary Deli.

Apparently, Imaginary Deli didn't have much more in common with his mom because after her one-word imaginary answer, she said no more. Jake sighed and fell backward onto the couch.

"I don't even know how I messed it up in the first place," he said aloud, to no one.

But that wasn't true, either. He still had all his pizza calculations. Jake looked around the room like a rat in a trap, which is pretty much how he felt. Kix only came on to him *after* the pizza trick, which meant that maybe she hadn't really come on to him at all. The idea of everything after the pizza being unreal was…well, frankly, he didn't want to think about it but his brain wouldn't stop.

What if she didn't even like him? What if she never would?

His eyes lit upon the cold pizza box. They had been too busy to eat that. He felt like eating the whole thing right now, but his stomach still wobbled from the shock of Eighty-Five-Cent, so he decided against it. Plus, it was probably all cold. He should put it in the fridge.

He thought about the fridge. In another reality, Kix had rummaged through that fridge. Then she probably got bored and went home. For a moment, he entertained the idea of leaving things as they were. The way reality worked right now, Kix had slept with him. That meant she liked him, right? At least a little bit?

Jake sighed a huge disappointed sigh. He may have won the game, but if he left things the way they were, he'd cheated to get there. Anything else he could handle cheating on—*TerrorCity* coding, winning the lottery, *Ascension*—any of that. But this was wrong. He didn't want to trick Kix into liking him. He wanted her to like him for real.

Double-double dammit, he thought before reminding himself that it would probably be *Dammit cubed.*

STEVE HAS A GOOD IDEA

FOR THE SECOND TIME IN HIS LIFE, Toesy experienced the shock and terror of being in a sack filling with water. He tried to jump away, to walk the thin boundary out of this strange pond, but he couldn't. Images from his kittenhood replayed in his mind, paralyzing him with remembered fear.

Thankfully, this time the water was not as deep. And it smelled less like rotting vegetation and more strongly of chlorine. His sat in the cold pool, trying to gain his balance on the strangely shaped bottom but failing because there was simply no place to move.

The sacking around him relaxed, and Toesy was just about to jump, when something hard and plastic hit him in the head, pushing him down. It closed him up in the soggy, strangely shaped box with a hollow *thunk*.

Toesy fought back by straightening his head up. He could not see out because he was still in the cursed sack, but the hard plastic thing gave way, and he was able to stretch his neck.

"Oh, no you don't!" The man's voice echoed slightly before the lid came crashing down again. Toesy pushed upward, but the lid did not budge.

"You are not going to ruin my chances with Connie, you horrible cat! You are going to stay right there, and when Connie comes home tomorrow morning, you are going to be the proof."

The weight pushing down on the lid lightened for a third time, and Toesy stretched his neck up—the only direction he could stretch. Another *thunk*, followed but the sound of water falling into a bucket drowned out all other noise. It echoed around the strange cavern. The lid over his head grew increasingly heavy. Toesy could not push against it for very long.

"There," said the prissy man, turning the waterfall sounds off. "That ought to hold you for now." Toesy heard the footsteps grow quieter as the man left.

He stayed still for a moment, weighing his options. Not only was he in a bag, but he was trapped in the cold, dank cavern. If he wasn't in the bag, he could get out of here in no time. But the cold water seeped through it, past his tummy fur, and chilled his skin. The memories played endlessly in his head, preventing him from concentrating.

A strange sort of calm overtook him then. Was this his destiny? To die in a sack, drowning in two inches of cold, smelly water?

We will not die, sir.

The voice in his head was respectful and polite with a just hint of superiority—a touch of which Toesy highly approved. He'd missed Steve. It had been a while since they'd spoke, directly.

How do you know that, Steve?

Because I believe we are only stuck in the toilet, sir.

Steve?

Yes, sir?

I will not have us die in a toilet. What are your thoughts on this?

The physical forces weighing upon us at the moment are quite formidable, sir.

What do you suggest, Steve?

How loud can you howl, sir?

Toesy growled low to stretch out his vocal cords. After a minute or two, he began to howl. The natural acoustics of Connie Caulfield's bathroom were a welcome surprise.

VITAMIN DEFICIENCIES

WHAT IF HE COULD UNMAKE the pizza? Go back and figure out what it was supposed to be, then rework the calculation so that it would return to normal. All systems can move backward and forward in time, depending on the pressures involved. So why couldn't he work against entropy to make the pizza change back? That could work, right?

Not really. No. Entropy is inevitable. Plus, the pizza had jalapeños. He saw it. He couldn't take that back.

Unless, of course, he'd been *wrong*. He hadn't been paying that much attention after Kix had uh...sat down. What if the jalapenos were really olives or pepperoni?

The idea intrigued him. If he introduced enough uncertainty into his calculations, could he change them? If he admitted he was wrong and worked from there, could he put everything back to normal? He had to try.

Jake began by reconstructing the environment. What factors had been at play when everything changed? The lighting? Possibly. He turned half the lights off, the same way they had been. Sound? What had they been listening to? The Korean movie. Jake grabbed the remote and flipped on the television. The DVD player blinked on, and he realized that the movie was still in it. He pressed *Play*.

What else? Drinks? Yes, he'd been drinking a beer. That was fortuitous because he was in need of a beer at the moment. He went to the kitchen and opened the fridge to see what he had. On the way there he noticed the answering machine for the Gloria Phone was blinking. That was good. It had been blinking last night as well.

Jake didn't like that he found solace in a bottle of beer, but since this was for science, he had no choice. Also, there was one IPA left and he loved IPAs, so that was good.

In an effort to reproduce the conditions exactly true to the evening, he grabbed a tumbler and popped the last of the mustache-shaped ice cubes into it. He poured a smallish shot of whiskey into it and brought it back to the living room with him where he sat it down next to the couch. Kix had been drinking whiskey, and the ice may have had some effect on the surrounding room temperature, you never know.

He made his way over to his command chair. The mess of papers surrounding his computer had ticks and symbols all over them, but he knew their order easily enough. He concentrated on setting his mind into the calculating groove.

Jake plugged away for thirty minutes before needing another beer. He went to the kitchen and opened the fridge. All the clean stuff was gone. Now he only had the muddy bottles of stout that he'd fished out of the shrubs. He grabbed one, brushed the mud off and cracked it open.

Walking back to his desk he caught a whiff of the whiskey sitting on the floor, waiting for someone to drink it before all the ice melted and it lost its edge. Jake did not consciously register the scent, but when he sat down, he remembered the rest of the evening with more clarity than before.

The fold of her legs as she sat on the couch. She had been wearing striped tights, and they made such intriguing patterns. He remembered her walking into the room with the confidence of a woman unafraid to be herself. He remembered how she'd teased him so much about being hungry, but when he showed her the pizza, she barely even looked at it. He remembered the smell of her sunscreen as she sat down—some sort of intoxicating fruity mixture.

He was halfway through remembering the soft pressure of her body against his as they kissed when a tiny red flag waved at him from the back of his mind.

Sunscreen?

That couldn't be right, could it? No one in Seattle wore sunscreen during the winter—they would die from vitamin D deficiency. The only people in Seattle who smelled like sunscreen at this time of year were California transplants and fourteen-year-old girls. And even the Californians usually stopped trying to block out the sun after the second month of straight rain.

Jake stood up very quickly and ran to his bedroom. He buried his face in his pillow and inhaled deep where the scent of her hair had worked itself into the sheet. It was overwhelming and delicious and had no SPF whatsoever. It smelled more like flowers and wood smoke than piña coladas.

He walked absently back to his desk as the gears of his intellect drove on. Something was staring him in the face. He could feel it. The answer sat right in front of him. He just needed to figure out the question.

STEALTH

THE TREE SHOOK with the kind of reverberation that Diabo understood. He was not a web reader, but he knew the language of movement. The way his tree shook told him that something small and nimble now roamed its branches. Diabo became very still in order to hear what the tiny scrambling something was doing. It seemed to be heading for the ground.

He was not a very skilled jumper, but it did not take much skill to jump downward. He skipped off the spiky leaves, his exoskeleton shielding him from the worst of them, and tumbled with a barely audible crunch onto the wet, rocky ground. It might have been a better landing had his tree not been so wet from the rain, but Diabo did not care. He had glimpsed the scrambling thing on the way down. It definitely looked tasty.

* * *

Pansy moved silently. It was no longer raining enough to cover her tracks, so she scampered along as quietly as she could. Considering her considerable skills as a nocturnal creature, this was very quiet indeed.

Once on the ground, she skipped over to where she might see the window that Thanatos had broken for her. She could see it, high up on the building, but the curtains were so heavy that they blocked out the light. She could not see any movement beyond them.

So intent was she on trying to see into the window that she did not hear the soft footfalls of Diabo until he was upon her. He moved with unnatural speed. Before she understood what was happening, Diabo filled her field of view. She saw nothing but the spider. Pansy had eaten spiders in the past but this one was too large to consider eating. This one was a monster.

He moved in undulating motions, hypnotic and terrible. The patterns he traced in the air switched off all her logical thought, and Pansy knew, with the keen certainty of an animal near the bottom of the food chain, that this might be the end.

But she was no mere *rodent*, was she? No! She was a marsupial, capable of higher conceptual thinking. And part of her tiny marsupial brain knew that if she could keep control of her thoughts, she might break this spell.

Facing her doom, Pansy forced herself to think of Connie and how much she loved her. Connie had grown into a shadow of her former self, incapable of loving Pansy back, but she knew it wasn't Connie's fault. She was probably clinically depressed or something. Pansy's death would certainly not go over well with Connie.

She thought of Thanatos, and her heart began to beat very fast. Toesy was a magnificent creature with many redeeming qualities and fine whiskers. He would save her if he could. But alas, he could not. No doubt that horrible man was doing something despicable to him at this very moment.

Thinking of that horrible man made Pansy's blood boil. For a moment, the spell of the monstrous spider lifted and she stumbled backward several paces.

But it was not enough. The spider anticipated her steps. By the time she registered that Diabo had moved at all, she was running directly at him. The last thing Pansy saw before they collided was a pair of blood-red fangs.

PLINK-BLOOP

SOMEONE NEXT DOOR turned the music back up. Nick would complain to the superintendent but for the moment, the bass line was covering up most of the insane beast's yowling. And also his bladder was so full, he couldn't really walk to the phone. Why had he put the blasted thing in the toilet? It was getting to the point where he strongly considered peeing in the sink.

Nick sat on the couch in Connie's living room, hunched over with his hands on his ears. He had no idea a cat could make that much noise.

A sudden knock at the door made him jump. His poor bladder couldn't take much more of this. The front door was at least twenty feet away. He walked toward it; bladder aching with every step. Another knock at the door and Nick opened his mouth to say *Hold on!* but closed it quickly. Who was at the door? Probably someone complaining about the cat yowling.

Nick assessed his situation. There was an excellent reason for the cat to be in the toilet, but other people might not see it that way. He kept his mouth shut and tiptoed to the front door as quietly as his bladder would allow.

He reached the door and stretched up to the peephole. The long-haired guy who had earlier told him to relax, the cat would be fine, stood on the other side of the door, rocking back and forth on his heels.

Nick did not move. He held his breath and hoped the guy would go away. He didn't go away. He knocked again. Nick's bladder reacted by shooting a pain right up his hip to his stomach. If he got a bladder infection from this, he was naming this man in the lawsuit as well.

"I know you're in there dude," the hippie said after a while. Nick did not say anything.

"I can hear Toesy over the party noise."

Nick kept silent.

"Okay, have it your way. But if I were you, I wouldn't be there when he gets loose. In fact, if he knows what you look like, it's a safe bet to say you should probably just leave now and not come back."

Nick still did not respond but that was because he was afraid to move his bladder, certainly not because he was scared of a cat. That would be ridiculous.

The man stayed for another thirty seconds before shaking his head and walking off.

Nick couldn't hold it anymore. He couldn't handle it anymore. The damn cat would not stop yowling, and his bladder hadn't been this full since the time at Disneyland when he was twelve. How could they expect a person to urinate in bathrooms like those? For Pete's sake, there were children eating food right near the entrance. Just thinking about it made his stomach turn which made his bladder complain even louder.

There was nothing for it. He was going to have to pee in the sink.

As slowly as possible and with minimal movement to his rib cage or pelvis, Nick tiptoed down the back hallway to the bathroom.

The closer he got, the louder the yowling became. When he reached the doorway, he could feel the reverberations of it in his brain.

"Hush *up*," he said to the yowling toilet. Much to his surprise, it did.

"That's better," he said. He wanted to say more. He wanted to say how angry he was and how much retribution would rain down upon that awful cat as soon as the 24-hour Animal Control hot line answered the phone, but the urge to empty his bladder overcame him. He crossed the cold tile floor as briskly as possible.

Behind the sink hung a round mirror, spotted with dried toothpaste. The sink was one of those pedestal types, white with a thin rolled edge around it. The plug at the bottom was crusted with dried toothpaste and that pinky sort of grunge that shows up when you don't clean often enough. Nick closed his eyes so he could try to focus on what he was doing. But as soon as he did, the cat began a series of barking wails that sounded very much like a dying Chihuahua. He jumped slightly and groaned as his swollen bladder jogged to the left with the rest of him.

"Stop it!"

The wailing stopped and was immediately followed by a deep, angry rumble. Nick had never heard another being make a noise like that. It was almost hollow in its fury. He turned the water on in an effort to drown it out, and also because even though he really *really* had to pee, for some reason he couldn't start.

It must be the sink. That was it. The sight of a dirty sink made Nick physically ill at the best of times—why would it not have an effect on him now? Although it was irresponsibly unsanitary, Nick turned to the bathtub. At least he wouldn't have to look at dried toothpaste.

With the sink still running, using one hand to cover his ear and the other to aim, he attempted again to urinate. The cat continued growling, hateful and eager. He tried to ignore it, but the intensity of its baritone made his ears hum and the noise had a way of drilling straight into the base of his brain.

He could not pee.

Drat that horrible cat, he had to pee.

"Shut up, you damnable beast."

He swung around, two long steps to the toilet and slammed his fist down on the handle. The sound of water draining out of the bowl made the growling come to an abrupt stop.

While he had his chance, Nick turned back to the bathtub and peed. He peed for a very long time.

When he finished, he zipped up his pants and stared down, into the tub. Just the thought of what he had done made him queasy, but the cat had given him no choice. He turned on the shower and let the water run hotter and hotter until he could no longer touch it comfortably with his hand. Steam filled the air. He let the water run while he went to the kitchen and washed his hands with dish soap.

He sang through the birthday song twice, dried his hands, and walked back to the bathroom. It wasn't until he turned the shower off that he realized the growling had stopped. The bathroom was intensely quiet.

Surely he hadn't flushed the thing…?

"Cat?" he said.

The toilet remained silent.

"Are you there?"

Nick bent over to peer through the small gap between the toilet seat and its porcelain bowl. He saw nothing. The lighting in Connie's bathroom was insufficient at best, probably due to dusty light bulbs. Connie didn't even clean the sink; he doubted she ever dusted the light bulbs. Between the plastic seat and the porcelain bowl, all Nick could see was darkness.

He leaned in half an inch closer. No shadows within the toilet bowl moved. Had he flushed that cat down the toilet? It seemed impossible. The thing was huge, how could it fit? Nick squinted and shook his head in confusion. There was no sound. There didn't seem to be anything at all.

He *must* have flushed it. There was no other answer. Nick relaxed. Thank the good Lord above, that cat was no longer his problem. He exhaled.

Then he heard a sound: the tiny *plink-bloop* of a single drop of water falling into a shallow pool.

It was the only warning he got.

A SMALL SETBACK

HOW COULD HE HAVE BEEN so stupid? He hadn't smelled sunscreen. He smelled something *tropical*. Pineapple is tropical. Jake made some mental calculations and began plugging numbers into his equations. After twenty minutes, he determined there was a ninety-seven-percent probability of the original pizza having pineapple on it. Including Canadian bacon in his equation brought that probability down to eighty-four percent—not a slam dunk but still enough to be mostly right. He continued working for what felt like a long time.

Jake finally looked up from the screen, lightheaded with fatigue and slightly confused as to a strange noise repeating itself in the background. After the third ring, he realized it was the phone. It broke his mathematical trance. He stretched himself out of the chair and sauntered over to the Gloria Phone on its table in the hallway.

"Hello?" he said into the receiver.

"How you doin' tonight, Seattle?!" Carl's voice was exhausted and exuberant at the same time. It made Jake want to smile, then kick him. Why the hell was Carl calling the Gloria phone anyway?

"Deli out of surgery?"

"You got it going on."

"Are you staying with her in the hospital tonight?"

"I said, I said, oh yeah!"

"Right, I'll see you tomorrow. Hope she's feeling better."

"The girl is all right."

"Of course she is, Mr. Blues. Why don't you take it off stage now? Show's over."

"Thank you! Good night!" said Carl with such heartfelt gratitude that Jake just knew he was punching his arms in the air. There was a loud *thunk* on the other end as Carl's phone dropped to the floor. Jake disconnected the call before he tried to do an encore.

He grabbed the shot of whiskey he'd poured earlier to simulate Kix being there with her drink. It was a poor substitute. It was also very watered down, as all the ice mustaches had melted. It didn't matter: Jake was almost to the point of figuring this out. He sat back down and rounded out the edges of his calculation. Dotting the obeli and crossing the taus.

After a few fiddly bits of parenthetical tidying, he had it. He knew he had it. He remembered the feeling of having the calculation so completely right that everything turned anxious. Double checking was his only way to relax.

He extended his logic in the direction of the right answer, along the probability curve, and found the edge of reasoning that he had stood on previously. Thinking himself down through the long equation, Jake made sure he was right.

He was right.

He felt around, testing the smaller data points to make sure they were correct. They were all correct. Everything was calculated to represent the exact situation from last night.

So how did he make it work?

He checked his notes again. They were right. He thought through the equation from back to front, starting with the answer. It should be there.

It wasn't. He felt nothing. There was no tension. There was no push.

He studied the room in confusion. What was off? The pizza box stood, untouched on the desk next to his monitor. The cardboard was cold and greasy, but that shouldn't matter because he'd cancelled out the temperature gradient on both sides. Maybe because the flaps of its lid splayed out on either side?

Jake didn't want to touch the box, in case any change of position put his calculations off, but he needed to make sure, so he reached out with a pencil and opened the lid carefully. Had it changed back to Canadian bacon and pineapple on its own?

He peered in. The pizza looked wonky. He opened the box wider.

The pizza looked wonky because it *was* wonky. Half of it was gone, replaced by a paper towel. On the paper towel was a note written in black marker.

Thanks for the pizza. Now we're even for the bike helmet crap. —S

Jake kicked the television stand, which sent tenuous wobbles throughout its framework. He loved Sacha like a brother, but there were times when he could stab him through the heart and laugh. This was one of those times. How the hell did that guy screw things up so thoroughly all the time? It was like a super power or something.

He sank to the floor. Underneath the carpet, the concrete foundation chilled him, but he didn't care. He sat there and fumed, trying not to hate Sacha for being such a complete idiot. And what was all this crap about a *bike helmet*?

Sacha was logged into the *TerrorCity* network as an admin which mean he had to be home. So why wasn't he answering his phone? Ugh, Jake was going to have to actually go upstairs to yell at him.

He slid his feet into a pair of old slippers and headed for the linen closet.

A PROMOTION

EXECUTIVE WINGMAN STEVE had really outdone himself this time. The only flaw that Toesy could see was that he *couldn't* see for most of the exciting parts. He heard it all in perfect detail, though. The water sloshing quietly in the small garbage can the man had balanced on top of the toilet lid. The faint increase of noise as he had nudged the toilet lid up just enough to get the water inside moving. The initial squeak when the garbage can slid through the condensation that had formed all around it. The slow, drawn-out scrape as the whole thing teetered and fell to the floor with an incredible crash. The sudden intake of breath as the prissy man understood what had just happened. Everything had gone so incredibly well that he promoted Steve to Executive Wartime Consigliore on the spot.

Truly, your work is masterful, said Toesy.

Thank you, sir. As is yours. I commend you on the expert way that you led the attack. Grabbing on to his nasal cavity so instantaneously was truly inspired.

The what?

I believe those fleshy bits you are tenderizing are called nostrils.

You don't say, Toesy said as he flexed his claws. *What is this hard part in the middle?*

Ah, that's the septum.

What does it do?

I'm not entirely sure. It seems to be some sort of volume control.

Toesy tightened his grip on the septum, and indeed the man's volume increased. He let go, and the screaming quieted.

That is quite amazing. Good deduction there.

He tested out the volume control a few more times until a loud clattering noise interrupted all the other noises in the bathroom. Toesy looked down to see that the man's phone had fallen out of his pocket.

He would have ignored it but Executive Wartime Consigliore Steve brought up a good point.

Sir, that man has referred to his tiny computer several times over the past two hours. I believe it may be his guidance system. If so, it would be advantageous for us to have access to it.

You want me to steal his electronical whatsit?

It may provide us with a way to find Miss Pansy.

Toesy yanked his claws free from the man's face.

Satan's whiskers, Steve! You're a Bast-blessed genius, he said.

Thank you, sir.

The man scrunched himself into a sobbing ball of shredded wool blend and began to rock back and forth. When Toesy reached out to swipe the phone from his side, he tried to shove himself into two directions at once. This resulted in him slamming his upper body into the underside of Connie's pedestal sink with enough force to crack the basin. Nick, the man who thought he could go up against Toesy and win, knocked himself out cold.

Thanatos grabbed the bleepy-whatsit off the floor. It looked like a smaller version of those computers the Holy Man was so fond of. The Holy Man! He could take this tiny computational machine to the Holy Man! He would know what to do.

Executive Wartime Consigliore Steve approved of the plan with all of his logic circuits. Toesy got a comfortable bite onto the thing so he wouldn't drop it, and prepared to go find His Holiness.

He made it as far as the bathroom door before he turned back to the bleeding, unconscious coward. Toesy knew which way the balance of power tilted, but he'd be damned if he left without this man conceding it as well. Fortunately, cats (and cat-shaped demigods) have a very simple form of communication that outlines this concept.

He climbed to the top of the man's unconscious chest and peed on him. Then he ran to find the Holy Man.

He took the stairs two at a time down to the basement apartment. If the Holy Man had returned from helping his Mistress, he would likely be there. With any luck, the Angel of Delivery would be there as well. She would understand his urgency. She would know not to let this toilet-trapping villain anywhere near Pansy.

At the secret bookshelf, Toesy jumped into the air, caught the copy of *Moby-Dick* on the way back down and let his weight pull the book forward. Unfortunately, like many of the custom-made fixtures in Horsey House, the internal locking mechanism inside the secret door had been made from pot metal. After many decades of abuse, it was no longer up to the challenge of a thirty-two-pound demigod. When Toesy's weight hit the book, the latch arm twisted and snapped off. Toesy, the electronic whatsit, and the tattered copy of *Moby-Dick* all fell to the floor with a *whump*.

JUST A LITTLE PUSH

TERROR AS OLD AS THE EARTH froze Pansy from the inside out. Not a whisker on her head twitched. The thing held her with spiny legs. As soon as she moved, it would strike.

Of course, there were worse ways to go. Bored and lonely, stuck in a cage with a clinically depressed human to worry about was one of them. She could have gone on like that for years, never knowing the taste of rain or the bite of cold against her skin. She would not balk at her ending now. It had been a short few hours of freedom, but they had been worth every moment. And really, this part was quick. She hoped it would be painless.

The laughing eyes, all eight of them, gazed at her with triumph. It pinned her to the ground with an instinctual fear that her body felt but not her mind. Her mind was free to think over the ending. She found her only regret to be that she would never see her Toesy again.

Pansy's tiny marsupial heart broke at the thought of Toesy. He was a gentle soul, with spiky claws, pointy teeth, and a mushy heart. He had risked his life to save her, and she had escaped. But without him now, she was caught. This evil thing, this slavering beast of an arachnid, stood victorious. If she so much as twitched her nose, it would end her life right now. She stayed absolutely still, while her mind whirled around, trying to find a way out.

She could no longer hear the angry howls of her beloved Toesy, and death lay heavy on her mind. She very nearly exhaled the last of her breath, but a loud crash brought her a tiny bit of relief. The crash was followed by a cry so vengeful and angry, it had to be Toesy.

Hearing her beloved Toesy one last time gave strength to her own anger. She rejected the idea of dying. She pushed it away like a rotten apple core. With every thought she had, she fought against the forces binding her to this fate.

Tiny though those thoughts may have been, in that one moment, they made a universe of difference.

JAKE'S REALITY

JAKE STEPPED INTO THE LINEN CLOSET angry at Sacha. When he opened the secret door within, he realized the knob was stuck again and the door wouldn't stay closed. No wonder the apartment was so cold. Jake grumbled, turned around, and kicked it shut with his foot. The force of the door hitting the frame was enough to unstick the latch bolt. Jake heard the metallic clunk as it popped back into place.

"This just keeps getting better," he said to no one.

The door at the top of the stairs didn't have a knob; it had a latch like a gate that fed through to the bookshelf on the other side. When Jake reached the top of the stairs and pushed down on the latch, nothing happened. More worrisome than that was the fact that the lever did not fall back down like it should, but stayed in the pushed-up position. He reached over and flipped on the light. There was nothing wrong that he could see, so he jiggled the latch a few times. It bounced within its housing, too loose to catch on anything.

Someone *broke* the bookshelf door? It was probably Sacha. Actually, Jake didn't care if it was Sacha or not—he was blaming him anyway.

He stormed back down the stairs, shaking with anger. He noticed that the door handle of the downstairs door looked strange, but he did not immediately understand why. Three steps farther and the primitive recesses of his brain woke up. Jake reached out to open the door and the alarm bells in his head started screaming. When he finally realized why, the bottom dropped out of his stomach.

Perched on top of the door handle, right where he was about to grab it, sat the biggest, creepiest spider Jake ever seen.

"*Gah!*" he said.

He had no way of knowing about the rubber tarantula Sacha had taped there earlier. If he had, none of this would have happened. All Jake knew was that on the door knob sat epic, spidery grossness on a level that almost made his heart explode. He did not *believe* in the spider because belief implies conscious thought. Jake simply knew the spider as truth.

Outside, in the gravel, Pansy had rejected the very idea of such a spider. But inside the stairwell, Jake's consciousness held the door open to a reality that accepted one. And because it was *Jake's* reality, that's exactly what he saw.

A gigantic spider.

DIABO WAS VERY CONFUSED

HE STARED INTO THE EYES OF HIS PREY, focusing his intent in its mind. Usually that was all it took. Most prey simply succumbed to his will and gave up. But as he stared into its eyes he thought perhaps there was more than just fuzzy snack staring back out at him. He saw fear there, of course. He saw uncertainty. He saw hope faltering. But he also saw the glint of something he did not understand.

It started as a tiny point of light. It tugged at him. It fascinated him. He could not look away. Neither could he shut his eyes, for spiders have no eyelids. By the time he realized his mistake, it was too late. He was entranced.

The point dilated. With his lateral eyes, Diabo saw the world go blurry. His dorsal eyes watched with mild hysteria as the spot yawned wider and wider until it consumed him.

When the world settled, his feet were struggling to hold on to the tiny ledge on which he sat. It was no longer raining, but neither did he have the tasty snack paralyzed within reach.

O que diabos just happened?

He found his center of gravity and calmed himself, clearing his thoughts. This must be a test. Mama Ayahuasca must have something in store for him. Yes! She has transported him to the spirit world, and was presenting him with a trial!

Something moved in front of him.

Diabo focused his dorsal eyes. The light was very dim, but that did not matter. He was a hunter. He was part of the night. He opened his mind to what he saw, and what he saw made his arachnid soul sing.

The Great Mother had charged him with a magnificent task.
She had given him his greatest foe.
At his feet, she had placed a *man*.

THE WORLD TURNED
UPSIDE DOWN

THE SPOT OF WHITE LIGHT overtook her and Pansy fell to what she assumed would be her death. The descent stretched on for a very long time. When she finally landed, it turned out not to be sudden death so much as it was a soggy holly tree. Now she sat among the spiny branches and wondered how she managed to fall *upward* from the ground to the branches. That certainly wasn't the normal order of things.

As she stood twitching her tiny pink nose into the wind, a thought struck Pansy right between the eyeballs. Such a big idea hitting such a tiny target made for quite an impact. For a moment, Pansy stood rigid, too stunned to do anything.

She was alone. *In a tree*.

Thirty-eight seconds later, she'd circumscribed the trunk enough times to have the basic layout of branches memorized. Her heart was wild with joy. How did squirrels do this every day and not die of shock? She longed to tell Toesy about this.

That stopped her, mid-scurry. How had she forgotten about her Toesy? He was trapped inside the house! She ran to the middle of the tree and climbed the westernmost bough. It hung high above her own window, and Pansy was confident that she could jump from that branch and glide through the broken pane with ease.

But when she reached the end of the bough and started to take aim, Pansy realized that it didn't matter how many times she'd made the jump in her mind, she would not be able to do it. Not for lack of skill; Pansy was an excellent glider. But no amount of skill would help her sail through a broken window that was no longer broken.

She stared at the glass, now completely intact, and wondered what she ought to do next.

ASHWOOD SUPER MALL
MEN'S ROOM

THE PILLS BRAD TOOK before he stole Thad's body were a prescription-strength sleep aid. He'd taken three. By all of his reasoning, Thad should be near comatose by now. Brad had no way of knowing that Thad's consciousness knew that particular drug—not as the powerful sleep agent that would kill him, but as an anti-anxiety medication similar to the one he used to steal from his mom's medicine cabinet when he was a teenager. Because of this, Thad woke up in the Ashwood Super Mall men's room feeling surprisingly optimistic about where he was in life and completely unconcerned about how he got there.

He stood up and looked around. He was back in the bathroom stall again. The door was still taped shut. It occurred to him that it was probably Brad that did the taping.

"What a dick," said Thad, peeling tape from the door. When he finished, he aimed a kick at the door. The tape on the outside came loose in a few places. He kicked it a few more times. The last kick ripped the tape free and caused the door to swing open with so much force it slammed against the wall.

Thad brushed himself off and strolled out of the stall. A senior gentleman with close-cropped hair and ample nostrils stood at the sink staring at him in the mirror.

"'Sup, Brah?" said Thad. The man left without drying his hands.

"Whatevs," he said and proceeded to inspect the soap dispenser.

TOESY PULLS RANK

THE RAIN BLANKETED EVERYTHING, masking movements and watering the smells down into the earth. He almost missed the scent at first. It wasn't until he'd run halfway across the back parking lot that it registered in his brain. He stopped running immediately.

Steve, do you smell that? She is here. I can feel it in my whiskers.

Yes, sir. May I advise putting the man's operating system down in a safe place first?

Good idea, said Toesy and opened his mouth, letting the tiny computer fall to the ground. It landed in a puddle.

Sir, I believe somewhere dry might be a better choice.

Yes, of course. Toesy picked the phone up with one paw and threw it, as far as he could, toward the steps that led down to the Holy Man's apartment. It landed on the top step and bounced several times on the way down. Toesy did not notice. He was concentrating on the yard. Underneath the holly tree, shadows consumed most of the light, but Toesy had more senses than sight.

The faint smell of cedar led him to the middle of the shadows. Something dark lay upon the ground and Toesy despaired that it might be her. It smelled so deeply of her fear that Toesy could not move. He stared at the dark lump on the ground for quite some time, until he was sure that whatever it was, it was not breathing.

Finally, Toesy willed his whiskers forward and approached the dark lump. At first he was confused. Then he was relieved. Then he got mad.

What is this?

I believe it is a novelty spider, sir.

Why does it smell so strongly of my Pansy? Is this some kind of horrible joke? I am displeased, Steve. Toesy was yowling his anger now, and getting angrier with each yowl.

No, sir, said Steve.

I will not have this, Steve, said Toesy. *It is one thing to mess with reality, but it is quite another thing to mess with my people.*

Toesy stood back on his hind legs. He picked up the rubber spider. The body was too large for him to get a comfortable grip on it, so he grabbed at it with his claws and shook it into the air. With his other paw, he made a fist.

Hear me, Universe, and be told. I am Thanatos, and this is my domain. I will not tolerate these shenanigans! They are not supposed to happen. There are too many happenings happening! Universe, you will straighten this out right now, or so help me, I will straighten you out.

Of course Toesy did not speak the words in English. He may be a demigod, but he still lives in the body of a cat. And cats, as everyone knows, have a notoriously difficult time with English. It is fair to say, however, that as he yowled his ultimatum into the night, he did so with the anger of gods and the wrath of titans. He yowled so loudly that emergency services received three consecutive calls to report coyote activity in the area. Next door, Etta Oslow, an exotic animal veterinarian for the Woodland Park Zoo, called the night staff to make sure the jaguar hadn't somehow gotten loose.

When Toesy finally stopped his yowling, he sat back to listen to what the Universe had to say for itself. The rain picked up with a gust of wind but offered nothing else in its defense.

I am waiting, he said.

The rain picked up one more time—a dramatic swell of raindrops drowning everything out. Then he heard it. The familiar noise of her car's engine. The Angel of Delivery had just turned down his alleyway.

I see, said Toesy. *A very wise choice.* He yowled this into the darkness, too, although anyone paying enough attention would pick up on the change in his demeanor. He no longer sounded angry.

Sir, if I may ask…what just happened? said Steve.

This Universe is a mess, Steve. I reminded it of its duty.

And Miss Welty?

Is she not the Angel of Delivery, Steve? She is here to deliver us from all this mess.

But what if she does not know how, sir?

Don't be daft, Steve. Of course she doesn't. We haven't taught her yet.

Executive Wartime Consigliore Steve did not follow the logic exactly, but he felt the increased endorphin output to every twelve millionth cycle and knew his overlord was excited for the future.

JAKE SCREAMED

ACTUALLY, HIS VOCAL CHORDS HAD CONSTRICTED with the rush of adrenaline and he squeaked more than anything. Under the circumstances, he wasn't too concerned with how much he had sounded like a five-year-old girl.

The gigantic spider sat in on the deadbolt, almost at eye level with him. If it had been a wolf spider, Jake wouldn't have minded that much. Wolf spiders may be creepy but they don't look like they could eat you whole. This was no wolf spider. This spider was huge and mean-looking and probably venomous as all get out. In a word, it looked…deadly.

Jake couldn't decide what was worse: the fact that all of its eyes seemed to be watching him or the way it moved, very slightly, as he moved. That couldn't be good.

"Ung," he said and slowly backed up one stair.

The spider's eyes followed him. Jake was sure of it.

"Ung," said Jake again because it had worked well the first time around. What was he supposed to do? That thing looked like it could actually kill him.

And as soon as the thought sprang to his mind, Jake knew it was true. He winced.

The spider appeared to understand wincing because it jumped into an offensive posture, waving its front legs at him menacingly. Jake did not scream again, but he may have groaned a little at that point. The spider then bared blood-red fangs. If he didn't know any better, Jake would swear it was smiling.

"*Gah!*" said Jake and backed up another step. That thing looked like Shelob and Aragog got together and had demonic spider babies. Where had it come from? Jake guessed that part didn't matter because if he didn't get out of here, he was going to end up like Frodo in the cave of Cirith Ungol—completely *screwed*.

He stared at the demon spider as it crawled down the deadbolt latch onto the door knob. Then it stepped off the door knob and fell to the floor with a fat *whap!* Jake gagged slightly. Panic seized his chest and constricted his lungs. His heart tried to climb up through his throat, and he found himself focusing on the spider just to keep from freaking out entirely.

What did he know about it? It was probably venomous. It was huge. It was mean-looking. It might be super-fast. But it was still a spider. Could he maybe…step on it?

He looked at the slavering maw of Aragog Jr., then looked at his own slippers. They were those fur-lined moccasin-type slippers with stupid little rubber treads sewn to the bottom. The rubber had worn away completely in the heels to expose the soft leather underneath.

No, squishing that thing with his foot was something he absolutely did not want to do. So what then? Could he wait for it to get far enough away from the door and step over it? What if it ran up his leg and bit him in the gnads?

Just the thought of that made Jake cringe, but he needed a plan and this was an important factor to consider.

The spider crawled straight up the riser to the step above it. When it stood on the next stair, it looked at him and began waving its forelegs in the air again.

Yes, that thing *definitely* looked like a gnad biter. Even if it wasn't, Jake would be damned if he was going to take that chance now.

Down on the floor, the spider swayed with malevolent rhythm. Jake's eyes followed it while his brain chased his possibilities down rabbit holes. Oh God, this was all his fault.

Why couldn't he just have asked Kix over for dinner and a movie? She might have said yes. If she hadn't, would that have been so bad? It may have been awkward, but at least he would know what the score was.

But no, he had to go mess around with space-time and turn her into some sort of strange version of herself. Jake thought about the last time things went this wrong. A lot of people got hurt and he accidentally made Toesy semi-immortal. Why did this crap always happen to him?

Now here he was, stuck in the back stairway, between a broken secret door and a venomous demon-spider. If he ever got out of this, Jake strongly considered taking one of Deli's bodu kura classes just so he could learn the proper way of kicking Sacha in the nuts for eating half of his goddamn space-time pizza.

None of that should even make sense, he thought and hung his head low.

From the corner of his eye, he saw a hairy leg poke over the stair riser, two stairs down. Jake found his feet again. He ran up the stairs to the top and tried the door again. It still wouldn't move. He threw his weight on it. It did not budge.

"Hey! Hello up there! Help!" he said, feeling incredibly stupid for doing so. Even in the cinder-block-lined walls of the secret passage, Jake could hear the party still going on in 2C. It must be past midnight for sure. Jake sighed. No one was coming to help him. Besides Sacha, everyone in the in the building was either at that party, in the hospital, or a nitwit with a sugar glider problem.

BACKYARD

IF YOU DIDN'T KNOW the entrance was there, it would be easy to miss because no one parks in the middle of a gigantic holly tree. A massive empire of razor-sharp landscaping all by itself, it spent the greater part of the twentieth century waging an unceasing (and very pokey) battle against stray cats, garbage trucks, and the property-line fence. Generations of gardeners had been employed to tame the horrible thing, but the only method of pruning that had ever won back any territory was driving a car through it on a regular basis.

Just on the other side of the monster holly was a small yard that started out as a kitchen garden but ended up an oil-stained patch of gravel. Kix pulled into the yard and turn sharply, so that Maxine faced the holly tree. Carl usually parked closer to the house, and she didn't want to take his spot if he was coming home any time soon.

She stared into the rearview mirror, listening to the tick of the engine as it cooled, trying to piece together a plan. If Jake would pick up his phone, this would be so much easier. Kix sat in the car, trying to figure out if there was anyone outside or not. Not because she was scared or anything. She just wanted to make sure she hadn't been followed.

Also, that was a lie. She was totally scared.

Reeeerrrrrrrrrrooooow.

Kix's hand flew up to make sure the door was locked before her brain could register where the screaming had come from. Outside, near the trunk of the holly tree, sat Deli's cat, Toesy. Jake had told her all about Toesy. How he wasn't a regular cat. He told her all about the nanobot and the thumbs and the ninety-nine-point-nine percent immortality, but all Kix had ever seen him do is sleep on the futon and drool when she scratched him too hard behind the ear. Not that she didn't like huge, fat cats, it's just that sometimes she wondered why everyone was so in awe of him.

"*Toesy*!" she said. She got out of the car and closed the door. Kneeling down, she whisper-shouted across the gravel. "You scared the pants off of me."

Toesy looked at her knees suspiciously.

"Well, no," said Kix. "Not really. But you scared me pretty bad. What are you doing out here?"

He walked over in a funny jog-hop that Kix mistook for a limp at first. When he got closer she saw that wasn't a limp. He was using one of his front paws to hold something close to his chest.

"Uh...whatcha got there?"

To her credit, Kix only mildly freaked out as Toesy stood up on his back legs, walked over to her, and handed her a tarantula.

"Ah! No thank you," she said and backed away a foot. Toesy stopped moving so she stopped moving. Then he offered her the spider again. This time Kix studied it under the weak glow of the streetlight and realized it wasn't real.

"Thank you," she said and took it gingerly. "I guess?"

It felt like rubber, but she grabbed it by one leg and shook really hard just to be sure.

"Why are you giving me this?"

Toesy chuffed at her and stared at the rubber spider. Kix couldn't guess what that meant. She was a little preoccupied with the fact that she was having a conversation with a cat.

"Okay," she said. "So... have you seen Jake lately?" She said.

To answer her question, Toesy walked across the parking lot to the front door of Jake's apartment. Kix followed. At the bottom of the stairs, she was surprised to find a phone laying on the ground next to the door, its screen was smashed in.

"Someone must have dropped their phone," she said and picked it up. As she did so, Toesy growled, low and menacing.

"Okay, I'm putting it back down. See?" Kix bent down slowly, to replace the phone and not make any sudden movements. As soon as she let it go, Toesy grabbed on to it and shoved it back in her hand.

"Or I can put it in my pocket." She stuck the phone in her jacket pocket and kept her attitude light, as though she had conversations with cats all the time. Then she knocked on the door. No one answered.

After a moment, Toesy nosed her out of the way. He stood on his hind legs and turned the door knob. It was unlocked. Then he stood aside and blinked at her in a way that was less blinking than it was winking simultaneously with both of his eyes.

"Thank you?" she said and walked inside. Toesy came in behind her and closed the door. Kix tried to ignore him because the alternative was to accept the fact that Toesy just opened the door for her and she wasn't quite ready to do that.

A lamp was on in the living room, so she walked that way, tripping over someone's shoes as she went.

"Jake? Are you here? I think we have a problem."

There was no answer. Something about this pissed her off. Sure, she'd broken into Jake's house, but it's not really breaking and entering if someone invites you in, is it? Kix was sure Toesy counted as 'someone'.

"I'm not stalking you or anything. I ran into Toesy outside. He handed me a rubber tarantula…and a broken phone. Then he let me in." After a small pause, she added, "I swear that happened. I'm not lying."

Still there was no answer. She surveyed the living room. It looked exactly as it had last night. Even the movie they—or maybe just she— had watched was playing. Her glass was sitting on the floor next to the futon, and she bent over to pick it up, surprised that it was still wet with condensation.

The computer screen caught her attention. It held a long list of numbers and symbols. She stepped forward to study them, but at that same moment, the screen dimmed and switched to energy-saver mode. How long did her computer wait before it went to sleep? Five minutes? Ten minutes? Jake must have been here recently.

She jiggled the mouse. The computer woke up from its short nap and asked for a password. The fuzzy calculations behind the popup window looked like the same ones he'd been working on last night. Kix couldn't tell for sure. She tiptoed toward the back hallway. The door to Jake's room stood open. The light was out.

"JAKE?"

THAT WAS KIX'S VOICE! She had decided to come over! Without thinking, Jake started to answer.

"Hey—"

At the sound of his voice, the gigantic spider stopped waving its legs. It paused for the briefest of moments then ran straight for him.

"Whoa! No, no no no!"

Jake whispered frantically and waved his hands around as if that was going to stop the thing. It did, sort of, but the spider was only three stairs away now which, in Jake's opinion, was uncomfortably close.

"Are you here? I think we have a problem," said Kix. She must be near the back hallway. Jake nodded.

You bet we do, he thought. *That spider has the most massive fangs I have ever seen, and it's going to bite my gnads off if I don't get out of here.*

"I'm totally not stalking you or anything. I ran into Toesy outside. He handed me a rubber tarantula and a smashed up phone. Then he let me in." After a small pause she added, "I swear that happened. I'm not lying."

Jake wasn't sure if he heard that right or not. It sounded right, but it also sounded ridiculous. This whole situation was ridiculous. He nodded his head slowly.

I believe you, he thought. *But it's all kinda unbelievable.*

And exhausting. The spider started waving its legs again. Jake had been keeping his eyes on it and trying to listen to Kix. Now he found it difficult to look away.

Sleepily, he nodded his head. He wanted nothing more than to see Kix, to talk with her and listen to her laugh. But he suddenly found himself too tired to move.

The spider continued making complicated and threatening movements, until the walls in his peripheral vision began to slip away. In his mind, he knew they would come back if he looked for them, but right now they were cloudy and irresolute—a mere suggestion of walls. His legs grew weary of standing.

"Jake, are you here?"

He tried to answer, but his head so swimmy that he couldn't think of any words to say.

PHOTOGRAPHIC EVIDENCE

THE FIRST THING NICK NOTICED was that his nose had stopped working. He coughed and sputtered and tried breathing through it, but it stayed stuck. He finally gave up and breathed through his mouth.

As soon as he opened his eyes, he regretted it. The light was incredibly bright, and he had to blink several times before his head would stop pounding. Why did his shirt feel all wet?

Nick spent a few blissful moments not remembering anything that happened, then reality came back to him, and all of his muscles tensed at once. This caused the lump on his head to graze the underside of Connie's cracked pedestal sink, sending a shock of pain through him, all the way down his legs. His list of defendants grew exponentially after that.

He scooted out from below the sink and felt the top of his head. It was sticky. His face felt stiff and sore. Carefully, in case he lost his balance, Nick stood up and looked at himself in the mirror. He did not scream at what he saw. He would not give in to that temptation.

Photographic evidence is what he needed. A minimum of three pictures from each angle, two of his legs and one of the bloodstains all over his shirt. And probably a few of the sink where he'd hit his head.

Nick reached for his phone, but it was not in his pocket. A quick search of the floor did not produce it, either. It *did* turn up several bloody paw prints near the spot where he'd fallen. The blood stains on his shirt looked a lot like paw prints too.

"Dear Lord forgive me. I am going to kill that cat."

WHERE WAS HE?

KIX FROWNED. Did Jake go to bed? How could he have fallen asleep so quickly? She tiptoed across the living room, just in case.

At the doorway to Jake's room, she paused. She didn't want to give him a heart attack if he was asleep so she tapped lightly on the door before stepping into his room.

"Jake? I don't want to frighten you. Your door was unlocked."

There was no answer.

A transom window let in the light from the street lamp in front of the house. It fought its way past the shrubbery and dappled the thin carpet. Kix's eyes were growing accustomed to the dark and she didn't need the watery streetlight to tell her something she could see clearly: Jake was not asleep. He wasn't even home.

Where did he go?

Outside, the crunch of tires on gravel announced a car pulling into the back driveway. Someone was here. Toesy headed toward the sound. Kix followed him.

The windows of the living room were cluttered with action figures and too high to reach easily. The kitchen window was blocked by holly shrubs so Kix ran over and peered out the peephole of the front door. Toesy sat down next to her as though he approved.

Most of the view was of the stairs leading down. Beyond that was darkness. But she could hear the car's engine out there, it must be close. Before it cut off, Kix reached up and slipped the security chain in place. If that was Carl, she would just unlock the chain. It would be awkward but Carl wouldn't make a fuss. He wasn't the fuss-making type.

She needn't have worried. Headlights flashed toward the front door as whoever drove into the back driveway made a tight turn. The engine noise grew softer, then it disappeared under the sound of wind knocking the shrubs against the kitchen window.

The backyard was again quiet except for the predictable weather. She stared out to the emptiness and reached for the safety chain. She almost had it unlatched when Thad appeared suddenly, dry despite the rain, and looking straight at her through the peephole. Kix bit down on her lip to keep from screaming.

Where had he come from? How did he know she was here? Could he see her through the spyhole? Probably not. But he might see movement. Kix willed her body to be as still as possible. Her heart thought that was a stupid idea and tried to jump out of her mouth. She had to gulp three times to force it back in.

She watched as he casually knocked on the door. Toesy stood between her feet, staring at the door. His ears had gone flat.

"Kix," he said. "Kix, I know you're in there. Your car is parked out here."

Kix did not answer. She barely breathed. Her heart was gearing up for another run at her tonsils. A low growl started near her feet.

"Listen you don't even have to answer the door. In fact, you probably shouldn't. But I want to apologize. I didn't mean to hurt you. I promise. I don't know what's going on. There was this stranger in my head. He said he was here to help me. I know that makes me sound crazy, but I can't really explain it any better. I have no idea how he got there. He forced himself in. And then he forced me out. You have to believe me, I had no idea he was going to hurt you. But I got back in, and I was able to hold him back. You saw me hold him back! I know you saw me. I just want to make sure you're safe."

Kix stepped back from the door and watched Toesy's hackles grow as Thad spoke. His fur puffed so far out that he looked nearly round.

This man is two men, and one of them is evil, he said, but to Kix it sounded more like "*MMmmrrROWOWReReRe.*"

"I agree," she whispered. "Something weird *is* going on."

"You need to leave before I call the cops," she shouted through the door and took a step back from the spyhole.

"I *knew* you were in there!" said Thad. Kix could hear the smile on his face. "I'm so sorry about what happened. Will you at least accept my apology?"

"I don't believe a word you're saying."

"I know. I'm sorry. But I'm telling the truth. There was this other guy and we fought. I thought he was going to kill me."

"Oh, I believe that part," said Kix.

"You do? Thank *God*. I was so scared, Kix. I thought I was never going to see you again. Please open the door. I won't hurt you. I promise."

Toesy growled louder.

"*That's* the part I don't believe."

For a second, there came no answer. Then the walls shook as Thad, or whoever was in his skin, kicked the door so hard that it bounced on its hinges. Toesy let out a murderous growl. Kix was a little afraid of Toesy at the moment, but she was afraid of Thad even more, so she stood on her tiptoes again and peered out the peephole.

Thad was at the front door, huffing and puffing, looking ready to blow. Then he disappeared as suddenly as he had appeared. Kix was so startled, she sneezed. When she opened her eyes, he was still not there. The growling now emanating from the kitchen told her either Toesy had found him or a mountain lion had.

"I know you're in there, Karen," Thad shouted. "That cat isn't going to save you."

Toesy snorted with grand derision. *Come closer so we may see about that, Kicker of Doors*, he said.

Kix nodded because even though the cat said no words that she recognized, the intent was clear enough. She leaned toward him and whispered. "Toesy, I'm going to try the secret way out. Can you hold him off for a bit while I disappear, too?"

The cat responded with a high pitched *roawroawroawr* noise that she understood to mean *I will kill this man if I can*. In this instance, she was one hundred percent correct.

She ducked to avoid being seen from the kitchen window and headed toward the linen closet.

"Look, I'm sorry about what happened. I didn't want to do that.

I never wanted to hurt you. That was very wrong of me. But you said you weren't seeing that guy, Karen. You *lied*. I know you two are together. And now you're trying to get rid of me. I'm not stupid Karen. It's just a piece of paper. It's not going to work."

Kix heard all this as she stepped into the linen closet. Shelves on either side of the closet held sheets and towels. The walls shook as Thad kicked at the door again.

"Karen, and you better get your ass out here. Do you hear me?"

She better *what* now? Kix turned to yell back, but Toesy came trotting up behind her and chittered at her in encouragement.

"Let's get out of here before I have to listen to much more of that."

She ran her hands along the back wall. When Jake showed her the secret stairs, they'd been squished together into the linen closet. Consequently, she hadn't been paying a lot of attention to how the door opened. Now she ran her hands all along the walls searching for hidden latches or possibly a button. She was mildly disappointed when she found just a regular old door knob hidden behind a towel. What a lame secret door.

She tried the handle.

It was locked.

THE BIRTH OF AN ANGEL

TOESY LOOKED AT THE ANGEL OF DELIVERY with greater respect than he ever had. Even with the evil Kicker of Doors outside, he did not worry. Of all the people in his realm, the Angel of Delivery had the most potential. Indeed, Toesy had long suspected her inborn abilities. It made perfect sense, given her holy stature. She was a worthy ally; the perfect human to help him quell these shenanigans and find Pansy. In return, he would help her gain Universal Consciousness.

"It's locked Toesy," said the Angel. "Is there an extra key somewhere?"

Toesy remembered seeing a set of keys near the Altar of Unopened Mail in the Holy Man's inner sanctum. He backed out of the linen closet and sprinted down the hall. The Angel of Delivery followed him closely.

They searched the altar, but the magazine gods, to whom it had been dedicated, were not very helpful in finding the extra keys. Toesy silently cursed their periodical wisdom.

"Maybe they're in the drawer?" said the Angel. Toesy opened the top drawer. There were many things inside it. Most of them were not keys. They tore through the drawer, unaware that their time grew short. So busy were they searching that they missed the first signs. The soft *spit-spit* sound of mud being squished aside. The tiny *scree* of a branch scraping across the window.

The hairs on the back of Toesy's neck rose up. He turned to the window. The Kicker of Doors leered down at them from above.

"Hello there," he said. Toesy bared all his teeth and hissed dramatically.

The Angel of Delivery looked up, temporarily lost in shock. She could not move. Toesy ratcheted his hiss down to a growl and struck up a defensive posture. He would not allow this man access to his angel. She turned to him, confusion marring her heavenly beauty.

"I can see you, Karen," said the Kicker of Doors. As he stared, the look on his face grew frustrated. He kicked the window, shattering it. Glass rained down on the carpet. The Angel barely had time to gasp in surprise before he reappeared in the middle of the Holy Man's bedroom.

"You should have opened the door like I asked," he said.

Toesy had wanted more time to study her natural abilities. Would she understand the jump? Could she see other realities? Did she get travel-sick? But it was not to be. This Boundary Walker would kill her if he had the chance. Toesy would not risk it.

He stood up on his hind legs and leaned into the Angel, positioning himself as close as possible to her backside. Then he bit down.

By the time the man lunged for them, they were already gone.

JAKE

WHEN THE DOWNSTAIRS DOOR KNOB SHOOK, Jake became aware that he was still standing in the back hallway, still staring at the big, fat spider, which was still waving its legs at him.

Somewhere, someone was shouting. Jake risked looking away from the nasty spider for half a second, toward the door. But as he looked, the door stretched away from him. Instead of six steps down, it now stood hundreds of stairs away. Jake blinked. When he opened his eyes again, the door snapped back into place.

That was not normal.

"Did you do that?" Kix said.

He was so glad to hear her voice that he almost answered but Jake did not want to scare the spider into running at him again. He kept his mouth shut and listened to the funny way Kix's voice carried around the stairwell. It almost sounded as if it came from *upstairs* this time.

"Did you *have* to bite me in the ass?"

He turned his attention to the top of the stairs. The walls, blurry and indistinct before, now became super-real. He could see every cobweb, every crack in the concrete, almost as though it were in extreme close-up. The volume of his surroundings increased. He heard more shouting and murmuring. Someone was very angry.

The noise confused his sense of direction, so he covered his left ear to hear downstairs better. A man was shouting. There was a man was in his apartment?

Jake covered the other ear and listened upstairs. Kix was there, talking with someone. He covered both ears. The noise grew dim. He uncovered both ears, and the noise grew louder again. He repeated this experiment quickly, three times in a row, until he became disoriented. Black spots began to float in front of his eyes, and he very nearly passed out. But Jake's consciousness wouldn't give up that easily. It grabbed on to the spots and rearranged them. Four black dots up and down, all in a neat little row. Black buttons on a white coat.

I meant here. *You aren't supposed to be* here.

Jake didn't throw up this time, but only because he didn't have anything left in his stomach.

"That isn't supposed to happen."

The sound of Kix's voice sent a shiver through the base of Jake's spine, and his heart started to pound. He resurfaced from his terror-induced trance. "Kix—" said Jake.

He didn't have time to say anything else. As soon as the word escaped his lips, Jake realized his mistake. The spider was at his feet in less time than it took for his stomach to try a daring escape through his neck and bowels at the same time. He didn't see where it went. Something moderately weighty had crawled up his pant leg to his sleeve, and Jake noted with disgust that he'd been right—it was a jumper.

Jake's arm started to implement the GETITOFFGETITOFFGETITOFF protocol for scary spider removal, but as soon as his hand came in contact with something that was definitely not sleeve, his heart tried to escape as well, and then the world around him went a little funny.

Later, Jake would tell people that the adrenaline was pumping so hard, he saw his life flash before his eyes. Because everyone knows when you're a split second away from death and full of adrenaline, that happens, right?

Well, at least it *ought* to happen that way.

But it didn't. Jake didn't relive the stutter he had in grade school. Or the time he accidentally burned the lawn mower up trying to trick out the motor. He didn't even relive the moment he first laid eyes on Kix. He saw many moments, yes. Perhaps a million moments. But they didn't add up to his life because they were all the exact *same* moment.

This moment, a million times.

All he could see were possibilities. An endless stretch of them, as though someone had squished his body between two mirrors, and every iteration of himself was just a tiny bit different. Which one was the real him? Better yet, which one would take him where he needed to go?

* * *

What actually happened to Jake in that back hallway is a bit less dramatic. Mainly this is due to the fact that the Universe, as previously discussed, likes to be tidy. But also because this particular region of the Universe knew Jake very well. It was used to this kind of tomfoolery and knew exactly what to do about it. It put him in time out.

That is to say, it dilated time all around Jake to create a bubble of improbability, then it parked him there—to reflect on how one shouldn't mess about with the space-time continuum unless one is prepared to get it *wrong*—until such time as one of his friends or the Great Void of Infinity came to collect him.

ASHWOOD SUPER MALL

THAD WALKED DOWN the long tiled hall again. He hadn't noticed the security cameras until now. He stared directly into the nearest one and gave it a thumbs-up as he walked past. Immediately, the phone at his hip started making beepy noises. It was an old-style flip phone, but no brand he'd ever seen. He flipped it open.

"Yello?" he said, cheery and chipper.

"What the hell happened to your face? And what are you still doing here? You better get gone before Gayle sees you on the security feeds, or she's going to have you arrested."

"I wish I could, Brah. I can't seem to get farther than the frozen yogurt joint."

"This isn't a joke, Brad."

"You know Brad? Tell me, is he always that much of an asshole?"

"You aren't funny."

"I ain't trying to be, Brah. That whole bathroom scene is really getting old."

"Have you been drinking?"

"What? No," said Thad, but he hadn't felt this relaxed in years, so maybe he had been? That might explain the bathroom trips.

"Brad, if you don't leave mall property in five minutes, I'm calling the ACPD myself."

"What is the ACPD?" said Thad but halfway through, his nose started to tickle and he sneezed. When he opened his eyes, he was back in the bathroom stall. The phone in his hand was silent.

"*Come on,*" he said walking out of the stall for the fifth time. "This is literally the worst friggin' cold in the world."

Thad walked out to the sinks and paused a moment to admire the goose egg on his eye. It looked like it hurt badly but there were so many drugs in his system he didn't realize that he should be feeling any pain.

Twelve steps down the tiled hallway, the phone at his hip started ringing again.

"What the hell was that?" said the guy on the phone.

"I *told* you I couldn't get past the Fro-Yo store, Brah. You didn't believe me."

BILLABLE HOURS

AUGUSTUS DRACOS TERKLE III, Auggie to his friends (and clients who made more than five hundred K a year), had been half asleep on the couch when his phone rang. When the familiar contact information popped up on screen, he reached over and answered it.

"Hello, Mr. Miller. What can I do for you this evening?"

"Firstly, I apologize Mr. Terkle. I realize what time it is, but unfortunately this cannot wait until morning. I have been assaulted, and I have been mugged, and I am going to take each and every one of these people to court. I don't care how we do it."

"No problem at all, Nick," said Mr. Terkle and indeed, he was not lying. At on-call service rates, Auggie would listen to anyone's story. "What's going on?"

"I am sitting in my car in front of the Clydesdale Manor apartments, and I've been reduced to using my tablet computer to make this phone call because my phone has been stolen. I am not in danger currently, but I do not discount future happenstance. You have no idea what kind of night I've had."

"Sounds like you've been through the wringer. Why don't you tell me about it?"

For five solid minutes, Nicholas Miller listed everything that happened to him since eleven that morning. Auggie listened patiently, making occasional scribbling noises with a pencil. At length, he interrupted.

"Have you called the police yet?"

"Obviously not. I needed to make sure you were available first."

"Wise move. Who did you say owned the cat?"

"That I don't know yet but—oh my dear Lord, *there it is*. Mr. Terkle, I am sorry to do this but I've just spotted the dratted thing. It's with a person now. Oh, am I ever going to give that girl a piece of my mind. With any luck, I will have more information soon," he said. Then he hung up.

Auggie Terkle sat on the phone, listening to the dead connection, until the minute was up. Then he noted his billable hours. He would have also added an Abrupt Conversation Termination fee, but *Clydesdale Manor Apartments* rang some bells, and he was busy trying to remember why.

A SHIFT IN PERSPECTIVE

TOESY BIT HER ON THE REAR END so hard that Kix would have yelped, but the pain made her nose tingle, so she sneezed instead. Kind of. Maybe. It was weird.

Later, Kix would remember it less like a sneeze and more like a fall or even a *jump*, but that sounded wrong in her head right now, so she thought of it as a sneeze. When she opened her eyes, the light was blinding, and she had to cover her face with her arm until she could see right. Once she could see, she took another moment to believe it.

Toesy sat behind her, purring and washing his face with a paw. When she turned around, his ears perked up, and his whiskers splayed out in friendly fashion. It made him look slightly apologetic.

"Did you do that?" she said, rubbing her behind. Toesy nodded.

"Did you *have* to bite me on the ass?" she said. Toesy chittered lightly and purred some more. Even his eyebrow whiskers were forward now, and one ear dipped in profound sincerity.

"Well, thank you for the…very strange rescue. Can you please aim for the calf next time?"

Toesy rubbed up against her knee and purred. Kix took that as a *yes* and pulled her phone from her jacket pocket. She dialed nine-one-one, pressed *Send,* and got an immediate busy signal for her troubles.

"That isn't supposed to happen," she said.

Her thoughts were interrupted by the sound of someone entering the security code at the front door. Kix looked up. "Toesy?" she said. He meowed at her from the top of the stairs.

"Good idea." She sprinted to the stairs. Halfway up the front door burst open and a man shouted.

"Hold it right there!"

Kix slowed down but didn't stop moving. Whoever it was, it wasn't Thad. The man ran up the stairs, pushing his way past her and blocking the next stair up.

"Is that your cat?" he said, pointing a bloody finger toward the floor.

Kix gasped. Whatever animal this man had encountered clearly had a lot of sharp claws. An acrid smell hit her in the nose then, making her gag. She turned away to see Toesy behind her, hackles raised and growling so low she almost couldn't hear it.

"Oh my God," she said scrunching her nose up and waving at the air. "You *stink*."

Toesy stopped growling. His ears perked up with glee. For half a second, he looked very pleased with himself. Then he flattened his ears and went back to threatening the man with all of his sharper parts.

"Is that your cat or *not*?" said the man, wincing when he turned his head too fast. The smell of him made Kix's eyes water.

"I don't think he's anyone's cat," she said.

"Don't mince words with me, *girly*. That cat ate my girlfriend's sugar glider and attacked me without cause. Then he stole my phone. If that is your cat, you can expect a letter from my lawyer within twenty-four hours."

Behind her, Toesy stepped up to rage-growling, making the hair on Kix's scalp itch. The man stepped back half a step but still refused to move out of the way. Kix really didn't have time for this.

"First of all," she straightened up. The man tried to stand firm but Kix simply walked into the space he occupied making him step backward in order to stay in front of her. "Don't call me *girly* again unless you want a broken nose."

"Secondly," she said, forcing him up another stair. "His name is Thanatos, not *That Cat*."

Step.

"Thirdly, *Get out of my way*."

They were at the top of the stairs now, the man trying to keep himself out of her reach but still not let her pass. She stepped up to him, but still he wouldn't move, so Kix gave up and pushed him out of the way. In a fit of supreme bad judgment, he grabbed her by the arm as she passed him.

"Now just a minute. You aren't going anywhere. I want your full name and a phone number where you can be reached."

Kix had been keyed up since Thad attacked her, and her reaction to the man's use of force may have been a little overzealous. She whipped her arm around, shaking him loose while simultaneously grabbing onto his right pinky. Then she twisted her body in an arc until he was kneeling backward on the stair below her trying desperately to free his hand from her vise-like grip before she broke his pinky in half.

"No," she said very calmly. "I am not giving you anything. What you just did was assault. And this—" she bent his finger back farther. "Is self-defense."

"Owowow. *Leggoleggoleggo,*" he said.

"I'm not going to warn you again. You come at me once more, and Toesy is going to turn this into justifiable homicide."

"Okay, okay! Just give me my phone back." said the man. His eyes shone with tears. "I know you have it somewhere."

"Your phone is dead. I found it smashed up on the ground. Toesy had nothing to do with it. Now leave me alone."

"You're lying. I know that cat took my phone. You have it somewhere. I know you d—"

Kix's other hand shot forward and made a neat little *whap* sound as she smacked him.

"Don't," she said and pointed at Toesy. The man's mouth worked itself up and down like a trout. She loosened her grip on his pinky and he shimmied away until he was just outside of her reach. Then she turned and started up the second flight of stairs. Two stairs up he found his voice again.

"You can't get away with this. I will find out who you are."

"Her name is Karen," said an angry voice near the front door.

Kix and Toesy both peeked over the banister at the same time. In the middle of the entryway stood Psycho-Thad. His feet were muddy and his jacket soaked through. He did not appear to care that he was making a giant mess.

"Oh sh—," said Kix.

JAKE'S ROOM

"—**IT. *CAN YOU WARN ME** next time you're gonna do that?*" said Kix as she rubbed at her leg. They were back downstairs in Jake's bedroom. Toesy huffed at her in exasperation and hustled her a few more steps toward the bedroom door.

"You don't have to push, I'm going." Kix fished her car keys from her pocket and ran toward the hallway. She intended to get in her car and drive straight to the police this time, but something about Jake's room in the dark brought a flash of memory so strong that she tripped. Toesy ran headfirst into the back of her knee.

"Hold up," she said.

Toesy growled lightly—not really a menacing growl, more of an irritated growl. A growl that tapped its foot and wanted to know *if they could please discuss this somewhere else.*

"There's an answer here, Toesy. I know there is."

He began pushing her out of the room using a special technique that involved lots of head-butting.

"Okay, never mind. I'm going." She made it as far as the living room when the feeling of familiarity hit her again. This time, a scene played through in her memory, cloudy and intangible but *right there.*

She'd stood in that exact spot. She'd said something to Jake. He'd said something back that had made her happy but also…impatient?

A small *crack*—not very loud, but worrisome—brought her back to reality.

"What was that?"

Toesy looked back to the shadows. His hackles raised immediately. He made a loud *chit-chit* noise and ran toward Kix.

"It's him, isn't it?"

Kix held her arm out for him to bite down like he'd done twice now, but something hit him as he ran, knocking him off course. Instead of biting and whisking her away to rescue, he could do nothing more than run a claw down her forearm with an outstretched paw. Kix watched in horror as Toesy hit the far wall and disappeared. Then there were hands, grasping at her hair.

Kix ducked and spun around, yanking her hair loose. Only then did she notice the blood dripping. Only then did the pain from Toesy's claw marks come alive.

It flew down her arm, directing her thoughts to a spot just beyond her reach. Kix found herself stepping toward it in a way that was much more meta- than physical just to catch up. She felt resistance push against her feet, or maybe it was inside her feet, or maybe she was just standing on something—it was hard to tell.

Around her, the rest of the world loosened. It melted. It flowed like water. The force gathering under her feet became a stone in the middle of the stream. When she stepped off to the other bank, she would be somewhere else. Kix thought very hard about what she wanted to see when she got there.

When she opened her eyes, she stood in the middle of Deli's living room.

Toesy, however, did not.

TOESY EVENTUALLY LANDED

IN A LARGE BATHROOM, empty save for the last stall. The door opened for a moment, then it closed. The person within seemed to be having an argument with themselves. Eventually they opened the door again and out walked the Kicker of Doors.

"Hey cat," said the villain and proceeded to admire himself in the mirror, poking at the massive welt over his eye. After a moment of this he turned back to Toesy and gave him a sideways grin.

"I'll see you," he pointed at Toesy and winked. "Later." Then the Kicker of Doors turned a jig and walked out of the room.

From this, Toesy determined that this man may not actually be the real Kicker of Doors. In fact, it was entirely possible that this was some alternate-reality door kicker who has been taking recreational drugs.

Toesy wasn't sure about the last part, but he did not care. The real Kicker of Doors was still with the Angel of Delivery and he needed to get back there with all haste. All this teleporting business was going to exact its toll on someone, and he wanted to be in the right place when it did. He jumped off the counter in the Ashwood Super Mall men's room...

...and landed on the Holy Man's kitchen counter. Immediately, Toesy noted a distinct the lack of obscenities being shouted. As he tiptoed to the spot where he'd been ambushed by the Door Kicker, he did not hear any angry thumps of fists pummeling the door. There was also a total absence of anyone screaming for help. He didn't even hear any breathing.

Steve.

Yes, sir?

I do not believe the Angel is here.

She may have jumped on her own, sir.

Great basking kittens, Steve! Do you think so?

It is a possibility, sir.

That would be a delight, would it not? said Toesy. *She is very close to consciousness. Let us go check.*

He jumped up to Jake's computer table...

...and landed on the counter in Deli's kitchen.

"Toesy!" said the Angel. She was standing in the middle of the room making *boop-boop* noises with her tiny computer. "What took you so long?" She smiled at him.

Huzzah, Steve! She is here!

You did suggest she could be taught, sir.

Yes, of course I did.

He had known she was a natural, but nothing could prepare him for the great swelling of pride in his breast at the realization that the Angel had not only walked a boundary between realities by herself, but she'd also come out relatively sane-looking on the other side.

He had done the impossible. He had taught this woman, this harbinger of pizza and other Italian foodstuffs, how to walk the thin lines. She was proof positive that a human—the least skilled animal in all of nature—could be taught. And also that Thanatos, Dark Lord of the Underworld and Everything within Six Blocks of Horsey House (songbirds excluded), was truly an excellent teacher.

It's the lack of self-awareness, you know, Steve. Most humans have very little, which makes it almost impossible for them to step through, you see? They never really know where they are, let alone where they're going. But our Angel has more self-awareness than a Manx. I tell you, she is quite capable.

Toesy broke into hearty fits of purring. The Angel reached out and stroked him behind his right ear. A small drop of saliva appeared in the corner of his mouth.

"I'm glad to see you, too, you big fuzzy monster." She rubbed his ears and Toesy almost melted into a small puddle. "Did you see what happened to Thad?"

Toesy did not stop purring, although his ears flattened.

"I didn't either. I was concentrating so hard on being here that I didn't see anything else. Speaking of that..." she said and disappeared.

She reappeared immediately on the other side of the kitchen.

"Are you contagious or something?"

Toesy blinked his eyes three times and purred harder. She walked back to him and rubbed him on the neck.

"Well, thank you. I guess? I'm not very good at it yet. I was trying for the hallway."

Toesy purred so hard that saliva dripped from his chin. He bumped her hand with the top of his head in pride and also to remind her to keep scratching his ear.

"Don't get pushy." She grinned at him and continued rubbing. "We need to find Jake. He's the key to all of this. I know he is. I just can't figure out how."

Toesy mewled again, this time in agreement.

"He told me last night he was going to Sacha's to work on *TerrorCity*. Let's try there."

Toesy mewled once more, this time with the pride of a demigod who has worked his first true miracle.

ANOTHER CONVERSATION
AT ON-CALL SERVICE RATES

"THEN THE MAN DISAPPEARED, TOO. I know it sounds ridiculous, but I swear to you that's what it looked like. I think they were making me high on some sort of hallucinogenic drug or something. I had a sneezing attack both times."

Auggie Terkle was beginning to think the same thing. The story Nick told him was getting weirder by the minute.

"What exactly did the woman do?"

"She attacked me! I asked for her name and a phone number where I could reach her, and she tried to break my hand! Then she threatened to kill me if I didn't leave her alone. I asked for my phone back. She lied and said it was broken but I know she has it. That cat took it. I know it did."

"And that's when the other guy showed up?"

"Yes, and then they both disappeared. Her first and him a second later."

"Explain that part again?"

"I told you, I didn't really see it. I think they drugged me."

"For the purpose of *what*, exactly?"

"To steal my fingerprint, of course."

"Because…why?"

"My phone has that Double Blind security system on it. You have to have my fingerprint and the pass code or you can't even access the keypad."

Nick droned on, but Auggie didn't hear it. He'd finally remembered from where he knew the name *Clydesdale Manor*. It housed the headquarters of Sanderson & Denny, Inc., a company he'd recently gone up against in court.

"Mr. Miller," said Auggie. "I'm going to give you a bit of friendly advice. Call the police, file a report. Tell them all you told me. Then go home and leave it alone. Unless you have some valid evidence that it attacked you *unprovoked*, you're not going to get anywhere."

"Oh, I can *get* evidence."

Auggie sighed into the phone. "Okay. Send me what you can, and I'll take a look, but I still can't guarantee anything."

THIEF

THE STALL DOOR OPENED in front of him with a squeak, and Brad opened his eyes.

How?

It was the only thought he had before a tidal wave of sleepiness hit him, washing most everything else away. Brad panicked. He scrambled toward the portal, pushing his consciousness away from the reality of the Ashwood Super Mall; pulling himself back toward his new home before Thad could realize what was happening. Back to his new life. Back to his new car, parked in the shadows, near a tree. It was not easy, but he was successful. When he opened his eyes, he saw the glistening spikes of holly reflecting light from the street lamp.

The sleepiness stayed with him for a moment, but Brad fought against it, knowing there were no drugs in his system here. Rain fell from the holly tree in great splatters on the roof. His car was dark and hidden from view. He sat there in the shadows trying to reconstruct what just happened. Something wasn't adding up.

The first time Kix disappeared, he thought he had done it, like how he'd pushed Danielle down the hall when he was angry. But upstairs, she disappeared before he could reach her. And when he finally had her by the arm, she pushed *him* somehow—all the way back to Ashwood. How could she have done that?

Maybe she found the portal. Maybe she was trying to take it over for herself. The idea seemed ridiculous at first. Karen wasn't smart enough to find it. But the memory of the stall door kept replaying itself in his mind. The last time he was there, he'd taped it shut, inside and out. There's no way it could have opened so easily unless someone had taken the tape off. Who could have done that if Thad was out cold?

It had to have been Karen. She found the portal. She was using it. It was the only way to explain her being able to pull him back there. She was trying to take it away from him. How had he been so stupid not to have seen that?

First she stole his trust. Then she took his dignity. When that wasn't enough, she took his job too. Now that bitch was trying to take the one thing he had left in this world. If she thought he was going to sit back and let her, she was in for a big surprise.

TIME OUT

THE MINUTE STRETCHED OUT to hours and years. Everywhere Jake looked, the world shimmered and split into more and more Jakes, each one a reflection of him, and each one a different reality. An infinite mirage, real and not real at the same time.

Some had obvious differences, like the one in the stupid orange jacket. He wouldn't wear a jacket like that. But the longer he looked at the orange jacket, the less sure he became about whether or not it was stupid. Didn't he have a jacket like that in his closet? He hadn't worn it this evening, had he?

Jake pulled his attention away from those Jakes and vowed not to notice anything else until he knew what was going on. That lasted until he saw that one of the Jakes had no scar on his cheek. Then he noticed that a lot of the Jakes were missing scars.

Jake tried to touch his cheek, to reassure himself that yes, he did have a scar, but he seemed to have lost all communication with his body. He couldn't remember where his arms went. What did that mean? Where did his arms go?

They're right in front of you, said the little voice in his head. He wasn't sure it was his own voice, but it sounded a lot like the one he argued with on a regular basis. He looked at the infinite sea of Jakes surrounding him.

Which one is the real one, though? Which head is thinking these thoughts?

All of them, said the little voice. *Which one do you want to be?*

All of the Jakes. Every one he saw was him. He would have to choose. Crap. What if he got it wrong? What if he stepped into a reality where he lived in Bellevue or was lactose intolerant or something? *What if he didn't know Kix?*

Jake didn't want to live in a world where he didn't know Kix. He also wanted to avoid any reality where he got bitten on the neck by a freakishly large spider, although he was willing to risk it if it meant that he and Kix could go back to hanging out and watching movies on his couch.

Circular arguments chased themselves through his thoughts, nipping at their own heels. They were all him. He could see that clearly now. They were all the possibilities forward from this moment.

Jake fell into himself, unsure of where to go, paralyzed with fear of making the wrong decision. He stayed that way for ten billion years. Or maybe it was twenty minutes, he had no way to tell.

HE FINALLY MADE IT PAST
THE FRO-YO STORE

THAD SAT AT THE BOOKING DESK and stared at the Sargent. He knew something heavy was going down, but he couldn't shake the chemically induced feeling that everything was going to work out for the best, so he went along with everything the cop-guy said because he looked nice. Also, he had a really big mustache. Thad could not stop staring at it. It looked a little like a guinea pig.

"Mr. Islenix, I understand Miss Wells has a court order of protection against you and that you were served earlier this afternoon with the paperwork."

"No kidding?" said Thad "Then I mustache you a question," he said, and struggled to keep a straight face.

"Mr. Islenix, I think you might want to show a bit more restraint, considering the gravity of the charges being leveled against you."

"Not me," said Thad.

"Yes sir, *you*. You are in a heap of shit."

"With all due respect, Officer Brah, *Brad* is the one in a heap of shit. I'm just the poor schmuck who happens to play him on TV. I don't even know where I am. Where am I?"

"Ashwood County lockup. You're being booked for violation of the court protection order placed against you this afternoon."

"Am I really? Well then, you should probably know that I may have to leave unexpectedly."

"I don't think so, Buddy. You aren't going anywhere for a while."

"Why does no one belie—"

"—VE ME?"

THAD OPENED HIS EYES to the accessible bathroom stall and the very startled gentleman currently occupying it. The man wore a tiny green hat, which Thad thought looked funny.

"Oh, excuse me," he said. "I'm not—"

He was going to say *staying long*, but something near the toilet paper dispenser tugged at his attention. Thad recognized the pull and started searching for the portal.

"Do you feel that?" he said.

"Son, you need to leave," said the surprised gentleman. He looked ninety years old if he was a day and about as dangerous as a wet hen.

"Hold on a second, Brah," said Thad. "It's here somewhere."

Behind him, the man abandoned his attempt at biology and started to fasten his trousers.

"Did you just call me a *bra*? As in a woman's *undergarment*?"

"Shh, I can feel it. It's here. Don't you feel that?"

The old man clucked in the background while Thad searched. He finally found the tear in the space-time continuum disguised as a bit of crumbling grout. He stared at it. The more he concentrated, the wider the portal opened. Soon he could see a gravel lot standing next to a familiar-looking car. The air around him grew cold and clammy. The lights went out. A *drippy-droppy* sound started up somewhere behind him, but Thad couldn't place it right away.

He stood next to a parked car. He knew the car, but to whom it belonged he couldn't say. It wasn't his car, was it? The thoughts in his head started to organize themselves better. No, surely he would remember something like that. Thad wanted to step forward, into that dark reality with the incredibly familiar car. When the hand came into view, he almost jumped for joy. It was wearing his favorite watch! He loved that watch.

A flash of light caught his attention and Thad saw the hand—*his* hand—now held something metal. Thad didn't care. He was so happy to see his own hand again that he took a step forward without even thinking. Instantly, the world around him started to boil. A cascade of anger and hatred came crashing down on him.

A sudden crack of pain made Thad's eyes close involuntarily. He fell back to the Ashwood Super Mall. Back to Brad's empty body now kneeling on the floor and clutching at the side of his head.

"What the hell, Grandpa? Did you just punch me?"

"Insubordination! You pervert! You gave me no choice. Now march your skinny ass out to the sinks right this instant."

The man looked pretty spry for being basically a human raisin, and Thad didn't want to risk another head shot, so he backed out of the stall.

"Look, you don't understand. I need to get back there. I was almost home. I'm not from here. I got sucked through some sort of interdimensional portal, and now I'm stuck in this bathroom."

"You expect me to believe that flimflammery? I know what you are. *You're a drug fiend!* You're not going to bugger me for money!"

The man stepped forward to swing his cane at Thad again, but it got caught up with the paper towel dispenser, and he stumbled forward. Thad grabbed him before he hit the floor.

"Whoa! Easy there, old man. You're gonna break a hip or something."

"Get your filthy hands off of me," shouted the raisin man. "You just stay right where you are. Now where's that wireless telephone of mine?"

SOMEONE IS FINALLY
TAKING THIS SERIOUSLY

NICK KNEW BETTER than to call Mr. Terkle back until morning. Instead he concentrated on gathering photographic evidence. Unfortunately, the camera on his tablet computer was not the best. It couldn't capture many of the finer bruises on his face or the scratch marks at all. He was able to get a good shot of the swelling, but it wasn't enough. He needed proof that the cat had done this. He needed to find that dratted cat and that vermin traitor so he could *show* Connie just what they were like. But he would need help.

"9-1-1 emergency services, what address are you calling from please?"

Nick read the address from the one of the many pieces of mail lying on Connie's kitchen counter.

"What is the nature of your emergency?"

"A feral beast from hell is what."

"Excuse me, sir?"

"I said there is a feral hell-beast roaming around this house, and I need it caught. I need the police here, to show them what it's done to me."

"Sir, could you describe the nature of the hell-beast?"

"It's a huge, rabid cat. It has large fangs and black, beady eyes.

It's already attacked me twice. It's trying to kill me."

"You say it's a large cat?"

"Yes, and it's trying to kill me."

"Can you please hold for a moment, sir? I think I have a related call."

"Oh, thank the Lord and Savior, *finally*. Yes, of course I will hold."

* * *

"Hey, Lou," Sol Underman leaned over his desk and whispered. "Where were those animal calls coming in from? Was it over on Capitol Hill?"

"Hold on, lemme check." Lou referred to his computer screen and nodded his head. "Yeah, three in a row. Bam. Bam. Bam. All scared to death of a big cat or something. We sent someone over to check it out, but he didn't see anything. Why? You got another sighting?"

"I might. Guy says he got attacked by it."

"No shit? Hold on. I'll get Ronnie."

Lou pushed some buttons and readjusted his headset. "Yeah, hey, Ronnie, I got a bunch of reports sighting a large cat—maybe a cougar or something up near Capitol Hill. Can you go check it out?" Lou read off the address that Sol provided for him. Then his mouth dropped open.

"What do you mean *you ain't going*? I got a guy on the line says he's been attacked by a cougar. We need Animal Control up there."

The headset squawked angrily, and Lou's face grew red.

"Now you listen here, Ronnie. You can't do that. I don't care if it's got laser eyes and a Kung fu grip, it's your damn *job*. You either go check it out or I'm writing you up—Hello?"

Lou stared at the headset. "That little pantywaist won't *go*. Says he seen that thing before, and it ain't a cougar. He says it has *thumbs*. What are we gonna do?"

"I dunno," said Sol. "We know anyone at the zoo?"

"Just my cousin, Burt."

"He's a custodian, ain't he?"

CASA DE SACHA

On the third knock, someone finally came to the door. Kix heard scrabbling at the security chain and smiled into the spyhole. When Sacha opened the door, a delicious aroma hit her right in the stomach. She hadn't eaten in a while.

"Wow! What is that amazing smell?" She said this in the lively voice of a friend who has been invited to dinner then pushed past Sacha into his apartment. Toesy slunk in behind her.

"Oh, uh, Kix. Come on in, I guess. I'm roasting pork for tamales." Sacha stood in the doorway, dumbfounded and Kix was afraid he couldn't move.

"Could you close the door, please?" she said, keeping her disposition very friendly and open. She smiled a lot. Sacha looked confused, but he was the type of guy who generally closed doors that women asked him to close, so he did.

"And could you please put the security chain back on?"

Again, he did as he was asked. But this time when he turned back to Kix, she could see he was trying to hide a smirk.

"So...uh...what's up?"

"Have you seen Jake? I haven't heard from him all day—not that I was supposed to or anything. But I can't get a hold of him at all, and I've been trying for a while. He told me he was going to come over here and work on *TerrorCity*. So I thought I'd ask you. Do you know where he is?"

The smirk sat at the corner of Sacha's mouth. "Sorry, haven't seen him," he said, crossing his arms over his chest and leaning against the wall. "He postponed the triage session until tomorrow, which is fine by me because I had a bunch of stuff to do."

"When did he cancel?"

"This morning. Said he needed a night off of zombies."

"Have you heard from him since then?"

"Nope," said Sacha, grinning wider now. "What's going on?"

"Everything. Deli broke her leg and Carl is up at the hospital with her. I'm being chased down by a homicidal maniac who thinks I'm his ex-girlfriend named Karen."

"Sure, sure. And how's Santa Claus?"

"You don't believe me?"

"Let's just say I'm not going to fall for another one of Jake's elaborate pranks, okay?"

"Look, I know it sounds crazy, but things are happening all over, and I can't explain any of them. My neighbor dove off the deep end of the sanity pool. Now he's murder-stalking me. And *he*," she said, pointing to Toesy, who had jumped up on Sacha's futon and was now licking the grime from his paw, "went all Morpheus earlier."

Sacha was almost laughing now. "Oh yeah, you gotta watch out for Thanatos. He does that sometimes."

"You still don't believe me?"

"Well, for someone being murder-stalked, you don't seem all that scared."

Sacha sneezed. When he opened his eyes, Kix was gone.

"That's because I can do *this* now."

Sacha shrieked. He whipped around to face Kix, who was standing directly behind him and whispering into his ear.

"I'm still getting the hang of it, though," she said.

"How did you do that?"

"Ask the friggin' Time Lord over there," said Kix, pointing to Toesy, who was now licking other parts of himself. "He showed me how."

"Thanatos, you gotta teach me how to do that," he said. Toesy stopped licking and stared at Sacha very hard in appraisal. Then he flicked his ears in apology, shook his head from side to side and went back to his impromptu bath.

"He can't," said Kix.

"What do you mean?"

"I think you have to be in danger or something. Look, forget about how it happens. Let's talk about my murder-stalker. He can do that little trick too, and I have no idea where he is at the moment."

Sacha stopped smiling. "This isn't a joke, is it?"

"No."

"So when you say *murder-stalker* you mean—"

"He's trying to kill me."

"Okay, you know what? We should definitely call the cops."

"That's a great idea! What part should I explain first? The sudden onset of split personality in my neighbor or the fact that we can both disappear at will? Or maybe I should start with the cat-wizard over there?"

"I see your point."

"Look, Deli told me to find Jake. She said he could fix this. She said to tell him his wig is all fuzzy."

"Fuzzy?"

"No, that's not right."

"Wuzzy?"

"No, that's not it either."

"Was it a bear?"

"Oh, ha *ha*. Shut up—I'm trying to remember." Kix closed her eyes tight and tried to think back over the conversation she had with Deli.

Sacha interrupted her with a snap. "It wasn't *wizzy*, was it?"

"Yes! That's it!"

"She had it backward." said Sacha. Kix looked at him sideways. "It's wizzy *wig*. As in *W-Y-S-I-W-Y-G*." Kix continued looking at him sideways. Toesy finished his bath and joined her.

"It's an acronym. It stands for *what you see is what you get*."

"Okay, but what if I'm not sure what I'm seeing?"

"I don't know. Look at it differently, I guess."

"Look at it differently?" said Kix. "That's your answer?"

"I don't know, maybe? Whatever happens, we should definitely call the cops."

Toesy sidelined his request by jumping down from the futon and walking over to Kix. He meowed twice and pointed his whiskers at her pocket.

"Oh, yeah! Do you know anything about this?" asked Kix and

pulled the rubber tarantula from her jacket pocket.

Sacha took one look at it and went still. "Where did it come from?"

"I don't know—Toesy handed it to me in the back yard. He also gave me this." She handed him Nick's smashed up phone. "Before he let me into Jake's apartment."

Kix looked thoughtful for a second before adding, "I *swear* that happened."

Sacha put the rubber tarantula down on the counter and studied the phone.

"Whose phone?" he said. Toesy started growling.

"That belongs to the guy who is suing me because Toesy ate his sugar glider."

Sacha turned sharply to Toesy. "You told me you weren't gonna eat that fancy squirrel."

Toesy's ears drooped under the weight of false accusation. He jumped up to Sacha's counter and grabbed the rubber tarantula. Then he turned away from them and stared out the window.

"I don't think he did," said Kix.

"Then where did she go?"

Toesy parked his behind in Sacha's kitchen sink, stretched himself up to the window sill overlooking the back parking lot and stared mournfully into the darkness. His ears were very low.

"I think he may have lost her," said Kix. "He handed me that rubber spider like it meant something. Where did it come from?"

"It was just a joke, I *swear*. I left it in the secret hallway. It was payback for the bike helmet garbage. Jake hates spiders. He's terrified of them."

"You sure it was *this* rubber tarantula?"

"Well, no. But it looked exactly like that one."

"You know what? I'm just gonna go check and see if it's still in the back hallway."

"Do you want me to go with you?"

"It's okay," she said. "I mean, I was just going to, you know...do that thing. And then come back."

Sacha looked disappointed, but instead of complaining, he grabbed his paring knife from the kitchen counter and handed it to her.

"Here. Take this," he said. "In case you run into your murder-stalker."

Kix smiled and took the tiny knife. "What am I gonna do, peel him to death?"

"Well, I don't have a gun, and it's the sharpest knife I own."

"Oh!" said Kix. "What am I thinking? *I* have a gun."

"You *do*?" said Sacha. He looked both terrified and impressed at the same time.

"Well, no, it's not mine. Marco made me take it. I didn't really want it, but he insisted, so I stuck it under the passenger seat of my car."

"Is it loaded?"

"I think so, why?"

"You left a loaded gun in your car when there's someone trying to murder-stalk you?"

"You know, that might not have been the best idea. I'll be right back."

SOMEONE VISITS LATE AT NIGHT

KIX THOUGHT ABOUT THE GUN, wrapped up in its blue, oily cloth, tucked under her passenger seat. She thought about the front seat of her car and what it felt like to be sitting on the passenger side. Before she opened her eyes, the air on her cheek dropped several degrees and the sound of rain hitting the metal roof drowned out any doubt. She reached down below the car seat and felt for the gun. It wasn't there.

She opened her eyes and reached farther underneath the seat, but still could not find it. She shoved her hand as far underneath the driver's seat as she could without actually getting in the back. Finally, her fingertips brushed against the oily rag. She was able to coax it forward just enough to get a firm hold, but when she pulled on it, the rag came away, completely gun-free. Where did it go? She'd shoved all those books back there so it wouldn't get lost.

Kix leaned over the seat and peered in the back. There were a few things on the floor, but everything looked just like normal stuff: a pair of running shoes, books, a few old receipts, a pen. She couldn't see anything particularly gun-shaped, although the backseat was in the shadows, and it was hard to see much. She slid the seat forward and sat down on the floor to try underneath it once more.

A footstep against gravel caught her attention. Kix kept her head down and looked up to the rearview mirror. Someone stood at the top of the stairs to Jake's apartment. The rain on the window made everything look wobbly, but even so, Kix recognized the shape as female.

KAREN KNOCKED ON THE DOOR

NO ONE ANSWERED after a minute, so she knocked again, this time a little louder. Still, no one answered. She didn't want to hang around too long, just in case Brad had followed her here. She couldn't see him, but that didn't mean anything. The hairs on the back of her neck were standing straight up. Of course, that didn't mean much either. They were always like that now.

Karen Wells, assistant manager of Peartree Athletics and recent ex-girlfriend of the sociopathic Brad Islenix, heaved a sigh. She shouldn't be here again. She'd been as invisible as she could, taking side streets and coming in from the alley, but it still wasn't the best idea. Visiting James twice in two nights would send a clear message to Brad, if the fact that she'd taken off work early to come here hadn't already. James deserved at least some sort of explanation for this morning. She hadn't meant to run out on him like that, but what was she going to say? *Gotta go, I have an appointment with the police in half an hour?*

Karen knocked one last time. If he didn't answer, she would text him from the car. He didn't answer.

She turned to head back to her car and freaked out. For half a second, it looked like there was someone sitting in the passenger seat, but she blinked and looked again. This time she could tell it was just a shadow. This back parking lot was creepy.

DRAMATIC WHISKERS

PERCHED NEAR THE SPONGE CRADLE like the disheartened King of All Pot Scrubbers, Toesy stared at his reflection in the window and tried to ignore what his heart was telling him. Somewhere out there, Pansy was cold, probably hurt, and possibly dead.

I promised I would find her, Steve. But the rain is heavy and her scent trail washed away. I confess, I do not know where to start.

Sir, I do not think her scent trail washed away.

What is this, Steve? You imply that I am feeble?

Not at all, sir. You are capable of detecting over twenty-six thousand aromatic compounds down to one-quarter part per million. Miss Pansy's scent trail contains twelve of these chemicals in distinct quantities. But beyond a thirty-centimeter radius of where the rubber arachnid was found, concentrations of those twelve distinct compounds dropped to undetectable levels.

This is all mathematical gibberish. What are you telling me, Steve?

You did not lose her scent, sir. It lost you.

For a moment, Toesy sat completely still, deep in thought. *By Sekhmet's Celestial Saucer, Steve! You don't think she's fallen into a different world, do you?*

Stranger things have happened this evening, sir. And you've stated that temporal shifts can be wildly unpredictable.

Toesy dropped the rubber tarantula and peered into the back parking lot. He could see the Angel of Delivery through the back window of her automobile, rifling around in the backseat. He kept an eye on her as he grew anxious for his Pansy.

Depending on where she landed, she may be in dire need of assistance, Steve.

He would have continued in his lament but was rudely interrupted by the curly whisker in his eyebrow twitching. Normally Toesy did not pay attention to that whisker, for it had a tendency toward melodrama, but Toesy was not too proud to admit that he needed some help. He followed his curly-whiskered instinct to a spot near the alleyway where he spied a suspicious shadow slinking around.

Hello there?

The curly whisker in his brow was now joined by three very straight and proper whiskers from his upper lip. Toesy tried concentrating on what was happening down below, but unease settled in his stomach, and he had to look away. Something was beginning down there. Something much like what had happened earlier to his Mistress of the Can Opener.

THE WINDOWS FOGGED UP
SLIGHTLY

KIX WATCHED THE MYSTERY WOMAN knock again and was secretly pleased when her shoulders slumped after a moment. She watched her trudge back up the stairs. When she walked into the glow from the porch light, Kix gasped. The jacket. The boots. Through the foggy window and the rainy darkness, Kix felt their eyes meet, and in that split second, she knew exactly who the other woman was.

"There are not enough swear words for this situation," she said, ducking out of sight. "What the hell is going on?"

Kix suddenly felt the need to know where the gun had gone. Why had she agreed to take the thing? Footsteps approached. She stopped moving but the harder she tried to listen, the quieter the footsteps got. In the distance, she heard a car door open.

"There's no one here but me." She whispered shutting her eyes tight. "And I am leaving as soon as I find that damn gun"

Kix began transferring shoes and magazines out of the way, dumping them in the spot behind the driver's seat. But the gun was nowhere to be found.

Overhead, Maxine's dome light blinked on and off, a stutter of light that made Kix's heart skip a few beats. She held her breath until the dome light stopped freaking out. *I am still alone in the car*, she thought but she didn't dare to say it out loud.

From somewhere close came the slam of a car door, and the feeling of déjà-vu returned. Or, sort-of returned. It felt different now—like she was remembering something as it happened or it was happening as she remembered it. That didn't even make sense, but she let it be because the experience of it was a scary enough—she didn't want to have to deal with it on an intellectual level too.

There was a noise. It was not a loud noise—not a noise that would cause anyone grief—just a tiny click. It could have been any number of things. A broken twig. A cat walking by. Hell, it could have been an extra-large raindrop hitting the ground for all she knew. She could turn around to look, but Kix didn't want to turn around. She wanted the click to go away.

He won't go away.

The atmosphere in the car changed in that instant. The air was heavier, the shadows were darker. Kix felt the weight of another person's attention. She wasn't alone anymore.

IN THE DARK

"WHY DID YOU COME HERE?"

Thad appeared at the driver's side window. Kix's hand flew to the door and hit the lock button. If he noticed, he did not say.

"Leave me alone, Thad. The police are already on their way."

"Did Danielle tell you to say that?"

"Who's Danielle?"

"I'm not in the mood for your jokes. Get out of the car."

She looked at the man, who was Thad and also *not* Thad, standing outside in the rain. He stood straight and calm. He almost seemed friendly. It made the hairs on the back of Kix's neck stand at attention.

"Where is Thad?"

"Gone. He left."

"Where did he go?"

Without warning, Not-Thad punched the driver's side window. When it didn't break, he screamed and took a swing at the side-view mirror. It flew obligingly into the holly tree. Kix slid down in her seat and conjured the image of Sacha's couch in her mind. Gun or no gun, if he broke through that window, she was out of here.

Brad did not break through the window. He calmed back down. Kix found this ten times creepier, now that she understood how crazy he was.

"Why don't you tell me," he said. "You were the last one there. Or did you think I wouldn't notice?"

"Notice what, Thad? Where have I been?"

"*Stop calling me that. My name is* Brad."

Kix flinched lower in her seat. The movement made Brad smile. This was a game to him. He was enjoying this. Fear crept into her thoughts, wild and irrational.

"Did you find him before the drugs set in? Did he tell you how to find it?"

He's going to kill us.

"Find what?" said Kix. "What drugs?"

"You should have left it alone. You got greedy, Karen."

"*No,*" said Kix, shaking her head. "I'm not Karen. Tell me where Thad is. What did you do with him?"

"I'm not going to let you steal it from me."

Casually, he shifted his weight from his left side to the right. He flexed his right arm gently. Kix felt terror climb up her throat, a razor blade of attention that Brad had held against her for months. She struggled under the pressure of it. It was too deep, too intimate. She remembered the breakup. The two a.m. phone calls. The increasingly strange threats. Her poor cat Mooshy, dead in her arms.

She remembered the court order. The one they told her to get. They said it would help. He would leave her alone. But it hadn't helped. All it had done was draw a bright red target on her back.

Hello? said Kix.

He's going to kill us, said Karen.

Us? said Kix.

"It's mine," said Brad.

Everything happened in slow motion after that. Brad's arm came up. Kix didn't need to see the gun to know it was Marco's. His arm tensed.

She closed her eyes a split second before Brad pulled the trigger.

TOESY ASKS FOR ADVICE

HE MADE IT TO THE PARKING LOT in time to witness the chaos boil over. As before with his mistress, once again Toesy could not approach. Reality flickered and waved around them, making it impossible to see what exactly was happening. There was the villain, talking to his Angel. Then she was gone and another was there. Then they were gone and the villain was someone else entirely. Then there were cows for some reason.

He could not risk stepping any closer until the tear in reality stopped whipping about like a deflating balloon. To do so would be like stepping in front of an oncoming bus, or in this case, an oncoming cow.

Through one wave of reality, Toesy smelled the clean, sharp scent of cedar, but it faded quickly, to be replaced by more nonsensical images and smells. He sat at the edge of the parking lot, witnessing the crazy turns of reality until a bright flash of light brought everything to an immediate stop. A split second later, he heard a very distant *pop!*

Toesy sat in the shadows of the tree and watched as worlds and images zoomed around the Boundary Walker like water circling a drain. They spun around him tighter and tighter, falling in on him until he himself became a living nexus.

This was very bad news. Not many now could touch him without repercussions, and those would be drastic, especially if the cows were still there. Toesy knew of only one way to stop such an anomaly. It was a dangerous path.

But they had to try.

Steve, you are Executive Wartime Consigliore. What do you advise is the best way to go about causing a great deal of pain if we only had one blow? After a suitable pause he added, *I am merely curious, of course.*

Sir, your actions during the Toilet Incident were impressive. It is possible that if you escalate the pressure on the nasal cavity, you may achieve a debilitating blow.

You mean that trick with the nose?

Yes, sir.

Right, I shall keep that in mind. Now we must send this villain back to where he belongs. This may get a bit dicey, Steve. I trust you know what to do.

*   *   *

Executive Wartime Consigliore Steve knew exactly what to do. For he had learned much in the 1.21e+16 nanoseconds he had known the Overlord. One of the first things he'd learned was that anyone messing with the Overlord's human subjects often found themselves on the wrong side of His Majesty's attentions.

Steve enjoyed those particular nanoseconds quite a bit although much of the time, they resulted in a generous need for dermal and muscular repair. He'd recently designed a preliminary protocol meant to counteract this need. It called for many things including (but not limited to) increased endorphin levels and the readiment of preliminary enzyme cascades necessary for collagen repair.

He referred to it as *Battle Mode.*

OFFICERS MUSTACHE
AND EDWARDS

THAD HADN'T RUN from the bathroom after the old guy threatened to call the cops. Why would he? Where would he go? He tried to keep an eye on the space-time portal for a while, but the anti-anxiety meds were in high gear, and he found it difficult to worry about anything. If he lost sight of the portal he could find it, easy peasy. He'd found it once before, hadn't he?

So it was that when the two Ashwood police officers dispatched to the call finally showed up, they found Thad relaxing on one of the Family Lounge sofas, discussing wing-suit training specs with a twenty-something kid sporting a hemp necklace and a blond goatee. The old guy stood at attention near the entrance to the bathroom, cane at the ready should he need it.

"Oh, snap, I think these guys are here for me, Cuz. Don't forget what I said now, right? Strength over flexibility." Thad held out a fist to the shaggy kid.

"But flexibility over flash," said the kid and gave Thad the ultimate cool-guy fist bump. "I hear ya. Later, Dog."

"Right on!" said Thad as the kid walked away. Then he turned to the cops and smiled hugely. Officer Mustache was back! And he'd brought a partner this time; a lady-cop with dark hair and stern-looking lip gloss. Thad addressed Officer Mustache.

"What took you so long, Brah? Did you have to like, drive across town or something?"

"You are under arrest," said Officer Lady-Cop.

"What kind of sneaky trick was that?" said Officer Mustache.

"I don't want to say I told you so, Brah but…I totally told you so. I *told* you that would happen. If you want to arrest me again, go ahead, but maybe don't haul my ass all the way across town again because I'm just gonna get sucked back here."

Thad said all of this in a conversational tone that put Officer Lady-Cop on edge. Her hand snuck itself up to her holster, and she took a step toward him. Officer Mustache patted the air in calming motions.

"Cool it, Edwards," said Mustache. "Von Grauer wants to hear what this scumbag has to say."

"Don't listen to that fathead. He's a peeping tom!" cried the old guy. He waved his cane around a bit for good measure.

"*For the last time,* I wasn't trying look at your shrivelly old wang. I'm just trying to get back home. I don't belong here. I keep getting sucked back here because there's some dude over *there* in my body. I want to get back there. I want my skin back."

Officer Mustache nodded Officer Edwards in the direction of the old guy. She had a brief conversation with him before taking his name down and sending him back to his senior group waiting at the coffee shop.

Officer Mustache then decided to move the whole show upstairs to the security office, leaving Officer Edwards to guard the bathroom should Thad suddenly get sucked back there again.

YOUR FUTON IS GOING TO NEED SOME HYDROGEN PEROXIDE

KIX THOUGHT SHE MIGHT BE having a stroke. Indeed, in some other reality she may have been. But not in *this* reality. In *this* reality, pain shot through her sinuses as she threw herself forward onto Sacha's futon. She landed in a crumpled heap and immediately felt the uncomfortable *drip drip drip* of something running from her nose. It must have been blood, for as soon as he saw her, Sacha screamed and ran to grab a roll of paper towels.

"Are you hurt? Oh my God, Kix, are you dead? Please don't be dead on my futon."

Kix had a difficult time answering. She didn't think she was dead. Her nose was bleeding all over and she felt like throwing up. But that was okay because you had to be alive to throw up, didn't you? She was pretty sure you did.

Sacha ripped paper towels from the roll and stuffed them around her so she didn't bleed everywhere.

"I've just been murdered," she said.

"What?" Said Sacha, pausing mid-rip. "*Who?*"

"Me, Brad just murdered me."

"But…" said Sacha. He continued ripping paper towels off the roll and tucking them around her legs. "You're…" he added.

"The *other* me. *That's* who Karen is. She's me. I went down to get Marco's gun. He must have gotten it from my car. I don't know. She was with me, inside my head. Then he shot her. He shot me."

"*Where?*"

"In the face."

"No, *where* did he shoot you?" Sacha waved his hands full of paper towels around the room.

"Oh," said Kix. "In the driveway."

"Kix, we need to call the police *right now*."

"No, not *this* driveway."

"Which driveway, then?"

"You don't understand. Not this driveway, *that* driveway. She's not here. When she's here, she's me. And when I'm there, I'm her. And she's just been murdered in the driveway that is here but over there."

"I am not following this at all. Who shot you—her?" Sacha was still tearing off paper towels, even though Kix's nose wasn't bleeding anymore. The wads began to spill onto the floor.

"Thad. Only he's Brad now. And she said Brad was going to kill *us*, but she didn't know I was there at first. I think she might have meant her and Jake."

"Wait, she knows *Jake?*"

Kix thought about this morning and all the strangeness that had been happening ever since. Knowing that she and Karen were the same person made large chunks of reality fall into place. She began to make sense of what she'd seen.

"I think he invited her over."

"What?"

"That experiment last night *did* something. That's when everything started. That's when she came here. That's when they…" Kix looked at Sacha and tried to convey a knowing glint in her eye.

Sacha stared back at her blankly.

"That's when they *met*."

"Met, like how? Did she stop by? Did you introduce her like, *Hey Jake this is the other me, her name is*… What's her name again?"

"Karen, and no. There wasn't a whole lot of conversation going on."

"Why? Were you all watching a movie or something?"

"No. I was half-asleep on the couch when I heard her come in.

Then they…" Kix made little you-get-my-drift circles with her hand, but Sacha just stared at her.

She raised her eyebrows. "How are you *not* getting this?"

"Oh my God," he said. His eyes grew wide very quickly. "Were they having sex?"

Kix nodded.

"Oh," he said. "That is…awkward."

"Yes. It was. I didn't understand at the time, but when I was in the driveway just now, I think I fell through, or maybe she did. Anyway, I saw her. She was me. We were close enough to know each other's thoughts."

"What did you hear?"

"It's not so much what I heard as what I remembered. I think she worked with Brad and they dated for a while. Not long, maybe a few weeks? I know he's been stalking her for months. Following her around, sitting outside her apartment. Stuff like that. She moved recently. Her cat went missing. She found it in a box on her front porch yesterday. He'd strangled it, then wrapped it up like a present."

For a brief moment, it had been her cat. The memory of its lifeless body stuck her through with sadness, and she paused, so she wouldn't start to cry.

"She filed a restraining order less than twenty-four hours ago," she said at last.

"Holy shit," said Sacha.

"And she said *us*. He's going to kill *us*. We need to find Jake."

BRAD WAITS

WHEN THE WIND WHIPPED UP into a crescendo covering the sound of his gunshot, Brad knew it was a sign that he was in alignment with the Universe. He was headed down the right path. Images shimmered at the edge of his vision. Blue sky, green grass, purple shadows, red sunsets—all of them hovering just beyond his senses. He could go anywhere, now that the thief no longer stood in his way. All he had to do was focus on those colors.

In front of him, the rain came down, just as dreary as before, but so close was he to those other worlds that he took no notice of it. He only stayed here so he could find James.

Brad stole back into the shadows of the holly tree and waited. He wanted to get going as soon as he could, but the colors were distracting and he needed some time to adjust to this new multiple vision. He studied the branches of the tree, trying to calm his mind. They were pebbly, not smooth. Someone had cut most of the lower branches away in one area, to make space for parking. There were several larger branches above him. Brad studied those too.

The images swirling at the edge of his dimmed and slowed. Brad was feeling more in control when a bright flash of purple caught his attention. Almost too late, he realized it wasn't an illusion but something flying straight at his head. His eyes snapped shut and he ducked. When he opened them again, there was nothing there.

What was that? He only saw it for a second but he was pretty sure it had fangs. It must have been a bat. Brad wasn't easily spooked. All the same, he stepped out of the shadows beneath the holly tree and crouched behind Karen's car.

He scanned the windows at the back of the apartment building to make sure no one was watching. Televisions flickered in the background of two, three were empty, but one framed a unicorn drinking a beer and chatting up a pirate. Soon Albert Einstein joined them, and Brad realized he was watching a costume party. Hopefully they were all too drunk to notice anything but it didn't really matter what they saw. He only needed to find James and then he could leave this place. Where should he start?

The guy on the second floor. That guy knew Danielle. He also knew James—or whatever name that dirtball went by here. *He probably knows where James is hiding too*, thought Brad.

Pain, sharp and unexpected, shot up the back of his arm. Brad jumped as if he'd been stung. At first, he thought maybe he'd leaned against a nail or a piece of broken glass. But he inspected the sleeve of his jacket and found a small hole near the elbow. It looked almost like a bite mark.

Brad turned around and looked at the holly tree. The shadow underneath looked creepier than before. He refused to get freaked out by a stupid tree though so he headed down the muddy side yard, toward the fence.

The farther he got from the tree, the more he calmed himself. James was here. That's what he needed to focus on. He would get this done. If he had to take a couple others out with him, then so be it. It didn't matter. He wasn't staying.

The attack was so fast he didn't see it coming. The thing landed on the side of his neck, definitely weighty enough to be a bat, and bit into his earlobe with razor-sharp fangs. Brad tried to hit it, but it flew away just as quickly as it had struck.

"What the devil was that?"

Brad nearly scaled the fence to get away. He would have teleported, as he was now confident he would be able to do, but he refused to be so easily cowed. Plus, the pain in his ear was distracting.

He found the latch, very high up on the fence, and let himself out in the front yard. At the front entryway, he keyed in the same apartment number as before. The girl having the party. She would let him in.

When she finally answered, her voice wasn't nearly as perky.

"Is this Sacha?" she said.

"Uh, yeah."

"Stop knocking on the wall, you creep. I turned the music down," she said and hung up.

Brad's first instinct was to call her back and scream at her, but he refrained. Keeping calm right now was essential. So he did what he always did to calm himself down. He reared back and kicked the bottom window of the door with everything he had. It wasn't until his foot connected with the glass that he remembered he wasn't wearing steel-toed boots.

Instead of screaming in pain, Brad gave in to his anger. He pulled the gun from his pocket and shot out the window. There was a very loud bang and glass shattered everywhere.

Brad reached through and opened the door. He did not notice a tiny, winged shadow follow him into the building. But to be fair, the shadow was really good at not being noticed.

LEARNING TO LIVE AGAIN

TOESY DID NOT BOTHER with subtleties for they had little time. He appeared on Mr. Sacha's coffee table headfirst, then his shoulders and tail, as though he'd walked through an interdimensional portal of his own making…which is basically what he did.

"Show-off," said Sacha.

"Toesy, where have you been?" said the Angel.

Toesy did not answer. He sat and stared at the Angel, trying to judge her measure. Would she be up to this task? It meant sending her to her death. He would accompany her, of course, to make sure she got back okay, but many humans had a strong aversion to death. If she had such an aversion, this would not work.

"Why are you staring at me like that?" she asked. "You're not going to hand me another tarantula, are you?"

Toesy reached out and put a paw on the back of her hand. He felt very bad about what he had to do next, but she would need the physical sensation to guide her back to this body.

"What are you doing?" she said.

He flexed his claws. The Angel screamed. Blood pooled around them. He dug in farther and held on. They were almost there.

"Let go—" she said but could not finish her sentence. She was too busy trying to move lips that no longer worked properly. Toesy sat in the driver's seat and purred at her very loudly.

"Osy uuht a uck?" she said.

He purred extra hard. She didn't really look convinced.

"Doan—" she made *pah-pah* noises, trying to make the lips form words. "Pah-urr at ma, yoo asstard. Whaa am ah doong here?"

Huzzah! She was getting the hang of it! He could hear it in her speech. He purred louder as he stood on his hind legs and leaned out of the broken car window.

"Doan you DARE leeb. Gek or ass ack here," said the Angel, but Toesy had already gone to fetch the other one.

* * *

Kix tried moving her head to see where the cat went but couldn't. It felt so wrong to be here. It was uncomfortable and useless and disrespectful to the *n*th degree. How was she ever going to live through this? Aren't you supposed to die in a dead body? Shouldn't she be worried about that?

All of these thoughts were punctuated by the throbbing pain in the back of her hand where Toesy had stabbed her with his stupid titanium claws. How did that hurt so badly? The pain would not go away, it kept throbbing and reminding her of where it came from.

"Ah," she said, mentally cursing her lack of vocal abilities. "Iss an anchor."

The pain in her arm was a bright red flag of where she was supposed to be, alive and healthy back home. Instead she was with Karen, or what was left of Karen, slumped over the middle console of the car.

Karen didn't deserve this. She deserved to be at home with her poor Mooshy. But she won't ever get to go home again. Toesy had brought her here for a reason and it didn't take Kix long to understand what it was. She started practicing.

"A kik bauwn ox umnped or a azy og," she said to no one.

"A kik. No, a ka-wick. Ka-wick. Ka-wick. Kwick. Quick. *Quickquickquickquickquick*."

VON GRAUER

CAPTAIN KAISER VON GRAUER sat at Paul's desk, asking the same four questions over and over. Paul was a little scared of Von Grauer but he wasn't embarrassed by that. Everyone was a little scared of Von Grauer. The guy looked like he'd been stitched together with steel wire and spite.

Gayle sat in the only other chair. Between staring at Brad and staring at the captain, Paul hadn't seen her blink for at least ten minutes. Paul stood next to her, near the window and listened as his former employee spun the biggest, stupidest lie he had ever heard.

"Okay, let me get this straight," said Von Grauer "You're telling me that you're from another dimension."

"Yes, exactly!"

"And that dimension can only be accessed by a portal that you found in the men's bathroom."

"I didn't find it. Brad found it."

"Oh, please excuse me. Brad, whom you are definitely *not*, found the interdimensional portal in the men's bathroom. And he *jumped through it* into your body. He then assumed your position as a sports writer—"

"Thrill documentarian," said Thad.

"*Thrill documentarian* to get close to your neighbor, Kix, short for Katarina, Welty and assault her. Additionally, you have never heard of Karen Wells and you quote-unquote *pinky swear* that you have not been stalking her."

"Cross my heart and hope to die," said Thad. He held up his

little finger.

"Mr. Islenix," said the captain.

"Thad," said Thad.

"Thad," said the captain. He sat back in the chair and crossed his ankles. "You see this?" He pointed to the eyepatch over his left eye. A thick rope of scar ran from underneath the patch to his left ear.

"I lost that on the Golmud Railway."

Gayle sucked sir through her teeth and Paul shifted uneasily from one foot to the next but Thad did not react. Von Grauer continued.

"Son, I have won three presidential commendations for devastating effectiveness in UCAV offensive maneuvering." Thad still did not react.

"I spent *three years* running anti-sniper point for the MALH. *Do you understand what that means?*"

"Uh..." said Thad, scratching his head. "My Aunt Lucy's House?"

Von Grauer slammed his fists down on the desk and stood up. "*It means I don't buy your bullshit story*. So either you tell me where I can find Karen or you're going to be eating through a straw for the next few weeks."

"I swear I have no idea! I've been stuck in the bathroom. You were there. You saw me disappear."

"Give me some flash paper and a rowboat and *I* can disappear too."

"Oh yeah? How did I get across town so fast then?"

The argument went on. Von Grauer would find a slip-up if Brad made one but so far, Brad hadn't missed a beat.

The blinds on the window weren't closed all the way. Paul stared out the bottom half inch of the window at the linoleum tile of the hallway and thought about the last time he'd talked with Karen.

She'd come in to complain about Brad. He was hanging around too much. He was acting in a threatening manner. Could she say how? No, she couldn't. Could she say when? No, she couldn't.

Paul brushed her concerns off. Brad had worked for him for two years, and he'd always been a reliable security guard. He was just heartbroken. Give him a few weeks and the kid will get over it. Thinking about his actions now made him sick with dread. They still hadn't heard from the officers assigned to find her.

A shadow crept across the hallway, coming to a stop just outside the office door. Something was standing out there. Quietly, so as not to draw attention away from the interview, Paul lifted one slat of the blinds to get a better view.

Outside the door stood the most massive housecat he'd ever seen. It looked unhappy about something. He was trying to figure out what a cat would be doing in the hallway when it reached up and opened the door to the broom closet.

Paul blinked. He opened the blinds wider to see what it may do next. Gayle cleared her throat and shot him a dirty look.

"Paul," said Gayle. She looked at him with her laser eyes. "There's a girl missing, and this man might be responsible. Can you at least pay attention for two minutes?"

The tone of her voice suggested he had better pay attention for longer than two minutes, but he couldn't get the image of that cat turning a door knob of his head.

"I'm sorry to interrupt, but I saw something strange, and I think I should go check it out."

"Oh, by all means. Don't let our little conversation get in your way. Please feel free to use this time for whatever you like," said Von Grauer.

"I'm sorry," he said, understanding full well what kind of shit-storm he just invited upon himself if he was wrong. "I'll only be a minute."

Paul opened the door to step out into the hallway and almost stepped on the cat instead. He bent over to shoo it away, but it ran past him into the room. Paul ducked out of the way on instinct and the thing jumped up into Thad's lap. Thad raised his hand to scratch the cat behind its ears. The cat responded to the man's ear scratches by purring so loudly that it tickled Paul's nose.

"Where did this asshole cat come from?" shouted Von Grauer.

"Get out of here. This isn't a circus," said Gayle. She made a move to pick it up but the cat let out a short growl and Gayle backed off.

"Hey, cat," said Thad. "*I'm* happy to see you at least."

The cat purred louder and grabbed onto Thad's hand with his forepaws. Then it bit down so hard Thad screamed. Paul would have flinched, but he sneezed too suddenly. When he opened his eyes, both the cat and Thad were gone.

"You all saw that, right?" said Paul, wiping his nose.

"That's exactly what he did at the station," said Von Grauer. He got on his radio. "Officer Edwards, our suspect has just disappeared again. Can you please search the bathroom premises for him?" They waited in silence until Officer Edwards came back on the radio a few moments later.

"I checked everywhere, Captain. He's not here."

EYEBALLS AND ALL

THE KICKER OF DOORS hadn't said the word *vampire*, but that mattered little. Pansy read it clearly in his eyes as she flew at them. She tasted it on the air as he ducked to the ground. She felt the power of his assumption mold the world around her. Her teeth grew long and needle-like. Her claws sharpened. The webbing she used to glide toward safety felt stronger, thinner…*battier*. In her tiny marsupial brain, there took hold a strong compulsion to fly into someone's hair.

Never in her life had Pansy been fearsome. She'd never even been mildly disquieting. Now this man called her *devil* and fell to the ground before her. Pansy loved it more than being alone in that tree. He wanted vampires? He would have one. A tiny one with a fuzzy head and great big eyes.

It should be noted here that Pansy's understanding of vampires came solely from watching old Vincent Price movies with Connie and therefore included much more *mua-ha-ha*-ing at ladies in silky nightgowns than actual blood-sucking. Still, she liked the fangs quite a bit.

The second attack had been more out of self-defense than anything else. The villain almost leaned right on her as she was trying to will her ears to become pointier. He now had a hole in his elbow half the size of a dime and would definitely think twice about leaning next to her again. For she was the fearsome *Pansarella*!

No, maybe not Pansarella. That was a little much. Perhaps she ought to stick with something more formal, like *Miss Pansy*. She didn't want to give anyone the wrong impression.

Before she could decide on a new name, the villain was on the move again. This time he headed across the parking lot. *Pansy the Terrible* (eh, maybe) followed him across the yard and down the side of the building. Where was he going? Surely not back inside? She would not allow that. When his arm came up to undo the latch, she struck.

With impossible speed, *Baroness Pansy* (absolutely not) flew at his neck, stabbing her razor-sharp fangs into what she thought was his jugular.

Unfortunately, Pansy knew even less about human anatomy than she did about vampiring. She did not stab him anywhere close to an artery. She did succeed, however, in finally biting most of his earlobe off. Then she flew away to safety before he could even react.

Now she sat near the hooves of a stone horse and watched the Kicker of Doors slowly freak out. It was frightening and immensely enjoyable to watch. *She* had done that. Pansy, *Sugar Glider of the Damned* (that *definitely* had possibilities) had sown fear in his evil heart.

Pansy liked this campaign of terror. It was very exciting. Maybe next she could try disappearing in a puff of smoke. Yes! that sounded like an excellent idea.

THAD IS DEFINITELY GOING
TO NEED SOME THERAPY

HE HAD BEEN SITTING in a chair when the cat tried to bite his hand off. Unfortunately, the chair hadn't come along for the interdimensional ride so when Thad popped into existence in the back alley, gravity took over and he fell, bum-first, onto the muddy gravel.

"*Cat*? What did you do that for? I was being nice to you, Brah."

The cat stood in the rain, underneath an old street lamp. Beside it stood a gigantic holly tree, like a force field of prickly leaves. There was a large tunnel through the foliage that led to the backyard of a house. The cat chittered at him and pointed his whiskers toward the tunnel.

"Are you crazy?" said Thad. "It's all dark and spooky in there!"

The cat chittered again and pointed its whiskers more encouragingly.

"Fine, but I'm not going first," he said.

It was probably the meds he was on but Thad could have sworn the cat rolled its eyes at him before starting toward the holly tree tunnel.

Thad followed, trying to keep his elbows tucked in and figure out what the heck they were doing. The night was cold and rainy and he sort of wished he had a hood.

"Soooo…cat. What's up with the spikey spooky?"

The holly tunnel led to a small gravelly yard behind one of those old gothic-type mansions. Across the make-shift parking lot, sat a car. It looked familiar.

"Is that Kix's car?" he said. The cat meowed at him then pointed his nose in the direction of said automobile. Thad squinted. Even through his medicinal haze, he began to feel a bit anxious.

"Why am I here, Mr. Cat?"

The cat gave him a stony glare, then growled in the direction of the car.

"Okay," said Thad. "I'm going."

He headed toward the driver's side. The window looked wrong somehow. He walked faster. As he approached, he could see something large draped across the front seat.

"Hey! Hello?" he said and broke into a run. "Kix, are you there?"

He approached the car and peeked in. Kix was indeed there. Her body was sprawled across the seats, the upholstery decorated in gruesome colors. There was a bullet entry wound on the left side of her face. It messed up her cheek so badly that Thad had to look away to be sick in the shrubbery. The pure shock of seeing his neighbor lying dead was enough to sober him into panic.

"Oh my god Kix," he said, mostly to himself. "Who did this to you?"

"You did, you asshole."

Her voice was so sudden that Thad screamed. It was shrill and high like a hyena, but he clamped down on it quickly, so it sounded more like a bark than anything. He turned slowly to face the car and found her lying there, staring at him. Even in her gory spectacle of death, Kix looked kind of annoyed.

"You shot me in the head and went to find Jake," she said.

Blood oozed from the wound as she moved her lips, and Thad had to focus on her right eye so he could look at her without hurling again.

"I swear I didn't. I've been stuck in the bathroom all day."

"Yeah, but no one knows that but you and me, do they?"

"What do you mean?" Thad started to pace. It was easier than looking at Kix or whoever it was in the car. He made a strange keening noise every time he turned around.

"Thad, listen to me. I know you didn't murder me, Brad did. And he needs to pay for what he's done. He has to be stopped. You and I can stop him before he kills anyone else."

"Why didn't you call the police?"

"Mainly because I'm *dead*, you idiot. The only living person who knows is you and you're the one who did it."

"Not me! I didn't, I swear! I would never do this."

"Then stop being a wuss about it and help Karen out."

Thad stopped pacing. He tiptoed back over to the car and peeked through the shattered window. "How am I supposed to help? I don't even know where I am."

"Put fingerprints on everything you can. Or better yet, get some of the gunpowder from my cheek and rub it on your hand. Hell, write his name on the window in bloo—"

"No way! I don't want to touch you. You're dead! That's like, bad luck or illegal or something."

"You know what else is illegal, Thad? *Murder*. And if you don't get over here and help Karen, I will make sure you remember that fact every day for the rest of your life. Now would you *please* get over here and implicate Brad?"

He moved closer to the window. Kix managed to tilt her head far enough to see him.

"I don't know about this," said Thad.

"You're helping bring a murderer to justice. You can do this," said Kix.

"You're not a zombie are you?"

"What? No. I'm not even really here. I'm sort of—balancing myself between here and there. I don't know what's going on back there, though, so can you please hurry up?"

"Can you get me back there?" said Thad.

"Yes," said Kix. She forgot to add *I think*.

"And you promise you're not going to eat my brain?"

"*Will you just open the car door?*"

Thad did as she asked. The dome light came on, illuminating a grisly mess inside. Holding his breath, he reached a shaking hand out to touch the powder residue on Kix's face.

As soon as he was close enough, Kix jumped forward, hurtling every last bit of energy she could muster through Karen's corpse. With dead arms and lifeless fingers, she grabbed Thad's arm and pulled herself up as far as she could. Thad fell forward into the car, screaming for his life. She couldn't let go or he'd run, so she did what she could. She leaned in as close as possible and bit him, right on the nose.

MEANWHILE, BACK AT SACHA'S

KIX HAD SCREAMED SO LOUDLY THAT Sacha almost wet his pants. Then she slumped over. Now she was unconscious. Sacha watched in horror as the back of her hand bled all down her arm. He looked around for Toesy to help, but the cat was nowhere in sight.

"Kix, wake up," said Sacha. "Kix, are you alright?"

He wadded up the paper towels and packed them around Kix's bleeding hand. With one arm underneath her head and another holding her shoulder, he tried sitting her upright. He had her halfway up to a sitting position when her torso went rigid, and her eyes shot open.

"Wick wick wick wick wick," she said.

Sacha's heart almost exploded with fright. He lost his grip on her shoulder, and she flopped back to the couch. When his heart stopped pounding, he leaned over and helped her up again. Her eyes were still open, but they were dilated and unfocused. He waved his other hand in front of her face, trying to get her attention.

"Kix! Are you there? Wake up!" But she didn't answer. Instead, she brought her hand up slowly and pointed at Sacha. Her lips started moving again, although no sound came out.

"I didn't hear that. What did you say?"

Her head lolled to the side as her eyes sought him out. When she finally saw him, she grunted and moved forward.

"Hng," she said and raised an arm to point at him, but her hand went limp at the wrist.

"Kix, are you okay? Can I get you some water or something? We need to get a bandage on your hand."

She stared, eyes still slightly off-kilter, like it was costing her too much energy to look directly at him. She leaned forward and almost fell off the couch.

"Whoa," Sacha said and jumped to catch her before she hit the floor. "Watch out there."

Kix's arms came up and grabbed on to his shoulders for support. He tried to put her back on the couch, but she kept holding on to him, so he figured she wanted to stand up.

"Okay, here you go." As soon as he balanced her on her feet, Sacha stepped away. Kix's eyes were still partially unfocused, but at least she looked more alive. He was about to say as much when they heard the gunshot.

Sacha ducked instinctively. Kix didn't even flinch. They heard the sound of glass being smashed on the first floor.

"I'm guessing that's your buddy. We need to get out of here," said Sacha.

"Nn-gry," said Kix.

"Oh, I'd say he's a little more than angry. Let's go."

Sacha grabbed her hand to try and hustle her to the front door. If they snuck out right now, they might be able to hide at the party next door while her murder-stalker tried to find them. Only they couldn't because Kix was walking dead slow. He didn't expect her to sprint, but he needed more than a shamble if they were going to get out of here.

"Kix, is there any way you can go faster than that? We don't have much time."

Outside in the hallway, footsteps pounded up the stairs. Sacha turned away from the door.

"Okay, new plan, we're going out the fire escape."

"Raaains," said Kix.

"Oh, good point." He said and grabbed his sweatshirt from the back of the futon. As soon as he moved, Kix moved. She was a lot faster this time.

"Did you bring a coat?" he said.

"Raaaaaaaaaaaaaains," said Kix.

Between the kitchenette and the bedroom side of his apartment was an oddly oversized window that led out to the fire escape ladder. Sacha opened the window.

"The ladder is about six inches to the left on the side of the building. It's a little scary to get out there, but it's not impossible." He stepped away to let Kix go first, but again, she moved at the same time he did, almost blocking him from getting away.

"You want me to go first? It'll be okay, I promise," he said.

"Hung-ry," said Kix and leaned so far forward, Sacha thought she was going to faint. He reached out to catch her, but she didn't fall. She grabbed his head and did not let go. For a second, all Sacha could think was, *crap this girl is strong*.

Three quick knocks on his front door made both of them turn their heads.

"He's here," she said in a completely normal Kix-toned voice. Then she growled loudly and let go of Sacha's head with such force that he fell to the ground.

"What are you doing?" said Sacha. "Don't answer that!"

But his words were lost in the explosion of sound. Kix's murder-stalker was outside trying to kick his front door in. Sacha contemplating heading out the window but he couldn't leave now. Kix was wounded and bleeding and he wasn't the kind of guy who would leave a person to die.

"Kix, don't go out there. He's going to—"

Like the rest of Horsey House, the substandard lock on Sacha's door was not up to much abuse. One well-placed heel cracked the door above it. Another kick tore the whole lockset away from the frame. The next kick sent the door flying wide and then there was Brad, standing in the door frame. Blood covered his left ear and the side of his neck and for one moment, Sacha thought he was dead.

"Oh *very nice*," said Brad eying Kix. "I'm going to enjoy killing you twice."

He raised his gun. Sacha ducked immediately. He tried pulling Kix down with him but she wouldn't bend.

"Braaaains," she said and lunged at him so fast that at first,

Sacha thought she tripped. Brad fired, but Kix had already plowed into him, and the shot went wild. She grabbed on to Brad's head just like she'd done to Sacha, only this time, she leaned over and bit him.

NOT THAD'S NIGHT

"YOU SAID YOU WEREN'T a zombie." Thad shoved Kix with as much strength as he could muster. She stumbled but gained her balance again easily. Thad backed up two steps and shook his head. His shoulders tightened.

"I'm not a zombie," said Kix. "Sacha, back me up."

"No, she's not a— wait..." he said. "That actually makes a lot of sense."

"What?"

"It was only for like, a minute. I wouldn't worry about it."

"Sacha, you are not helping," said Kix.

"Where am I?" said Thad.

"Sacha's apartment. You came here to kill me," Kix said, pointing to his arm.

It was then that Thad realized he'd been holding something heavy. He turned to see it, shocked that it was a gun. He looked at Kix. She nodded. He looked back to the gun he was holding.

Thad wasn't feeling so super anymore. Now that he was no longer hopped up on anti-anxiety meds the long, cold shower of sobriety hit him. His foot hurt badly and for some reason his left earlobe had gone numb. He reached a hand up to feel his ear and discovered that most of it was missing. He took one more look at Kix then he threw the gun to the floor and ran.

"*Catch him*," said Kix. "We need to make sure he's the right Thad."

Thad took the stairs two at a time. Halfway down the stairs, something purple flew at him, smacking him in the cheek. He jerked sideways and stumbled to the bottom of the stairs, barely managing to stay on his feet. At the landing, he straightened himself up and turned to run for the door. But Kix ran around him, blocking his path. He stopped himself before he ran into her.

"Don't come any closer," he said.

"It's okay, Thad, we're back now. You're *you* again," said Kix. She held her hands up in surrender as she took a few more steps in his direction. Thad waved at her to stop.

"Y-you were dead. I saw you." He stepped backward. "There was b-blood everywhere, but you talked to me. You were dead, and you *talked* to me."

"I'm not dead," said Kix. She put one hand over her heart and took a small step toward him. "I promise."

"*I said don't come any closer. You can't have my brains.*"

"I'm not a zombie, Thad. We were in an alternate reality. I had to make contact with you somehow to get you back here. I'm sorry if your nose hurts."

"What about my ear? What's your excuse there, huh? Just a little snack?"

"I don't know what happened to your ear. I only bit your nose."

"Oh God," said Thad. His eye glazed over with terror. "You bit me. I'm going to turn into a zombie now, aren't I? *That's how it works.*"

At that point, Thad's brain hit the *Panic* button. He ducked to the left. Kix tried leaning left to stop him but he veered right at the last moment and got around her to the door. He even succeeded in not colliding with it. He did, however, run straight into the man walking through it.

It really wasn't his night.

NOT LETTING ANY OF THESE
WEIRDOS OUT OF HIS SIGHT

NICHOLAS MILLER COLLIDED with the man running out the door, but basking as he was in the glow of self-righteousness, he didn't even feel the impact. He simply stood still and let the big bloody oaf fall over. When the guy finally tried to stand, Nick brought the wide-barreled gun right up to his face.

"I don't think so, Tough Guy. You just march right back there."

The guy backed all the way into the foyer but stopped before getting any closer to the woman.

"Keep going," said Nick. The man shook his head and refused to budge.

"I'm not going anywhere near her." He nodded in the woman's direction. Then he covered his mouth and stage-whispered, *"She's a zombie."*

"No, I'm *not*," the woman said through gritted teeth.

"Is that a flare gun?"

Nick turned to see the curly-haired guy from earlier standing in the middle of the grand staircase. He spun around and pointed the gun at him.

"Listen you...*hippie*, don't argue with me when I've got a gun pointed at your face. Just shut up, and be quiet."

"It's *Sacha*, and that's totally a flare gun," said Sacha. He did not put his hands up. Nick was about to say something more when the oaf that had run into him started inching toward the door.

"Don't you *dare*! You make one more move toward that door, and I swear I will pull this trigger." Nick pointed the gun in the oaf's direction now.

"Please, you have to let me go," he said. "She tried to eat my brains, Brah and *you're gonna be next.*"

The woman's arms shot up in the air. "How is this even fair? You *murdered* me, you dick."

Sacha started to laugh. "What are you gonna do, signal us to death?"

"*Will you all please shut up?*" said Nick. His ears had gone red and the abrasions on his face were swollen and scratchy. "*What is wrong with you people?* Have any of you got a lick of compassion? Can you see what has happened to me this evening? That cat ate my girlfriend's pet, and none of you even care."

"That's not true," said Sacha.

"That's a lie," said the woman.

"*It was probably her,*" said the oaf in his stage whisper.

"That. Is. *It,*" said the woman. The bloody oaf yelped in surprise when her fist connected squarely with his nose.

Nick was rapidly losing control of the situation. Keyed up on adrenaline and anger he aimed his flare gun at the stairs and pulled the trigger.

"Watch it!" said Sacha and jumped out of the way. The flare shot across the room, hit a stair riser halfway up, and bounced high into the air. It came down near the bottom of the stairs and rolled toward the mailboxes.

"What the hell did you do that for?" yelled Sacha. He waved his arms around in the thickening smoke.

"I'm tired of you people jerking me around," said Nick. "I want answers."

"Well, I want for my apartment building to not burn down, you moron. Get some water or something."

"I will do nothing of the sort. You people are all going to hell anyway. *I want answers,*" he said and did not move.

* * *

Kix spied the lump of castaway carpeting in the breezeway and pointed at it. "Grab the mat!" she said.

Thad moved on her command. He ran at the mat, and for a

moment it almost looked as though he was going to scoop it up and bring it back to help smother the flare. But when he reached the breezeway, he flung open the outer door and kept running.

"Oh, you *jerk*," said Kix.

"There's an extinguisher on the other side of the bookshelf door in the back hallway," said Sacha and pointed to the bookshelf. Kix closed her eyes and tried to visualize the stairwell, but nothing in her mind could show her what it looked like so she just walked over to it.

"Sacha, I can't remember what the hallway looks like. How do I open the door?"

Sacha looked up from stomping. "Tilt the book forward," he said, punctuating his sentence with extra stomps.

"What book?" said Kix.

"*Moby-Dick*. It's on the left. Tilt it forward." said Sacha.

Kix searched the shelf. She found an atlas, several gardening books, the complete works of Shakespeare, and a suspicious gap. On the ground at her feet lay a hardbound version of *Moby-Dick*. She picked it up. A short length of metal protruded from the back edge. The end was twisted and broken.

"I don't think that's going to work," she shouted to Sacha. He was now swinging the front door back and forth, trying to clear smoke from the air. Nick stood in the middle of the entryway, still pointing the empty flare gun at him.

"Don't worry about it. I don't need the extinguisher anymore. We just need to get the smoke out." He turned to Nick. "You know, you could help me here. You're the idiot who's responsible for this."

"I take no responsibility *whatsoever*. I did what I had to do to get you people to start taking me seriously. I have been attacked, vandalized, scandalized, maimed, mauled—"

The two men began to bicker, but that wasn't as important right now as the broken latch. All of Kix's instincts told her it meant something. That it was significant somehow. But how?

The books were just books, nothing special about them. Still there was something about this that Kix felt was important. It could be nothing. It could be rats. It could be a cow for all she knew. Snippets of an earlier conversation came back to her.

What if I'm not sure what I'm seeing?

I don't know, Look at it differently, I guess.

But how else could she see it? She couldn't get inside the stairway. With this door broken and the downstairs door locked, the entire back hallway was sealed shut.

Completely closed off.

An idea popped into her mind. It was a funny little idea, ephemeral and strange. It flitted around as though any sudden movement or stray thought might scare it away.

Kix grew very still. She concentrated on her idea, turning it this way and that, giving it weight. It was an interesting idea, a hopeful idea. And, if she thought about it *just right*, it might be true.

"Watch out Pizza Wizard," she said. Then she lifted her foot and kicked the bookshelf right in the *Illustrated Guide to Chicken Farming*.

The shelf fell down. Once the back was exposed, Kix turned around and donkey-kicked it hard enough to dent the wood. It should have made a loud thump, but as soon as her foot made contact with the door, everything went quiet. Noise, smoke, movement—all of it stopped. For a moment, there was nothing.

Then a delicate *tink* broke the spell. Another *tink* followed. And another. The tinks turned into a rattle as the secret locking mechanism within the secret door fell to the ground. The bookshelf creaked and swung forward an inch. Then the volume turned up on the world and everything went nuts.

PRESSURE

AT THE SOUND OF HER VOICE. Pressure in a spot where ears should be. Warmth flooded into his mind. He felt a twinge of tension in an outstretched arm. Then a loud bang startled his mind from its paralysis. Once more, Jake became aware of the infinite. The endless Jakes around him. It was too much. He tried to go back to where he was but something prevented him. Things were happening.

Far off, from beyond all the Jakes he could see, there came a hollow *tink*. The Jake wearing orange popped out of existence. Another *tink* and two Jakes with dark hair were gone. A third *tink*, and four more Jakes disappeared. *Tink*s came on faster then, growing into a rattle. The rattle came closer and closer still, getting louder every moment. More and more Jakes were gone. Soon huge swaths of Jakes disappeared, as though they were simply blinked away—which was silly because he still wasn't sure where his eyelids were.

With equal parts fascination and horror, Jake witnessed the infinite collapse back to the finite. Iterations of himself winked out like fairy lights. What if he winked out too?

The rattle became deafening. The world boiled and jumped as realities shifted around to claim their part of the Universe. Silence hit him at the same time as consciousness did, and he slammed back into his body, arms mid-flail, stomach mid-heave, legs mid-scramble.

Above him, a faint sigh of air sealed his fate. The creak of a hinge gave life to his feet. He became aware of his body, trying to remove its own shoulder and the hairy beast upon it. He felt fresh air and ran for it, getting all the way to the top stair before tripping over his feet.

MAMA AYAHUASCA'S
PRETTY WORDS

DIABO HAD THE MAN in his thrall. He was about to claim his victory when the wall to the Infinite Realm shook with a holy rattle, a harbinger of the great and mighty. When the world stopped shaking, the wall cracked open. Diabo had been very surprised at that, but he kept his cool and paid attention. It seemed important to do so.

When he saw who had opened the door to the Infinite, Diabo immediately fell to prayer. For there, in the doorway, stood Mama Ayahuasca herself. She had fewer legs than he expected, but Diabo knew it was her. Only Mama Ayahuasca could have broken that trance.

Mama, I am here! I have almost completed your task.

The door to Heaven opened wider and the man found his spirit. He broke free of the trance and ran. It did not surprise Diabo when, at the doorway to Heaven, the man tripped over his own feet.

Instead of falling with the clumsy bananito, Diabo used the momentum to propel himself high into the air where he executed a standard double flip, adding a slight nuance with his back legs that allowed for the airflow to spin his cephalothorax horizontally. He landed, legs splayed and fangs out, in the middle of the human hive. He then spun to a graceful and controlled stop, facing his victims. It was a very impressive move, and Mama Ayahuasca gasped. Diabo was exceedingly proud of himself.

"My God, what is that?" she said.

"Jesus, gah!" said a bananito near the hive entrance. "That thing looks evil. Where did it come from?"

"Demon spider," said the clumsy bananito but Diabo was no longer paying attention. He was too busy rejoicing at his own blessedness. Mama Ayahuasca had just invoked her own *personal* god. A god like that must be ancient indeed.

He turned a slow and menacing circle, basking in the light of their terrorized adoration. He had only begun his second turn around when another bananito spoke up.

"Kill it," said the man.

Diabo heard him clearly but had no fear. He did not even stop turning his circle for it was nothing less than what he expected: a challenge. There is always a challenge.

He searched his audience for the source and found the man standing near the door, holding a weapon. Of course he was holding a weapon. Challengers almost always held weapons. They thought human weapons could kill him.

"No," said Mama. "Do not mess with that thing. I don't know what it is, but it looks deadly."

If Diabo had cheeks, they would be blushing with pride, so enamored was he of her pretty words. He loved Mama Ayahuasca more every moment.

"Nonsense, it's just a wolf spider."

A collective gasp ran among the hive as Diabo spun around with lightning speed. There followed a minute of desperate footsteps and shouting which he enjoyed greatly. And then he was upon him—the man who had dared to utter the words.

Wolf spider.

He ascended the man's mane to his crown with one single purpose. Once there, Diabo raised his front legs high.

Great Mother, in your honor, I am victorious.

He finished his prayer with a flourish of his front legs and then, using his fabulous blood-red fangs, bit down hard on the man's forehead.

That's when the fun really started.

A CALL TO
EMERGENCY SERVICES

"IT BIT ME! Get it *off*! Where is it?" Nick Miller danced around the base of the stairway trying to tear his hair out. From the noises he made, it should have been clear that he was in a significant amount of pain but everyone just stood there, staring.

"Don't just stand there, *call emergency services*. If I have a reaction to this, I am suing your pants off," he said.

"That's not really making me want to call emergency services for you, man," said Sacha.

"You d-damned hippie." Nick was trying unbutton his shirt, but it was proving too complicated for his fingers. After the third attempt, he grabbed one side of the collar and yanked. Buttons flew in all directions. He threw the shirt on the ground and started in on his trousers.

"This is y-your fault you know," he said. "If you had gotten that s-sugar b-bear back when I asked you t-to—"

But Sacha wasn't listening. He was crouched over his phone with one hand on his other ear to muffle the background noise.

"I think he's going into shock," he said into the phone and turned to inspect Nick again. "His head is swelling up pretty bad. Definitely *not* a wolf spider. I've never seen anything like it." Sacha paused to listen and soon began nodding his head. "Okay, I'll ask him."

He turned to Nick. "Hey, did you see what it looked like? They need to be able to identify the spi— Oh *gross, what the hell*? Put your pants back on, man."

But Nick couldn't put his pants back on. They might have a spider in them. Plus, he was feeling sort of oogy and out of sorts. He wanted to sit down but something was making it very uncomfortable for him to do so.

* * *

Kix ran to the heap of Jake in the corner. He'd fallen at the top of the stairs and was trying to stand.

"Jake, are you okay?" Kix tried to help him up but his eyes were fully dilated, and she had a hard time getting his attention.

"Am I wearing an orange coat?" he said at last.

"Uh…no."

"Do I have a scar on my cheek?"

"You mean the one you got from being shot?"

"Yes! That *happened,* right? It's there?"

Kix reached her hand out and traced her finger along the scar. "It's right here," she said.

Gradually, his eyes focused in on her. Tears gathered at the corners, but he made no move to wipe them away. "How did you find me?" he said.

"I assumed you were stuck in the hallway, and I worked backward from there."

He stared at her. "What if you were wrong?" he said. "What if the Jake you know is lost, and I'm some random, crazy Jake?"

"You'd better be the Jake I know, or I'm locking you back in the stairwell until you find him." Jake barked out a laugh.

"Plus," she said. "I'm not wrong. Not about this."

Tears fell from his eyes and ran down his cheek. He snorted a huge, sniffling snort. With all the gravitas he could muster (which, after experiencing the vastness of the Universe for about an hour, was quite a bit) he looked her in the eye and said, "Thank you, Kix. I owe you my life twice now."

"Are you feeling okay? Did that spider bite you? Do you need to go to the hospital?"

"No, I'm fine. I can't say the same for him though. What is going on over there?"

He pointed to Nick, now completely naked (except for his socks), shouting and pointing in the corner.

"What's wrong with him?" asked Jake.

"Karma, I think," said Kix. "Oh, wait. Maybe not."

"What is *that*?" asked Jake.

Nicholas Miller turned to face them. He looked like the starring role in a pornographic horror movie. Covered in blood and cat scratches, his head had begun to swell from the top down. He looked like pitiful rag doll until you looked farther down and realized that rag dolls weren't usually anatomically correct. They weren't generally fully erect either.

"Is that dude...?" asked Jake.

"Yep," said Kix.

Above his bloody knees and bruised thighs, Li'l Nick bounced up and down, saluting them joyfully each time Big Nick pointed a finger at someone—which was quite often because Big Nick was very angry at the moment.

PARAMEDICS ON THE SCENE

CYNTHIA LAVISH WALKED THROUGH the broken glass of the doorway, immediately in charge of the situation. She didn't even say anything, she just crunched her way in and everyone breathed out a sigh of relief.

On the floor a naked man sat hugging himself and rocking back and forth. He panted heavily, every so often shouting a streak of near-profanity at anyone who would listen.

"I take it he's our man?" she said, pointing to the rocking figure. Everyone in the room nodded. Cynthia knelt down to the victim and adopted her cheery-grandma tone.

"How you doing tonight, Mr..." She looked up to the others. "What's his name?" Most shrugged, but the blond guy looked thoughtful for a second.

"Miller?" he said. Cynthia gave him a warm smile and turned back to the vic.

"Mr. Miller, it's nice to meet you. I heard you had a run in with a creepy crawly. You mind if I just take a look-see?"

Mr. Miller stopped rocking back and forth long enough to point a finger in her direction. "I want you to arrest every single one of these people. They have done this to me. It is their fault this happened." Cynthia walked a few paces toward him.

"I am certain that's true, Mr. Miller, but right now, I am more concerned with your health than their legal status. If I may say so, honey...you look like you've been ridden hard and put away wet."

Nick stopped rocking for a second. He regarded her with a look of disbelief.

"I *have*," he said. "You have no idea what's going on here."."

Cynthia smiled and knitted her brow in sympathy. "Your friend says you've had a pretty rough night."

"He is *not* my friend. He is a criminal and a *thief*." Nick lowered his head back to his knees. As he did so, Cynthia studied his crown.

Mr. Miller then turned his head sideways to look at her on the sly. When he spoke, it was from the corner of his mouth. *"He's in league with those two demons. So is she, but I don't know about the blond guy."* He wiggled what he could of his eyebrows to show how serious he was but his head was incredibly swollen and he started rocking back and forth immediately. Probably because the eyebrow wiggle hurt.

Cynthia rubbed her hands together lightly. "I tell you what. I'm gonna go have a little chat with those people and tell them not to leave. While I do that, Kevin is going to come over here and take your vitals. I want you to tell Kevin every single thing that has happened to you this evening. It is important that we get details. Can you do that for me?"

With the promise of a sympathetic ear, a light came on behind the man's eyes.

"I have *notes*," said Mr. Miller.

"Oh, that's super! You hold tight now, Kevin will be right over." She walked back to Kevin near the front door.

"From what I can see there are two puncture wounds, badly swollen. Edema all down the sides of his face. Let's get his BP. Then probably two mgs of morphine and one hundred fifty Benadryl."

Kevin, a wiry-looking guy with short, dark hair and a studious attitude, busied himself with the blood-pressure monitor and Mr. Miller's sob story, while Cynthia turned to address the frizzy-haired man.

"Did you see what bit him?"

"We all did. It was a huge spider."

"What about the abrasions all over his face? Did it do that?"

"No, that happened to him earlier," said the woman.

"How do you mean?"

The woman stepped forward to speak. "He had a tangle with a...a cat. He thinks the cat is out to get him. I'm not sure, but he may have tried to drown him."

"Drown who? Mr. Miller?"

"No, the cat. I think Mr. Miller tried to drown the cat. He's been trying to catch him all night. He thinks Toesy ate his sugar glider."

Cynthia processed the information for a moment. "Do you know if Mr. Miller has any mental health issues that we may be dealing with?"

"Yeah," said Sacha. "He gets off on spider bites." Cynthia gave the frizzy-haired man a stern look.

"How do you mean?"

"I'm on the phone with you guys, and he's over here taking his clothes off. The next thing I know, *bam*! There's his junk all up in our faces. What is that about?"

"You mean he had an erection?" She didn't wait for an answer before calling over her shoulder. "Kevin, can you check for priapism?"

Kevin went quiet for half a second, then called back, "Uh…that's a pretty big positive," he said.

Cynthia turned back to the frizzy-haired guy. "Do you know if that happened after he received the bite or before?"

"I have no idea. He was shooting up the place with a flare gun, then everything stopped, and he was over there yanking off his clothes, showing us all his massive boner. That's what I know."

"Has he vomited at all?"

Over on the stairs, Mr. Miller didn't wait for anyone to answer on his behalf. He made a *herk*ing sound and threw up all over Kevin's shoes.

"I guess he has," said Cynthia. "Folks, if you could please keep your eyes out for that spider, it would be an incredible help to us. Whatever you do, don't touch it. You probably don't want to end up like Mr. Miller."

"What was it, like a hobo spider or something?"

"Can't make an identification based on symptoms. You've got to *catch* the thing before you can say for sure. But I'll tell you this for nothing, I've never seen a hobo spider do *that* to a man before."

INSURANCE POLICIES

THEY FELL TO SEARCHING as the medics worked on calming Mr. Miller. That is to say, no one wanted to be caught *not* searching. There were quite a few toes poked into dark alcoves, and many corners of rugs pulled up by hesitant fingers. Sacha even ventured toward the heap of broken shelf near the secret door. Meanwhile Kevin, the assistant paramedic, dosed Nick to the gills with morphine. Nick was still trying to sue everyone.

"You know what?" said Jake after a minute of halfhearted searching. "We *could* just burn the house down. I'm okay with that. I haven't read the policies in a while, but I think we're still covered for exorcisms."

"Anyone sets this house on fire, and I am *not* putting it out this time," said Sacha, sounding only partly serious. Then he said, "Kix, could you give me a hand for a second?"

Kix, who had been poking her toe around the soot-stained lump of welcome mat looked up in surprise.

"...Sure?" she said.

Jake stood up to go with her, but she walked past him without a second glance, so he didn't. Instead, he climbed to the middle of the grand staircase and sat down.

"You got the *other* guy back, right?" said Sacha. He was trying to whisper, but Nick's list of grievances was quite loud so he didn't try that hard.

"Which guy — Thad?" said Kix. Sacha nodded.

"The one that's *not* trying to kill us."

"Yes. He is definitely back. Brad is gone," she said, sliding her hands away from her to express just how way-gone Brad was.

"Are you sure? How do you *know*?"

"Because when I dragged Thad home, I met Karen coming back the other way."

"I thought you said she was dead."

"Not anymore."

"How does that work?"

"Braaaains," said Kix and brought her arms out stiffly. Sacha jumped.

"Be serious. That didn't really happen, did it? This is all a joke, right?"

"I can still taste blood."

"That is so *sick*," said Sacha. He made a fist and bit his knuckle but his eyes still sparkled with curiosity.

"What about that thing?" he said. "Can you still do that jumpy-jumpy thing?"

Kix shook her head. "I don't think so. I think everything is back to normal now."

"All right, folks, we'll be on our way." Cynthia, the lead medic, snapped her first aid kit closed with authority. Kevin had strapped the blathering Mr. Miller onto a gurney and started wheeling it toward the door. The first time he hit the wall, it looked like an accident. But after Mr. Miller named him in his litany of defendants, it became clear that the second and third bumps were less accidental. He rolled the gurney up to the breezeway as Cynthia gave Kix, Jake and Sacha the run-down.

"We're taking your pal here to Harborview, if you happen to catch that spider you'd be doing him a favor to bring it in and be identified. Remember, don't touch it. Put a glass over it or some— *Good gracious me, what is that thing?*"

She stopped just shy of the smashed up door and pointed to the top of the frame. Above her sat a tiny...something. It was definitely a something. It had black leathery wings and large bloodshot eyes with vertical pupils that glowed like they were on fire. It also had a fuzzy head. When it noticed everyone watching, it opened its tiny mouth to reveal two needle-like fangs. Then it sneezed and disappeared in a tiny puff of purple smoke.

"Where is Ronnie when you need him? Kev, get on the radio and call Animal Control."

Sacha noticed the corresponding puff of smoke near the secret door and leaned back as nonchalantly as possible to make sure he was seeing what he thought he was seeing. He was.

He made a play of tying his shoe in order to bend over. Then he scooped the tiny creature up into his hand and shoved her in the pocket of his hoodie.

"Uuuh, nope. You don't have to call Animal Control. It's fine. It's just a shu—" His eyes went up to Nick, strapped to the gurney. Nick's head was swollen and lolling to one side but his eyes were still very litigious.

"—ampire squirrel. It's a shampire squirrel."

"It had wings," said Kevin.

"It's a *European* shampire squirrel."

Kevin shrugged. "Never heard of them. They bite?"

"No. They're very tame." As if on cue, a soft purring noise started emanating from the pocket of Sacha's hoodie.

"We'll have to take your word on that," said Cynthia, and with a nod to Kevin, they were gone.

ALWAYS OBSERVE PROPER
SAFETY PROTOCOL

A NORMAL HUMAN would have left an empty corpse. Their life force would have been absorbed back into the Universal thread, to manifest elsewhere, perhaps into a mouse or a tree. Surely something physically logical.

But the Angel of Delivery was not a normal human. She was a Boundary Walker, a being so aligned with the rhythms of the Universe that she could slip between the planes of reality. And part of her had just suffered a gruesome, traumatic death. Even if she hadn't spent the last half hour training her other self's corpse how to speak, Toesy knew it would happen. He was slightly disappointed to be missing out on the nostril trick though.

He watched as the car rocked to one side. A short scream filled the back parking lot then cut off abruptly. In the front seat, Karen Wells, the Angel of Delivery's other self, took her undead revenge upon her murderer. The crunching sounds coming from the car were disgusting, yet oddly satisfying.

There was no saving this world now. Toesy mourned the loss, but things like this were bound to happen when you ignored basic safety protocol.

Let us learn from this, Steve.

How, sir?

Messing around with realities is not to be taken lightly. If you do not know what you're doing, you will end up with a zombie apocalypse. No one likes a zombie apocalypse, Steve. It can get very messy.

Is there anything we can do to stop it, sir?

It would be folly to try. This world has been doomed by his greed. The Kicker of Doors tried to game the system but he had no idea what the rules were. This is not only a stupid thing to do but it is also incredibly unsafe. The Universe seeks balance always, Steve. Remember that. If you don't know what you're doing, bad things can happen.

Toesy shook his ears against the rain and walked toward the holly tree. The crunching sounds coming from Karen's car were now accompanied by slurping sounds.

If that is so sir, then how did the Holy Man escape the same fate?

The Holy Man sought to test the Universe so he could understand it. The Kicker of Doors sought to tame it so he could harness its power for his own means. But no man can tame the Universe, that's just silly.

If I may ask, Sir, why is it silly? said Steve.

Because there are far too many things in it! Trees and plants and mice and ants, to all these things, Steve, there is no end. They exist in every dimension, an infinite amount of times. One man thinking he could bend all that to his will? Definitely not the brightest.

Across the parking lot, the squeaking noise of Karen's car rocking on its axles died down. Then the dome light blinked to life as the passenger side door opened.

We have done what we can here. We must return to our friends to make sure they are safe.

Toesy concentrated on getting back to their own world while Executive Wartime Consigliore Steve analyzed all his recent data as per the Overlord's request.

Steve understood balance; it was another way of saying *ratio*. But the idea of infinite mice put his circuits to the test. Eventually, he found enough logic in it to make a good approximation and filed it away for later.

In the end, that's all anyone can really do.

A VERY FURRY END

AS SOON AS THE AMBULANCE PULLED AWAY from the curb, Sacha turned to Jake and shouted at him. "Swear to me this isn't a joke!"

"I swear this isn't a joke," said Jake.

"I know it isn't," said Sacha. "I just wanted to make you swear because seriously, if this was a joke, I would have to kill you."

"Funny, I was coming upstairs to do the same."

"What do you mean?"

"You ate my damn space-time pizza you idiot! I could have fixed this if you hadn't eaten that pizza."

"It's not his fault, Jake." said Kix. She was standing at the base of the stairs, between the two men, the only person actually trying to find the spider. "He thought you were playing a prank on him.

"Why would I play a prank on him?"

"Uh, *hello*? What about all the Jell-O? I had to replace all the condiments in my fridge after that. It cost me eighty-seven dollars, you butt-face."

"You have eighty-seven dollars' worth of condiments in your fridge?"

"Shut up. Mustard is expensive."

"Will you *both* please shut up?" said Kix. Jake and Sacha looked at her as though they'd forgotten she was in the room. "Help me look for that spider. We need to find it."

"No, we don't." said Jake.

"Yes, we *do*. If that Miller guy dies, I'm going to feel horrible. So get up and help me look for it."

"No, I mean we don't need to *look* for it." He pointed to the front door. Just inside the breezeway sat Toesy, listening to their conversation. Sticking out of his mouth were several long hairy legs.

"Toesy! Don't eat that spider. It's not good for you," said Kix.

Toesy opened his mouth immediately, and the spider dropped to the floor. It was so huge and fat, it made a soft *thud* as it hit. For a moment, it looked as though it was dead, but Sacha moved toward it, and it shot back up to standing, forelegs waving in attack mode. Everyone gasped. Kix took a step back.

"Please don't let it bite anyone else, though," she said.

Toesy blinked at her warmly and took a step forward to catch it again, but the spider had other ideas. With incredible speed, it flipped around and darted forward, biting Toesy right on the nose. Toesy hissed, flicked his ears once, and sat down again. It assumed attack position, ready to strike again if necessary.

Toesy glared at the spider in stony silence. He looked at the people in the room, then back to the spider. Then he stretched his whole body out and began to purr. When he was limber enough, he walked around the spider in a circle. It moved as he moved, watching him intently. When he neared Kix, Toesy turned and walked a few paces in her direction. Then he backed up and sat down, right on top of the thing.

"Sacha, maybe you can get a glass before it bites Toesy again?" said Kix in as neutral a voice as possible.

Sacha ran past Jake up the stairs to his apartment, returning ten seconds later with a clear glass bowl. He walked over to Toesy, leaned down to inspect the situation, and stood back up. He walked a few paces to the left and bent down to inspect him from that angle. He stood up again. He walked a few paces to the right.

"Sacha, just give me the bowl," said Kix. Sacha gave her the bowl. She walked over to Toesy.

"Okay, Toesy, you get up, and I'll trap it for you. We need to get that thing to the hospital." Toesy mewled at her and did as she asked.

The spider scurried from Toesy's furry underside as soon as he stood, heading directly at Kix. It was quick, but she was determined. She slammed the bowl down and stepped back, trapping it neatly underneath. Immediately, it went into attack stance again.

"What do you think it is?" said Jake.

"I have no idea. Look how huge it is." She leaned over to study it through the glass. As she did so, it ran at her, slapping its massive abdomen against the side of the bowl. Kix flinched and jumped backward.

"*Kix!*" said Jake. He jumped up, shocked to see her very suddenly *not* where she had been standing.

"You have to be kidding me," said Sacha. "*You just did that thing again.*"

Kix opened her eyes to find herself halfway across the room, too stunned to respond. She closed her eyes and stepped forward, this time appearing on the stairs right next to Jake.

"How did you do that?" he said.

She was about to explain when they heard a faint *Ark*! coming from Sacha's pocket, and Toesy's head was suddenly enshrouded in a poof of purple smoke.

AN APOLOGY

KIX TURNED AROUND and sat down next to him on the stair. As she did so, her hair spilled between them. Without thinking Jake leaned into her and inhaled deeply.

"Don't do that again," she said.

Jake immediately sat up as straight as he could. "I'm sorry. I wasn't trying to smell you. It's just that your hair was in my face and—"

"I don't mean that, I mean the disappearing act," she said. "I've been trying to get in touch with you all day Jake. I called. You never answered."

"You tried to call me?"

"Several times."

"My phone never rang at all. Kix, I swear. I never got any calls. I checked it about a billion times."

"How long were you stuck in the back stairwell?" she said.

"I don't know. It felt an eternity but that can't be right." Jake's eyes went all glassy. She coughed softly and his attention snapped back to her.

"Kix, I owe you a huge apology. All I wanted was to hang out with you. I didn't mean for things to get so messed up."

She held a hand up to stop him and noticed for the first time, that her arm was smeared with blood from where Toesy bit her. Jake gasped. Kix shook her head slightly.

"Tonight has been long and weird," she said. "And I don't want apologies. At least not yet. Right now I want answers."

Jake nodded. He didn't want to ruin this thing twice so he kept his mouth shut until he was supposed to talk.

"Who was at your house last night?"

"You were at my house last night."

"What did we do? Do you remember?"

"Of *course* I remember," he said. "We talked, had drinks. You watched a movie while I did that experiment."

"The phone rang at one point, right?"

"Yes, you offered to pick it up but I told you it was probably my mom, so you left it."

"What happened after that?"

Jake's cheeks grew hot. He tried to sum up the next few moments as succinctly as possible. "I finished the experiment. I told you I figured out the equation and you asked me to show you the pizza. I did. Then you…uh, sat down."

"Where?" She looked him directly in the eye making it difficult for him to speak. He cleared his throat.

"On my lap." he said.

Kix's eyebrows went up. "Then what happened?" she asked.

Jake blushed. In the corner, Sacha was busy trying to turn himself invisible by stacking all the fallen books into a pile.

"You kissed me," he said.

"Kissed you, like *how*? Was it like, a peck on the cheek…"

"It was definitely not that."

"Right," said Kix. He noted that she did not sound surprised. "Did we have sex?"

Jake's heart began to race. The tips of his ears burned and his mouth grew very dry. "Are you asking because you don't remember?" he said.

"I'm asking because I want to know your answer."

"Yes," said Jake. "We did. I thought that you…" but Jake didn't know what he thought anymore. All the thoughts he could come up with were sad and depressing. Of *course* she didn't remember last night.

"I don't know any other way to tell you this so I'll just say it outright: that wasn't me."

Jake wanted to disagree with her but he stayed quiet. Instead, he gave her as much of a smile as he could muster. Kix *had* been here last night, he was sure of it. It just wasn't her *anymore*. He'd expected this but knowing it was true didn't make it any easier. Jake ran a hand along his forehead so he had a reason to look away for a moment.

"Kix, I am so sorry this happened. Thank you for saving my life, *again*. I did not mean to make anything awkward for you. If you want to go, I totally understand. I wouldn't blame you for wanting to get out of here."

"*Will you stop?*" she said. The fire in her eyes told him that he should go back to keeping his mouth shut. "This isn't high school, Jake. I'm not going to storm out of here because I don't like what happened. You say you slept with someone last night and I believe you. But I'm telling you, *that person wasn't me*." She softened her voice and stared straight ahead.

"I fell asleep in the middle of the movie. When I woke up, I heard another woman talking. I thought it was Deli at first but then I heard her whispering and I knew it wasn't. I couldn't believe the nerve you had, with me less than twenty feet away. I was so angry I wanted to scream. Instead, I decided to leave and never come back. But when I stood up to go, you weren't making out with another woman at all. You were asleep at your desk."

Jake stopped looking sad and started looking confused.

"I'm confused," he said.

"I was too. But that was when I thought everything was still normal. It wasn't until I talked with Deli that I figured out something was seriously wrong. I tried to get in touch with you but you wouldn't answer so I went to see Marco. Unfortunately, Thad got to him first."

"Thad attacked Marco?"

"No, it was the other one, Brad." Kix was talking faster now, trying to piece it all together in her mind. "I came here after that, to try and find you. I didn't, obviously. But I found Toesy. Then Brad found us and that's when Toesy showed me how to jump. He saved my life."

"Wait, *Toesy* showed you how to teleport?"

"Don't ask him to teach you how," said Sacha from the book stacks in the corner. "I already tried. Apparently you have to have PTSD or something."

"Jake already knows how."

"*What?* Is that true? And you never showed me?" said Sacha.

"No," said Jake. "I've never done anything like that."

"I think you have," said Kix. "In fact, I think that's what started all this. Look, when I did it, I concentrated on where I wanted to be and what it would look like when I got there. Then I sort of stepped *around* everything else and when I opened my eyes, I was in a different place."

"That makes no sense," said Jake.

"I know it doesn't but it worked. And what's more, I think when you did your experiment last night, you did something similar. Only you didn't concentrate on going to a different place, you concentrated on a different place coming to you. You concentrated on a different *reality*."

He stared at her, unsure of what to say.

"With different people in it," she said.

Jake continued staring. "So the girl last night was—"

"Her name was Karen."

"How do you know?"

"Because we were here together, sort of. It's more like we were so close that we were the same person for a while. I heard her thoughts. I knew her memories. That's how I know her name was Karen. I saw her life, what had happened to her. She came to see you this evening, to tell you to watch out for Brad, just like I did." Kix said this in a way that emphasized the past tense.

"What happened?"

"*Brad* happened," said Kix. He opened his mouth to ask how but she shook her head tightly. Jake looked away. How much damage had he done here?

"Is she dead?" he said.

Kix squinted as she searched for words. "Sort of? It's kind of complicated. For now, let's just say she's *gone*." Then she brightened a little. "But so is Brad."

"Is that the guy who ran off?"

"That was Thad."

"What's the difference?"

"One of them is an idiot and the other one isn't coming back."

"What happens if the idiot one comes back?"

"I don't think he will," she said. "But if he does, someone needs to tell him to stay away from Pizza Joe's. Marco has a gun and a long memory."

"Marco has a gun?"

"Yes, but only one for now."

"Well, thank goodness for that. Let's keep it that way."

Kix gave a half-hearted chuckle but didn't say anything else. After a moment, Jake started getting anxious. What could he say to apologize for all of this? He wanted to stay here talking but he couldn't figure out how. Sweat broke out on his forehead. What if he tried and ended up saying something really stupid and she left? What if he couldn't think of anything to say at all?

The moment grew fragile and thin. Kix sat up straight. Jake started to panic. Any second now she was going to stand up and leave. He had to say *something*. What was it going to be? He took a deep breath, twisted around to face her and gave it his best shot. He wanted to reach out and hold her hand too but he chickened out at the last moment and dropped his fist in his lap.

"Kix, I know that it didn't happen but, last night was incredible. You're incredible. And funny and super smart and I know of at least twelve other guys you could have been with but you weren't. You were *here*, with *me*. I'm not exaggerating when I say it was the best thing that's ever happened in my life. Although it didn't. And it probably wouldn't have if I hadn't messed everything up so completely. So please let me say I'm sorry," he said. "I didn't mean to overstep boundaries, or cause any sort of tear in the space-time continuum. I just wanted to hang out with you."

He would have said more but he'd run out of breath so he stopped and studied her reaction in case it was really bad. Not being the best at this sort of thing to begin with, Jake couldn't interpret the look on Kix's face. She was smiling, which seemed like a good thing, but her eyes were sad somehow.

"That's all you got?" she said at last.

Jake sputtered something that wasn't a full word. His eyebrows scrunched together in confusion and he stared at Kix, unsure of...well, everything really.

"What?"

"*Probably wouldn't have if I hadn't messed everything up so completely? Twelve other guys I could be with?*" Kix leaned away to rest on her elbow.

"Which twelve guys, Jake? Can you point them out for me?"

"That was just—I was just illustrating my point."

"What, that I'm out of your league?"

"Well," said Jake, suddenly on the defense. "Sort of, yeah."

"Which league do you think I'm *in*, Jake? You think I'm one of those snooty cheerleader types that reject everyone outright?"

"No, you're obviously not like that but…"

"Because as far as I'm aware, I've *never* turned you down. I can't have, even if I wanted to, because you've *never asked me out.*"

"That's true but I…"

"So when you say *probably wouldn't have*, you're making an assumption aren't you?"

"Well, I…"

"You're supposed to be brilliant. You know what happens when you assume, right?

"Is the answer that I make an ass out of myself?"

"Yes. A Royal Ass," she said turned to face forward.

In the background Sacha had gone back to stacking books, this time by color. Kix was clearly upset but she didn't leave. Jake wasn't sure what to think about that. She just sat there, staring straight ahead, not doing anything, almost like she was waiting for Jake to say something.

"Oh—" said Jake. "I need a do-over."

"A what?" said Kix.

"A do-over. Forget that last part. It wasn't what I meant to say. Please—just one do-over."

"Okay", she said. "But only one." She shook a finger at him but her eyes had gone soft. Jake continued before he could chicken out again.

"Thank you," he said. Then he cleared his throat.

"Kix, when I walk into a room you probably think *Oh, there's Jake.* But it's not like that for me. When *you* walk into a room, I don't see anyone else. I can't get comfortable. I am aware of everything you do, everything you say, where you sit, things you touch."

"I've tried not caring, not worrying about what you think. But then I see you again and it knocks the wind out of me. You are so beautiful that it makes me want to do stupid things just so you'll pay attention to me."

"Like science?" she said, scrunching her lips all the way over to the side of her face in an effort not to smile.

"Like a lot of dumb things," he said. "You know how I always order light garlic?"

"Yeah. Marco thinks you're a wuss."

"I *know*," said Jake. "I'm not a wuss though. I'm *allergic* to it."

"You aren't." she said but her eyes went wide and she had to scrunch her mouth farther to the side to keep from smiling.

"I am."

Kix snorted and immediately covered her mouth but she couldn't hide the laughter in her eyes.

"Look, I had jack up space-time in order to get the courage for this so you can't laugh until after I'm done, okay?"

She kept her mouth covered and nodded. Jake sat up straighter. "Kix, would you like to come over and have drinks with me? No science this time, I promise. Just drinks and a movie."

"Now?" she said from behind her hand. As promised, she did not laugh.

"Yes," said Jake. "I, Jake Denny, King of All Assholes, am asking you to come over for a date, *right now*—as long as you're okay that it's beer and a movie because it's super late and that's all I have."

"Can it be a zombie movie?" said Kix.

"Yes. It can be anything you want," said Jake.

"Okay," she said. "But don't think it's going to end the same way as last night you horn-dog."

Jake's breath caught in his throat and he started to cough. Kix couldn't hold it in any longer and busted up. Jake exhaled. His shoulders relaxed.

"I should have asked you out months ago, shouldn't I have?"

"Yes, you should have."

"Would you have said yes?"

"What do *you* think?" she said. Jake thought about it for less than a second.

"I think we should take care of *that* thing so we can go downstairs and have a beer." He pointed across the front entryway to the gigantic spider now trying to claw its way out from underneath the glass bowl.

"*I got this*," said Sacha. Actually, he almost screamed it. He'd stacked the books neatly in order of size and he was working on ways to stick the shelf back together without making noise.

"Really?" said Jake.

"Please, go away," he said.

"That thing is nasty-scary, Sacha. You sure you don't want help?" said Jake.

"I would rather deal with a gigantic poisonous spider than listen to any more of this conversation." Said Sacha. Then he added, "Please."

"Well okay. Thanks, man. I owe you."

"Yes, you do," said Sacha.

Kix smiled at him as she stood up. "Thanks Sacha," she said.

"You're welcome," he said and pulled out his phone to call emergency services for the second time that night.

QUESTIONS

"**WHAT IN THE NAME** of *Jesús Christo* is going on here?"

She wheeled her suitcase through the shards of glass in the entryway and stared wide-eyed at Sacha. Her curly dark hair had been pulled back in an unruly ponytail. There were tired circles under her eyes, but Sacha didn't see them. He stopped sweeping up shards of glass.

"Oh...hey. It's Connie, right?" he said, trying to sound like he didn't know.

"Yes." She said warily. "Do you know what is going on?"

"I'm Sacha," said Sacha. "I live down the hall."

"I know," she said. "Why is the door all busted up?"

"There've been some...*things* going on. Your boyfriend—"

"Who?" She stepped closer to Sacha, her wheeled bag trailing shards of glass behind as she went.

"Uh, your boyfriend? The guy that was watching your apartment while you were gone?"

Connie's eye got all squinty as she tried to figure out who Sacha was talking about.

"You mean *Nick*? He is not my boyfriend. He works in accounting."

"Oh," said Sacha, cocking his head to one side. "He told me you two were dating. Well anyway, you can tell him that I found your sugar glider, and she's safe, so you don't have to worry about her."

"Pansy? *Dios mío*, what happened? If she's hurt, I will kill him." Anger flashed in her eyes and Sacha knew she meant it.

"Don't worry, nothing bad has happened to her. Toesy wouldn't let us put her back in the cage but he promised to keep her safe until you came home. He'll be around soon."

"What do you mean, safe? Where is she? Who is Toesy?"

Sacha looked at the ground. He looked back up to Connie. She stared at him with sultry, disapproving eyes. "I can answer most of your questions, but you're not going to believe me."

"*Start talking.*"

Sacha talked. He told her about Toesy and the fancy squirrel-hat. He told her about the couch cushions and the yowling and the flare gun. As he spoke, he picked up her suitcase and carried it up the stairway. Connie followed him, listening to his lunatic story, until they stood right outside her front door where he set her suitcase down.

"I don't believe any of this," she said when he finished.

"I told you, didn't I tell you? I'm not lying, though. I promise." Sacha stood at her door, unsure of what to do next. This was the longest conversation he'd ever had with his neighbor. "So, if you need to check on your, uh...friend, they took him to Harborview."

Connie didn't say anything else. She just stood there staring at him.

"Right. And if you have any questions, you're welcome to come on over. I'm just right down the hall. Busted up door. Can't miss it."

"I don't think I will have any questions. It is well past midnight. Good night," she said.

There was nothing else he could do. He said good night and walked back down the hallway to his own apartment. The pork roast, long since abandoned in its medium-low oven, filled his head with savory smells as soon as he neared the door.

"Oh crap, the roast." He hurried to the kitchen, abandoning all thoughts of his beautiful, angry neighbor and her sugar glider problem. If his roast got ruined because of all of this, he was going to be really ticked off.

The roast was not ruined. Sacha set it on the cutting board to cool before he pulled it apart. He was elbow-deep in pulled-pork grease when he heard someone knock at his door. Thinking it might be Jake, he didn't bother to look through the spyhole before he moved the chair holding it closed.

Connie stood in the doorway, wearing pink pajamas. She held a large piece of porcelain in her hands. It looked a lot like a broken piece of sink.

"I have questions," she said.

LIFE GOES ON

THE NEXT DAY, Kix tried to return Marco's gun. Marco was still convinced that Thad was a mafia hit man and refused to take it. She kept it for the same reason she'd taken it in the first place: one less weapon in Marco's hands made the world a safer place.

No one knew what happened to Thad after he took off that night. No one really cared. Kix came home from work one afternoon to find his apartment empty and the landlord putting up a *For Lease* sign. He offered her another fifty dollars off rent if she didn't move. She said she'd think about it.

Jake spent several days apologizing to Kix for all the damage he'd caused, even though most of it never happened. Or rather, it *did* happen, just not in the same way everyone thought it did, whatever that means. Kix forgave him, reasoning that his mistake may have caused a lot of grief, but she basically had super powers now, and that was pretty cool.

Deli came back from the hospital in a walking cast. She had no memory of being pushed down the stairs by a dangerous psychopath. She claims to have slipped on the freshly polished grand staircase. Gloria Denny became aware of the situation and offered Deli free rent for a year if she didn't sue. Deli talked her up to eighteen months and agreed not to sue because eighteen months of free rent was a damn good deal. To everyone's relief, Carl stopped trying to sing. He still wore the fedora occasionally, though.

No murder charges were ever leveled against anyone, since,

as far as anyone could tell, no murder had been committed. But Kix knew better. She eventually told Jake the whole thing, zombie apocalypse and all. Jake urged her to seek help for PTSD. Kix declined therapy but spent most of the winter curled up under a blanket watching zombie movies with Jake. After Christmas, he asked if her to move in with him. She said she'd think about it.

Contrary to his lawyer's advice, Nicholas Miller filed suit against Denny Holdings, LLC, asking for more than three million dollars in damages. It took the prosecuting attorney two days to present the entire folio of evidence Mr. Miller had collected from that evening. It took the Honorable Judge Bustamante twenty minutes to find the defendants not guilty on any charges. Fifteen of those minutes were spent searching the Internet for information on European shampire squirrels.

Although the new and improved Pansy was pointier and more fearsome than before, Connie still attempted to keep her safe by locking her in her cage at night. Unfortunately for Connie, Pansy also retained the ability to disappear in puffs of purple smoke. After her third trip to Sacha's apartment to retrieve the smoking sugar-glider, Connie gave up and started leaving the cage open. Eventually, she took to leaving the front door unlocked too because Toesy still has a difficult time with keys.

The following May an independent filmmaker out of Portland, Oregon, calling himself Brother Thaddeus released a short film titled *Beer and Serenity: The Life of a Monk*. As part of his promotional tour, he sat down for a live interview on a popular website. Unfortunately, most of the questions were not about his movie but rather, how he lost his earlobe. When Brother Thaddeus refused to say, things turned ugly. Within the hour, several angry, earless monk themed internet memes went viral.

A MOST PRECIOUS GIFT

THEY WERE GATHERING OUTSIDE. He felt their footfalls on the ground. He heard whispers of nervous chatter. Soon they would come for him but Diabo was ready.

"Kids, this next fella is known for being the most venomous spider in the world. His proper name is *Phoneutria fera* but we call him Duke because he likes to put his fists up. Now some of you may have read about Duke in the papers. He came to us in a very interesting way! He was found in an old mansion up on Capitol Hill after he bit some poor shmo, *right in the forehead.*"

The gasp through the crowd told Diabo it was almost time.

"As we learned at the black widow station, the only sure way to identify a spider bite is to capture and identify the spider that bit you. The guy that Duke bit was lucky to have quick-witted friends that day. And *Duke* here was lucky that those friends called our night custodian Burt.

Now, Duke can't get out of the enclosure so don't worry, but he is pretty aggressive so you little ones in the front might want to take a step back."

There came the sound of smaller footfalls. Diabo readied his leg spines. His fangs were slick with venom.

"Alright little missy, but don't say I didn't warn you."

Flash! The curtain opened. Thirteen human hatchlings stood in front of his window, wide-eyed and eagerly searching him out. They could not see him until he moved and he would not move until they came close. A plump one with hair the color of fire was the first to step up. And after that, another hatchling stepped closer. One by one, they approached. As they did so, Diabo began his prayers.

Mama, you gave me a man, and I became brave.
Mama, you gave me a hive of men and I grew strong.
Mama Ayahuasca, I thank you for this most precious gift.
You have given me heaven and I now rejoice.

As he finished, the last hatchling overcame her pink and frilly fears and crowded in around his window. Up went his forelegs. Out came his blood red fangs. He zeroed in on the frilly hatchling and ran at her, waving his leg spines.

They scrambled over themselves to get away. The frilly one had started to cry and giggle at the same time. Diabo selected a different one, a taller one that had not screamed, and ran at it. It fell onto the ground as it jumped away.

Diabo was almost sick to his cephalothorax with glee. The shrieking was tremendous. It was delicious. And since he'd come to this sanctuary, he had been supplied with fresh victims at *least* twice a day, sometimes three.

Truly, this was heaven.

ACKNOWLEDGEMENTS

FIRST AND FOREMOST, I'd like to thank the four incredibly skilled women who gave every bit of their attention to this project: Stephanie Konat, Magdalen Powers, Renee Garcia and Karen Alcaide. You all have done a super job. A heartfelt thank you to Shari Ryan for stepping in at the last moment so one of our super team could become a super mom. To wee baby Ilario, thank you for letting us have your mom for so long. You're a good kid.

Brian, you have kept me sane, entertained, fed and watered while I grouched and crabbed my way through this. I could not have done this without your love, support and all those late night cheese sandwiches. Thank you for those. You are truly a master of the grilled cheese arts.

Thanks to Monica Pagano for help with spider translation; to Art and Lara Grauer for buying what I thought was a goofy auction item but which turned into a super fun character; to both the CK8 and the BNS communities for such support, I am incredibly lucky to know all of you.

Thanks also to Candy Sunick and April Magrane for letting me talk their ears off; to Jennifer Mills for the all the advice, it's amazing what sisters know if you shut up and listen to them; to Madelyn for the writing sanctuary; to all my friends who turned into readers because they were curious about my mental health; and to Sherry Edwards for her tireless cheerleading.

Thank you Sherry, you can stop meowing at me now.

www.ingramcontent.com/pod-product-compliance
Lightning Source LLC
Chambersburg PA
CBHW021202250626
47155CB00008B/2638